Unplanned Obsession

Amara Holt

Published by Amara Holt, 2024.

Copyright © 2024 by Amara Holt
All rights reserved.

No part of this book may be reproduced, distributed, or transmitted in any form or by any means, including photocopying, recording, or other electronic or mechanical methods, without the prior written permission of the author, except in the case of brief quotations in book reviews.

This is a work of fiction. Names, characters, places, and incidents are the product of the author's imagination or are used fictitiously. Any resemblance to actual events, organizations, locales, or persons, living or dead is coincidental and is not intended by the authors.

Prologue

Zoe

Boston — Massachusetts

At Seven Years Old

She holds my hand, squeezing it tightly, and without needing to say anything, I know she is as sad as I am.

We talk a lot.

Every day, in fact, since I moved here almost a year ago. Pauline is the only person who can make me smile. My mom died. She was the only person I had in the world since Dad went to heaven a long time ago.

I tell stories to my friend because I've learned to read. Mom used to do that with me, mimicking the characters' voices. It was very funny. I'm not very good at it, because I read slowly and sometimes I even stutter, but she never laughs at me, unlike Aunt Ernestine, her mother, and the owner of the house where I live.

Pauline is older than me—much older, almost twelve and says she's not a child, but a teenager. Even so, being almost an adult, she can't get out of bed because her legs don't have the strength to walk. She had an accident when she was younger than I am now.

I wish I had the power to make her get up, run, and play, but as my teacher said the other day: *"Sometimes we can't understand God's will, Zoe."*

I don't know what that means, but it's not fair.

1

I've found a way to make her happy: I do things for her. When she wakes up and says she wants to take a walk in the yard, I run outside. I come back with my lungs bursting, out of breath, but when I see her smile, it's worth it.

The first time she said I was crazy, but then she started to love the idea; she always asks me for things.

"Zoe, go outside and catch some rain for me."

"Zoe, tell me about the cutest boy at your school. He's going to be my secret boyfriend."

"Zoe, what's it like to jump really high?"

I swing my feet, sitting on her bed.

They don't reach the floor yet because her bed is high. "*It's a hospital bed, and it cost a fortune,*" Aunt Ernestine always says, as if it's Pauline's fault she needs one.

We used to play, betting on when I'd be tall enough to make my feet touch the floor.

Now we'll never know because I'm leaving.

"Promise you'll come back for me when you're rich?"

I look at her and smile, which helps ease the pain I feel in my chest.

It's been a week since I've been crying secretly. Since I found out I'd be going to live in an orphanage again, I've been very sad.

My pretend aunt called the government man and said she would *return me* because the money she received to keep me wasn't enough. She also has other children here, so I don't understand why I'm the only one being returned.

"How am I going to be rich, Pauline?" I ask. "I only have two dollars in the piggy bank I got that time I helped Mrs. Nole gather the leaves from the yard."

"Remember our game where you're me, doing things for me? I dream of becoming a *famous top model*. Beautiful, walking the runway with all the men in the world in love with me, but that will never happen because I can't walk."

"What's a *top model*?" I ask, testing the name on my tongue and finding it funny.

"They're very beautiful girls who walk on a runway or are photographed. They get clothes and travel all around the world."

"It must be really cool."

"Yes, Zoe. The best job in the world. Promise me you'll do it for me and that, wherever you travel, you'll remember my wish."

"I know your mom is sending me away, but does that mean I'll never see you again, Pauline?"

She looks at me strangely, as if she knows a secret and doesn't want to share it.

"I'm not sure, Zoe, but anyway, when you're sad and alone, look up at the sky and think of me. I'll always think of you too."

Chapter 1

Zoe

Barcelona

Eleven Years Later

Oh, God, how uncomfortable!
Pauline, I love you so much because this idea of traveling the world is proving to be harder than I imagined.

A Mediterranean cruise might be the dream of every girl my age, but right now, I'd give anything to ditch this sticky uniform and throw myself into the snow in Boston. But even if I were back home, that wouldn't be possible, of course, since it's summer there too.

I try to see the time on the clock inside the ship, but it's really hard from here. Since we're prohibited from checking our phones during work, all I can do is hope to get back to the air conditioning soon.

With the same force that the thought of discouragement comes, I push it away by remembering my best friend and how she would give anything to be living even this experience on a damp summer day, trapped in a uniform that makes anyone feel like a banana: covered up to the neck.

I hate turtlenecks and would love to have a word with the designer—if there was one—who came up with such a garment for the ship's assistants.

"What time can I take a picture with the handsome captain, dear?" an elderly lady approaches me and asks.

"Good evening. Welcome to Dream Cruises," I reply with the memorized phrase. "The captain will be available half an hour before the gala dinner tonight and will be available for photographs with passengers for fifteen minutes."

"Only fifteen? I need at least an hour with that *hunk*."

I hide a laugh.

She must be around eighty or older, and the captain about fifty, but who says love has an age?

Personally, I didn't like the guy the one time we were in the same room because he looks at all women as if he considers himself a gift from the heavens to us.

Another girl, who was also hired for this week-long cruise and has worked on others, told me that he usually ends every voyage with the ship's staff fighting for his attention. And that a good portion of them—or all—take a *little spin* in his cabin.

The lady says goodbye, and I take the opportunity to check if the photographer's materials are all in order.

When I read on the *internet* a few months ago that *Dolphin Cruises*, the largest cruise line in the world, was hiring young people with no experience to work on a Mediterranean voyage, I thought: now is the time.

They gave us two weeks of training, and since I had just finished high school, it would be a perfect gift for myself.

I passed the training with ease, and the company even provided my passport.

My adoptive parents, a kind couple who finally took me out of the orphanage permanently when I was eleven, could never have provided me with something like this. In return, they gave me a lot of love, and even though they couldn't piece together all the broken parts of my heart, they made me feel wanted after so many temporary homes.

Only about a year ago did I meet a distant cousin of my biological mother, but although I liked finding some blood relatives, they never tried to get close.

They have money, which is very different from the life my biological parents led, and when they invited me to family parties, I felt like an outsider and was looked at with superiority. Only one of that cousin's daughters, a girl as shy as I am, Madeline, who had dyslexia, was kind to me.

I tried very hard to get along with them, but I reached my limit when her mother, at a dinner I attended as a guest, asked me if I could help the maid serve the meal because one of the staff had not shown up. I said yes, because I think I didn't fully understand what that meant at the time. I mean, when my adoptive parents host people at their home, everyone helps set the table, wash the dishes afterward, so I didn't think much of it.

Only when she handed me the uniform her staff was wearing did it hit me.

I made up an excuse, saying that my mom needed me, and never went back to them.

Aunt Adley saw me—and I understood too late—as a nuisance, someone who wanted to enjoy the privileges of her wealth. I couldn't be further from the truth. I just wanted to be part of a big family since my adoptive parents don't have any other relatives.

I watch as people begin to circulate around the ship in their fancy clothes. The women's dresses, long and sparkly, and the men in *tuxedos*, just like we see in movies.

Sometimes I daydream, wishing I could live that for at least one night, like Cinderella at the ball with the prince.

But that dream is practically impossible to come true, so I really need to stay focused and replenish the water bottle the photographer warned me about from the first day that couldn't be missing.

The good thing is that once I finish my shift here, I'm off. I usually wander around the ship, but tomorrow morning is my day off, so I decided to take a walk around Barcelona. Nothing too spectacular. A stroll through the city streets and a visit to *La Sagrada Familia*, Spain's most famous church. Mom never traveled, but she recommended I visit it because it's one of the world's landmarks.

I grab a box of paper napkins and place it near the water. The photographer sweats a lot, and I always leave tissues or napkins nearby.

My mother used to say that a lady should never appear sweaty in public. I think that recommendation goes for gentlemen too.

Funny how this is one of the few things I still remember about her.

I feel sad occasionally because when I think of Mom now, most of the time it's not the biological one, but Mrs. Macy, the adoptive one. It's been so long since she and my dad passed away that I've forgotten almost everything we lived through. As for the time I spent in the orphanage, to my sorrow, I remember it perfectly.

Of the requests Pauline made of me the last time we saw each other, this is the first I'm trying to fulfill.

Even though my body is suited to try a modeling career, standing at one meter and seventy-seven, my shyness ends up making me hide from the world.

In my head, I'm very extroverted. I talk a lot to myself and am also ironic, but when it comes to putting it all out there, it changes.

"Zoe, are you up for making some extra cash?" Tamara, a colleague hired with me and also from Boston, asks. We share a cabin in the crew quarters.

"Always," I reply, smiling. "I want to buy some souvenirs for my parents, so any extra money is welcome."

"They need a waitress for the gala dinner in the captain's cabin. There will be only a handful of guests, but they will be powerful people."

"Look, that's quite an opportunity, but I really don't think it's a good idea. The chance that I might spill something on these elegant people's clothes is high. I'm pretty clumsy."

"Don't be silly, the tips will be substantial. I've worked a few times at events like this."

"But why me?"

"I was the one who suggested you be called. I know your situation isn't the best."

I'm not offended by what she says because it's nothing more than the truth.

"Are you sure? And what if I mess up and end up causing trouble for you?"

"Don't worry. Relax and trust yourself more. Everything will be fine."

Chapter 2

Christos

Barcelona

Earlier That Day

"What do you have to offer me?" I ask, desperate for him to give me a reason to get up and leave.

"You're not being reasonable, Christos."

"I've never been accused of that. You have five more minutes."

"I thought our negotiation was moving forward."

"So did I, until I discovered you inflated your profits this year. Do you have any idea what could happen if this gets to the shareholders?"

He paces back and forth, and once again I regret having to negotiate with someone like him. If my analysts hadn't projected such an obscene profit if I acquire his company, I'd send him straight to hell.

Frank Morrison is everything I despise in a man: weak character, malleable, acting according to what he thinks others expect of him. If you want to be a bastard and act like one, you should embrace the role and not fear anyone. But if you need to adapt to situations, then, to me, you're nothing.

"What do you want me to do?"

"If, and I'm emphasizing the 'if,' we're going to negotiate, you'll have to undergo an audit of the past ten years. My analysts took only an hour to find inconsistencies in the numbers you sent me."

In fact, I've already instructed the audit to be done and have the results in my *email*, but I like making him sweat. Besides, I want to know if there are any more skeletons in the closet. Data that my employees might not have been able to uncover, though I doubt it. Frank isn't a financial genius but a small-time crook who tried to defraud his own company and failed miserably.

He nods, but I see that he pales.

"And what else?"

"If there are any other signs of fraud, the deal is off."

"There weren't any, it was the first time..."

"Your luck is that the fiscal year hasn't ended yet. According to my lawyers, there's time to fix it." I cross one leg over the other and stare at him. He looks about to faint. "Did you really think you could fool me? Do you believe I would invest in a business of nearly a billion dollars without being sure of where I'm stepping?"

"No... I mean, you don't understand. I was... I am desperate."

"No, it's you who doesn't understand, Frank. Lie to me again and you won't get another chance. I'll let the banks seize all your assets. Before long, even that expensive watch you're wearing will have to be pawned."

"That won't happen, Christos. You have my word."

I get up without responding because his word means nothing to me anymore. Once a liar, always a liar.

I despise white-collar criminals. They gamble with the lives of thousands of families.

"What will your next move be?" he asks, looking anxious.

"I want to see one of the ships. You told me there's one docked here in Barcelona, so let's go. Take me to see it."

"I can't clear a ship with over two thousand passengers."

"I didn't ask for that, but I want to talk to some of the employees. Not the temporary ones, but the permanent staff."

"Why?"

"I would never go into a business like this without studying it first. There are things only they can answer for me, things no specialist can attest to, but the ones who are in daily contact with the crew and passengers."

"Can I ask for an example?"

"No."

Later

AS I WALK ACROSS THE ship surrounded by my security, people move aside to watch me. There's nothing I hate more than this, but I was the target of an attempted robbery about a month ago, and since then, the head of my security team has been somewhat paranoid.

It's the price you pay for being rich, but nothing that makes me regret the path I've taken to get here.

The story my father tells, ever since we immigrated to the United States, has marked me forever. My grandmother, his mother, died in Greece because she couldn't afford her medical treatment. That led him to leave the country of his birth and seek a better life in America.

I was still a child, but I remember how dad would come home late, never having a day off, full of ideas and plans.

He learned the trade of tailoring and soon became highly sought after, to the point where the business grew enough to require hiring employees and opening branches.

To cut a long story short, by the time I turned eighteen, we were already rich. My father's motto is to grow and multiply — and it has nothing to do with grandchildren, although I am sure he wants them — but with the balance of our bank account.

Today, I own the ten largest high fashion and accessory brands around the world, in both men's and women's segments, but true to my father's motto, I've expanded my business by investing in various sectors.

And that's precisely why I'm attending this dinner tonight.

My mother went crazy at the idea of me buying a fleet of cruise ships, and one might think I don't own a gigantic yacht. The problem is, inside Danae Lykaios, there's still a simple girl from a small island in Greece.

No matter how many jewels and fur coats she owns, she's a woman with not a shred of arrogance and who loves to talk to people — anyone — so being on a cruise, or several, because if I know her well, she'll take a *tour* around the world if this deal goes through, seems to be her idea of paradise.

"We'll be dining in a room on the top floor, with the captain, but if you want, you can visit the ship afterwards," Frank says.

I nod.

"Wouldn't tonight be the gala night? From what I understand, the captain needs to be present."

He looks at me, seeming surprised.

"Yes, it is, but he won't be dining with the guests. He rarely does. On our ships, only first class is admitted to this dinner, and even then, the captain is often pestered, especially by women. To avoid issues, he dines alone or... in special company."

"I won't be long."

In fact, I don't even plan to have dinner. I have an actress waiting for me in a presidential suite at the Oviedo Tower. She's a casual fling whenever I'm in Barcelona. This would be the second time we've met.

Although I have an apartment in the city, I don't bring girlfriends there. It could give the wrong impression of commitment. Like every Greek, family is important to me, and of course, I plan to marry one day and have descendants, but I've never met anyone who made me think about anything more than enjoyable nights of sex.

"Alright. As you wish."

HALF AN HOUR OF CONVERSATION and I'm already ready to leave.

In fact, at thirty-five, I don't need much more than a few minutes of conversation with someone to make a complete read of their personality, and the captain, Bentley Williams, is nothing but a vain asshole. What I really want to do is take a tour and chat with some staff members randomly.

I'm preparing to get up when I notice, at the entrance of the room, a delicious pair of legs in a miniskirt.

Yes, a pair of legs, because she's carrying a tray twice her size. Unable to see her face, I follow the reverse path.

She's tall, but has delicate feet in *horrible* high heels, though they look very *sexy* on her. Her hips are smooth but somewhat hypnotic, as she has a sensual sway when she walks.

For a moment, I forget who's around me, eager to see more.

Chapter 3

Christos

I have a vague sense that someone is talking to me, but I'm too intrigued by the goddess to pay attention.

Long legs and blonde hair are my weakness, and that's all I can see right now, eager to find out who they belong to. Almost platinum hair, fine and shoulder-length, and endless legs. That's all the woman needed to show me to have me completely captivated by her.

The tray she's holding seems impossibly heavy for someone with such a delicate frame, which is confirmed when the glasses on it sway dangerously.

Another girl helps her, and then I finally get to see the whole picture — from behind, because in a game of hide and seek, she turns around before I can see her face.

And yet, the little I observe makes my pulse race.

I'm not the poetic type, but I swear to God I feel like I'm in the presence of an angel.

My main business is fashion, so I have a keen eye for bodies, and the girl, whose name I have no idea of, would make an excellent runway model. With a frame like that, they could dress her in garbage bags and she'd still be the only one seen by the audience.

The hair I imagined shorter falls in a rounded cut down her back, a cascade of delicately wavy strands falling over her narrow shoulders.

I estimate that, without the high heels, she's about fifteen centimeters shorter than my one meter ninety-five, but her body is all woman.

I'm completely focused on her, and that's not common for me. I love sex and women, but nothing distracts me from what's happening around me.

Even before she turns around, I take out my phone and send a message canceling my date. I don't want more than one woman at a time, and there's no chance of spending the night with the model I was scheduled to meet when my attention was caught by the mysterious blonde.

I type quickly.

"Enjoy yourself in the suite. Order whatever you want. Something came up. I'll make it up to you."

I make a mental note to ask my assistant to send her a piece of jewelry.

I turn off the phone immediately because I don't handle complaints or demands well, and from the time I've spent in this world, I know that's what will come.

"Christos, do you want to take a tour of the ship?" Frank asks next to me.

"What?"

I finally become aware that there are more people with me, but just then the blonde turns around, almost in slow motion.

Her beauty leaves me dizzy.

She is stunning.

Delicate nose, full lips, and eyes that are almost oriental but blue, creating an exotic contrast with the whole.

I'm used to seeing beauty every day, and to be honest, after a while, it gets tiring; in fact, it's boring.

But the woman in front of me is perfect and unique. I've never seen a face with such striking features. Translucent skin but with Japanese-like eyes.

Her breasts are small, from what I can see of her ugly uniform, but she's very sensual, as if her body was made for pleasure.

The predator in me is awakened, the need to make her mine echoes strongly.

"Look at me," I command, as if my thoughts had the power to make her obey.

"Christos?"

"Yes, I'd like to walk around the ship," I reply, just to get him to stop talking.

What's the matter with the girl? Even while talking to the other staff member, she doesn't lift her eyes from the floor, doesn't make eye contact with anyone, and I need her to see me.

The woman who's helping her takes the lead and starts serving us, while, frustrated, I watch the object of my interest move away.

I STALLED AS MUCH AS I could during dinner to see if she would return, but nothing happened, so minutes later, I announced that I was ready to tour the ship.

I have no desire to continue in the company of the two of them, each despicable in their own way, but I don't go back on my word, even though I'm dying to leave.

I barely hear Frank or the captain's explanations, though I occasionally stop to speak with a crew member.

I'm about to end the night, incredibly frustrated knowing I'll have to use other means to find out who the blonde is, when I see a platinum cloud exit through a door onto the deck.

I tell my men to wait for me for a moment and make it clear by my tone that I don't want any company.

Like a crazed stalker, I follow what I imagine is the woman who awakened my libido. I believe that opportunities should not be wasted, and if she's the one there, I won't lose sight of her again.

I walk slowly so as not to startle her.

She seems to be taking selfies with the ship in the background.

The temperature has dropped, and still dressed in her waitress uniform, she seems to be feeling cold, but she still tries to get a good angle.

She also talks to herself from time to time, shaking her head, arguing, and I've just discovered a voyeur within me.

I'm not used to waiting for things to happen, but this time I stay in the shadows, just watching her, hands in the pockets of my suit pants.

The deck is deserted at this hour because there's a party going on downstairs. In fact, from what I gathered from Frank's explanations, she shouldn't even be here, as only authorized staff can circulate on this floor.

As if sensing she's not alone, she looks back and, startled to see me, drops her phone on the ground.

She bends down to pick it up and seems about to run away.

"No. Stay," I command.

Chapter 4

Zoe

Minutes Earlier

I climb the stairs to the upper deck with wobbly legs. I know I shouldn't be doing this. Coming to this floor disobeys the rules I agreed to when I was hired, but the upper deck, outside, has the most beautiful view of the ship. I need to take pictures, as I promised Pauline.

I hold the little doll I always carry with me, which represents her, so that we both appear in the photo, but it's hard to find a good angle. I need a *selfie-stick*.

The fact that my heart is pounding like a drum doesn't help either. If they catch me here, I'll be fired.

I adjust my arm a bit, and finally it looks like we'll both be in the shot. I'm ready to press the button when, through the camera viewfinder, I notice someone — a man — behind me.

I turn to look at him and, startled to be caught, my phone falls. Oh God!

I crouch down at lightning speed and, like a madwoman, prepare to run — yes, I'm not thinking straight. I should apologize for being in an unauthorized place and try to salvage the rest of the trip.

"No. Stay," the man commands, and as if trained for it, I freeze in place.

I'm looking at the floor, dying of embarrassment, but there's something in his tone that makes me want to obey him.

"You don't need to be afraid of me," he says, and I believe him, even though I have no idea who he is.

"I'm sorry. I shouldn't be here," I finally force myself to say, still not looking at him.

"What's your name?"

I see him through my lashes because my damn shyness won't let me make *eye contact*, even though I'm a bit curious now. His voice is nice, though it sounds harsh. There's no doubt that it belongs to someone used to being obeyed.

The first thing I notice is his broad shoulders, almost a straight line. And when I say broad, that's the exact definition. The suit he wears seems molded onto him, with not a crease of fabric left over.

Curiosity overcomes shyness, and I lift my face to observe him. Maybe it's not very polite, but I do a study of his features.

He has a softly tanned skin, and I guess it's natural. He gives the impression of having so much energy inside him that I doubt he'd sit around sunbathing.

He must be over thirty.

Dark blonde hair, cut short, with not a strand out of place — the opposite of mine, which, being very fine, are always flying around. His nose is straight. The square jaw and needing a shave complete the picture. In a weird way, I like that, because it breaks a bit of his perfect aura, making him more human.

"Closer to me," a voice without sense says in my head.

Closer? I don't think so. From his appearance, he could perfectly be royalty. His posture is that of a noble.

I've never been so impacted in the presence of a man before, and I can't stop watching him.

I reach his eyes. They are blue, deep, and they look at me as if allowing my examination.

Without saying another word, he manages to keep me in place.

"Name," he repeats, and this time there's a rougher tone in his voice that sends shivers down my spine.

"Zoe Turner."

He takes a step closer, but I don't feel fear. On the contrary, I feel anxious, but before either of us can speak, I hear a door opening behind him, and, nervous thinking it might be a superior from the ship who will call my attention, I run away.

Barcelona — Spain

The Next Morning

I CAN'T BELIEVE I'M here! It's like being in a movie... Seeing in person a building I've observed so many times on *tourism sites* on the *internet*.

From Boston to the world, Pauline.

When I was approved to work on the ship, I made a list with my mom of the places we would dock so we could discover the best tourist attractions in the cities.

We didn't have money to buy tickets in advance for all the museums I wanted to visit, but from what we read, at least for *La Sagrada Familia* I needed to, because they are limited and sell out quickly.

When I arrived, there was a huge line of tourists outside waiting to get in, and I thanked God for being prepared.

I read the brochure in my hand.

"... *La Sagrada Familia is a large, unfinished basilica in Barcelona, Spain. Designed by Spanish architect Antoni Gaudí, it is part of the UNESCO World Heritage.*

Construction of the Sagrada Familia began on March 19, 1882, under the supervision of architect Francisco de Paula del Villar. In 1883, when Villar resigned, Gaudí took over as chief architect, transforming the design with his architectural and engineering style, combining Gothic forms and curvilinear Art Nouveau. Gaudí devoted the rest of his life to the project and is buried in the crypt. At the time of his death in 1926, less than a quarter of the project was completed.

Relying only on private donations, construction of the Sagrada Familia progressed slowly and was interrupted by the Spanish Civil War.

In July 1936, revolutionaries set fire to the crypt and raided the workshop, partially destroying Gaudí's original plans, drawings, and plaster models, leading to 16 years of work to piece together the master model. Construction resumed with intermittent progress in the 1950s.

Advances in technology allowed for faster progress, and construction passed the halfway point in 2010. However, some of the project's greatest challenges remain, including building ten more towers, each symbolizing a significant Biblical figure in the New Testament..."

As I walk through the church nave, I see people photographing the walls of the building. I prefer to look and then buy a book about its history, because if I keep stopping to take pictures, I'll miss the real thrill of being here.

When I leave, however, I'll take my photograph with Pauline. She's inside the bag. So far, on this trip, we have two dozen photos together, and we're going to give our album a major *upgrade*.

Before this trip, I had photos *with her* right in Boston. At the science museum, at *Quincy Market* — which I love visiting, even without money to buy anything — and at *Boston Harbor*, my favorite place of all, outside of summer. During this season, tourists crowd the streets, and it's hard to even reach the harbor.

"No *selfies* today?"

My heart races at the question because I know exactly who the voice belongs to.

The gorgeous man I ran away from yesterday.

Chapter 5

Zoe

I turn to him with my hand pressed against my chest. It's not so much the shock, but an attempt to calm my racing heart.

What is it about this man that makes me feel this way? I'm inexperienced, but I lead a normal life. I even had a boyfriend in school, though nothing intimate ever happened between us.

It's not like I live on a deserted island and have never seen a handsome man in my life. Especially since I started working on the ship. Not only are many of the guests charming and interesting, but so are several of the crew members. But there's something about this one that makes my legs shake.

Last night, after I fled from him and the fear of potentially being caught by my superiors for doing something against the rules passed, I spent a long time unable to sleep, staring at the ceiling of the stuffy cabin I share with Tamara.

The man's face wouldn't leave my mind, just like the tingling sensation throughout my body.

I'm sure he doesn't work on the ship — he doesn't seem to work for anyone but himself — and he's not one of the usual guests, as I know the *VIP* guests in first class, who aren't as numerous as those in the economy classes.

And I don't doubt for a second that this man standing in front of me doesn't need to save anything. He gives off such a powerful aura that it's intimidating, though, when it comes to me, it's not hard to make me feel shy.

"You're not much of a talker, are you?"

His voice shows irritation, which ends up stirring my own.

"Not with strangers," I reply, lifting my chin. "What are you doing here?"

"I had someone follow you."

I open and close my mouth, but no sound comes out. I'm stunned by the confession.

"Aren't you going to say anything?"

"I don't know what to say."

"A pleasure to meet you would be a good start, Zoe Turner."

"I... um... don't even know your name."

"Xander Megalos," he says, extending his hand in greeting.

I look at it. It's huge, and a sudden desire to feel his skin overwhelms me. I hesitate before offering my hand, but as soon as I do, he takes it, holding it.

A delicious shock runs through my body, and I'm breathless.

His thumb caresses the back of my hand, and the simple touch makes my pulse race.

This lasts only a few seconds because, forcing myself back to reality, I pull away and take a step back.

The man is a stranger, and I'm usually quite guarded in situations like this — I mean, not like this one, because I've never had such a stunning man pursue me before, but I've had quite awkward encounters with people who mistook my kindness for openness to something more.

"Why did you follow me, Mr. Megalos?"

"Why does a man follow a woman?"

"There's a name for that in the United States," I say, rather than answering directly. Not that I'm sure and I'm afraid of embarrassing myself.

I try to appear more confident than I am because, to be honest, I'm excited by the possibility that someone like him took the trouble to come after me.

"Am I imposing on you, Zoe?"

I look at him tempted to say yes, but I'm not a liar.

"No, but I'd like to understand why you had someone follow me."

"Because I want to get to know you better."

I pretend I didn't hear that part, even though my heart is pounding in my chest.

"I don't understand. How can you get to know me *better*? We don't know each other at all, except for that moment when I went to the upper deck and encountered you."

"You were serving dinner to the commander, and I saw you, but since you didn't lift your eyes from the floor, you probably didn't notice that I was watching you."

Oh my God, what a straightforward man!

Why does what he's saying, instead of scaring me, make me feel like there's a revolution of butterflies in my stomach?

"There's nothing wrong with being shy," I argue, risking a glance.

A corner of his mouth lifts with the shadow of a smile.

"I didn't say there was, Zoe."

I feel my cheeks heat up. I've been acting like a rude person since yesterday. My mom would give me a serious talking-to if she found out. Starting with sneaking up to the upper deck and, with that, breaking several rules.

"I don't usually run away from people, and I'm sorry for leaving like that yesterday. I was rude, but I was scared. I shouldn't have been there," I say before I can stop myself, and then quickly add, "but I wouldn't miss the chance to take a picture in that place."

"Do you usually seize opportunities, Zoe?"

Is it crazy that I love the way he says my name? It sounds like caramel dripping from his mouth. He stretches the syllables, as if savoring each letter.

"I've never had so many that I could think about it. Are you a guest? I'm almost sure you're not, but I want to clarify because, if you are, we shouldn't even be talking."

I look at his hands and don't see any wedding ring, but when I focus back on his face, I know I've been caught in the act.

"Not for both questions."

The heat in my face increases.

"I didn't understand," I play it off.

"I'm not a guest. I was on the ship because I might buy the fleet. And I'm not married."

I don't even try to save my dignity, as I don't think he'd believe it anyway.

"I can't talk to guests, except to serve them," I explain.

"We're not on the ship."

"That's not all. Most of the men there are married, and it wouldn't be right to talk to you..."

"You —" he commands.

"Okay. It wouldn't be right to talk to you anywhere, if that were the case."

"But I'm not. And I'm not a guest either, so we can skip that part."

"I don't understand."

"Have lunch with me."

"It's still morning. Besides, I came to visit the church. I haven't finished yet. I don't know when I'll have another chance like this in my life," I explain. "But if you want, you can keep me company."

I can't even believe I said something like that, but the truth is, I'm very attracted to him.

Chapter 6

Christos

I can hardly believe what I've just heard.

She wants me to walk alongside her through the church?

Zoe Turner is definitely not even close to belonging in my world. I don't need to bother approaching women I'm interested in. A look usually takes care of everything, and now, as I walk with her inside *La Sagrada Familia*, I wonder what I'm doing here.

In the daylight, the girl looks even younger than I initially thought, and for a moment, I consider backing off because it's obvious she's inexperienced. The problem is, Zoe has kept me thinking about her ever since she ran away yesterday.

No, she captured my complete attention the second I saw those long, perfect legs balancing in those ugly shoes.

"Is this your first time in Spain?"

"My first time outside of Boston," she replies, turning to look at me.

And in that moment, I understand why there's no chance of me backing off. She's too beautiful.

"Your name, Xander Megalos, is Greek? Don't laugh if I'm talking nonsense, but it sounds Greek."

"It is," I reply, not elaborating further.

Purposely, I only gave my middle name and my mother's surname when I introduced myself to her because I'm very well-known worldwide. Since I wasn't sure if anything between us would come of it, I preferred to remain anonymous.

But after five minutes here, I think it was foolish. Zoe probably doesn't know anything about high society—which only makes her even more attractive to me.

"Was I being indiscreet by asking that?"

"What?"

"I'm not very sociable, so I'm not sure how to make conversation."

"Is that what we're doing?"

She shrugs.

"You offered to see the church with me, so I thought..."

"I already know this church. I'm here because I want you. That's also the reason I had someone find out if you'd be leaving the ship today."

I see the movement of her throat as she swallows.

"That's a little scary."

"Probably."

"But also flattering. Thank you."

Is she thanking me for desiring her? Doesn't Zoe have a mirror at home?

"Let's have brunch. It's Sunday, the day you Americans do that."

Again, she avoids answering.

"How did you get a *ticket* to get in here? I bought mine ages ago."

"Everything has a price. Money, connections, you just need to know how to leverage what the other desires and you can get anything."

"That sounds a bit cold."

"Direct, I'd say. I always prefer honesty. Cards on the table."

We're almost at the exit now, and I feel like we haven't made any progress.

"What time do you need to return to the ship?"

"It doesn't leave until five, so I just need to be there by three. I need to walk because I have to buy some souvenirs for my mother."

"Come with me to my yacht."

"Thank you for the invitation, but I don't know you. However, I'd be delighted if you joined me for an espresso."

I look at her to see if she's joking, but her innocent face tells me she's being very serious.

"I have a counteroffer."

"Is this a negotiation?" she asks with blushing cheeks, and I finally see that she's just as interested as I am, but maybe doesn't know how to show it.

"Everything in my life is a negotiation, Zoe."

"What would your proposal be?"

"A coffee to start. A lunch later. I want to get to know you better."

"But I'm leaving today."

"Maybe you don't want to go."

But instead of scaring her off with my usual arrogance, I address her doubts.

"One thing at a time, Zoe. A coffee, and then we decide the rest."

We leave the church and, after navigating through the crowd with my bodyguards just a few steps behind, I spot my car.

But apparently, Zoe also sees it and stops walking.

"I thought we were going to walk."

"Not to where I'm taking you."

"I..."

"Are you an adult, Zoe?"

"Yes."

"Then you'll have to make a decision. I want to get to know you better, but I won't force you. I'm inviting you for a coffee, but not in a place where we'd have to shout to hear each other. It's up to you whether you come with me or not."

"I don't know anything about you."

"You know my name." I extend my hand towards her, asking for her phone, which she holds like a treasure. "Unlock it."

She hesitates but eventually complies.

I open her contacts and save my name and phone number.

Then I call myself.

"And now you have my number too. Share it with anyone you want if it means you'll come with me."

"I'm not a child," she says with a stern face, and even that doesn't lessen her beauty. "I can very well go for a *coffee*"—she emphasizes the word to make it clear to me that it won't go beyond that—"without needing anyone's permission."

"A rebel?"

"Not even close, but I don't like being challenged, Mr. Megalos."

I'm sure she called me 'Mr.' again to provoke me, and it only excites me more.

I don't like pointless arguments, so, placing my hand on the small of her back, I guide her towards the car.

I can't remember the last time I felt so stimulated by a woman.

When you've been in the game of seduction as long as I have, it gets to a point where everything becomes boring and predictable. With Zoe, however, I don't know what's going to happen. Despite her shy nature, she makes it clear she has a personality, and that's making my blood boil.

The driver is waiting for us with the car door open. She turns back and says to me:

"I need to come back here before going to the ship. I haven't bought my mother's souvenir."

"I can take care of that."

As she settles into the back seat, I turn to one of the bodyguards.

"Go to one of those *souvenir* shops and buy one of everything with 'Barcelona' and *'La Sagrada Familia'* on it."

"Yes, sir."

I get into the vehicle, and she's fastening her seatbelt.

"I'm accepting a coffee. Nothing more."

"I don't remember offering anything else, Zoe," I reply, hiding a smile.

Chapter 7

Zoe

Half an hour later

"You're making me talk, but you haven't said much about yourself."

In fact, he's looking at me as if he wants to see inside me. If I weren't so attracted to him, it might scare me, but being the focus of his attention gives me a delicious thrill.

We're on the terrace of a restaurant, alone — just a waiter besides us. He invited me for lunch later, but here we are in a suitable place, and he didn't ask if I wanted a full meal. I think it's because he has plans for me.

Of course, with how eager I am for his presence, I wouldn't be able to eat anyway.

"Maybe I'm a better listener."

"Are you?"

"Usually not, but I like your voice. Actually, everything I've seen in you so far."

I focus on the espresso in front of me.

"You're very direct."

"Life is short, Zoe. I'm not the type of man who beats around the bush. When I want something, I go after it."

"Like me."

"Yes," he replies, and a sense of unease spreads within me. It's not his bluntness, but the casual way he says it.

One doesn't have to be a genius to understand that this isn't the first time he's pursued a woman he wanted.

With that, my bubble bursts. My Cinderella dream, feeling special to him, vanishes in a flash, and the reality behind the picture I wanted to see isn't pretty at all.

Xander wants sex.

For whatever reason, he found me attractive and decided to pursue me.

To mask how much I feel like an idiot, I check the time on my phone.

When I look back at him, I know he immediately realizes that our meeting is over.

"A prolonged lunch on my yacht is out of the question, I suppose."

I nod up and down.

"I need to go," I say, already reaching for my bag. "I have to go back and get my mother's *souvenir*. Besides, it's not just lunch you have in mind."

He doesn't deny it, and as the needy fool that I am, I feel my heart sink.

Before I can stand up, he positions himself behind my chair and helps me up.

Not only is he handsome and fragrant, but he's also very polite.

He doesn't move away, and the warmth of his body against my back makes me shiver.

I don't move but look back.

Sweet Lord Jesus, the man is scandalously good-looking. If I weren't a dreamer hoping to find a prince charming someday, I'd accept without hesitation being his... mistress? Yes, I think that's what men like him have.

I look into his eyes, mentally saying goodbye to the most *sexy* man I've ever met.

The problem is, I may not know much about life, but I know myself. When it's all over, which would be this afternoon since I have to go back to the ship, I'll feel alone and rejected once again.

All the love I received from my biological mother is becoming increasingly distant in my mind. And although my adoptive parents, my earthly angels, have helped heal many wounds, the years in which I barely got used to a family and was then returned left me with a real fear of abandonment.

I'd have to be very crazy or stupid to willingly choose something like that.

He lowers his head and speaks close to my ear.

"My intuition says it would be delightful, Zoe."

His mouth is so close that the temptation to kiss him is overwhelming.

Feeling a bit more confident because I'm resolved to leave, I look him in the eye.

"So do I, but believe me when I say that despite that, neither of us is what the other is looking for."

WE RETURN TO THE CAR, and there are at least three bags with dozens of *souvenirs* inside. I felt really awkward when he told me he had sent his employee to buy them for my mother.

I said I couldn't accept them, but he didn't take no for an answer, so the only option was to thank him, get in the car, and enjoy the ride back to the port.

To my disappointment, he won't be joining me, only instructing the driver where to drop me off.

With the door still open, he's looking at me with such intensity that, for the first time in my life, I want to take a chance, and I do something I never imagined I'd be capable of.

I unfasten my seatbelt and get out of the car, my body almost pressed against his, as he remains by the door.

He doesn't move, looking at me like a predator.

I feel beautiful and desired, and I follow through with my plan. In a burst of boldness, I wrap my arms around his neck and press our lips together.

I don't even know how to kiss a man like him, but I don't think about it; I just know this is my last chance to taste his mouth.

The intention was for it to be a light kiss, but as soon as our lips touch, he wraps his hand around my waist, pulling me against his body.

His fingers tangle in my hair with enough force to tilt my head back, but without hurting me.

"I don't do anything gently, Zoe. Want to kiss me? Let's make it enjoyable."

And then, all those movie descriptions of starry skies, ringing bells, and butterflies in the stomach happen at once as he takes control of the kiss.

True to his promise, his lips devour mine, sucking, biting, his tongue demanding entry, and the intensity of his grip on my hair increasing.

I melt against his body, my skin on fire. My aching breasts, sensitive against his solid chest. My hands come alive, losing themselves in his hair, nails lightly scratching his neck.

I'm so surrendered that I forget everything around me, but he apparently doesn't, as he pulls away, though still holding me by the waist, perhaps sensing that I might not be able to stay upright.

Seconds later, he steps back.

"Changed your mind?" he asks.

"I can't. I want to so much, but I've had my share of abandonment in life."

I quickly return to the car before I lose my nerve, because I know there's a good chance I'll regret missing this chance to dream.

I rest my head against the seat, eyes closed, and hear the door close.

This afternoon will stay in my memory.

You don't meet a man like him and forget it.

Everyone else will fade in comparison to his beauty and masculinity.

I've always been attracted to older men, but never to someone with as much power aura as Xander.

And thinking about that now reminds me of what he said about being interested in buying the cruise fleet. Just another small sample of the chasm between us.

It's not just age or experience that separates us, but wealth as well.

The car drives through the streets of Barcelona, and normally that would excite me — people smiling and chatting carefree, a different scene from my dull life in Boston — but at this moment, all I can think about is our kiss and his gaze on me.

Chapter 8

Zoe

I walk up the ramp to return to the ship, feeling like I'm leaving a dream behind. Yes, I know it's crazy and that there's a good chance this feeling is just a result of my own longing, but what if there's more to it? What if, out of fear, I've let go of something incredible?

The crew members greet me as I walk. According to my calculations, there are still about three hours before the ship departs, so instead of heading straight to the tiny cabin to drop off the bags with the souvenirs, I make my way to the deck to look at the sea.

Some people talk to me, and I recognize a guest or two among them, but I avoid eye contact, both because I'm not one to initiate conversation and because I want to be alone and think about today.

I lean my elbows on the railing and watch the sea.

I'm an adult now, but I haven't experienced much yet. Would it be foolish to dive into something purely physical with the gorgeous Greek?

God, the man's kiss blew me away.

The force of his lips against mine. The urgency and the way his body, without forcing or saying anything, made me surrender to desire.

What would it be like to have someone like him as a boyfriend?

The problem is, he doesn't want a girlfriend. From what I could gather, he was looking for an afternoon of sex, and that doesn't fit into my life.

"Are you going to the crew party tonight?"

I turn to see who spoke to me.

It's one of the first-class waiters, who had never greeted me before. In fact, I've only seen him twice up to now.

"Good afternoon. Party?"

"Yes, this is the penultimate port before we head back home. You're American too, right?"

"I am."

"So, this is my tenth trip, and there's always a pretty lively little party before we get to the last port, just for the crew."

It takes me little time to realize two things. I don't like the way he says that, and I especially don't like the way he's looking at me: like I'm a piece of meat.

In fact, I don't think I like him at all. The whole package.

"I didn't know about any party," I deflect, partly because it's true, partly because I don't want to be in the same place as this guy.

"It'll be much more fun if you go, Zoe. There will be recreational substances there that make everything colorful."

Am I crazy, or did he just imply that there are drugs on the ship?

"Hmm... *okay*. I'll consider it," I lie. "Now, if you'll excuse me," I say, starting to walk away, but he grabs my arm.

"There's nothing to think about, girl. Don't be silly. Our parties are unmatched."

I pull away with a jerk and take two steps back.

"I've said what I wanted, and I understand. Don't touch me again, or I'll report you to the captain."

To my surprise, the threat makes him laugh.

"Good luck with that," he says enigmatically.

I walk away from the unbearable man, incredibly frustrated that he ruined the rest of my afternoon.

I head straight to the cabin, thinking about taking a shower and resting a bit, but when I arrive, it's a mess, with Tamara's clothes scattered everywhere.

I leave my bags on the bed and head to the tiny bathroom with my phone in hand. Ten minutes later, I hear voices coming from the room.

Did Tamara bring someone into our cabin? I mean, I know she's *been with* some crew members and I don't judge, but we agreed she wouldn't do that in our sleeping space.

Thank God I brought the dress and underwear I'm going to wear. I usually do this because she doesn't have much sense, and once she walked in on me while I was changing and left the door wide open for more than a minute, allowing someone passing by the hallway to see me nearly naked.

Since then, I don't change in the room anymore.

I quickly change, but when I'm about to leave, I hear what sounds like moans.

I hesitate, unable to believe what's happening. It's impossible that she's having sex in our dormitory, but the sounds leave little to the imagination.

God, what now?

I'm not a baby, but I don't want to be part of a porno movie.

I take a deep breath while thinking of an escape plan.

Open the door and get out of the room as quickly as I can.

But when I do, I'm nauseated by the scene.

My bag was on the bed, so it's impossible they didn't know I was here. Did they do it on purpose?

Tamara is kneeling, performing oral sex on the captain, who, from what I can see, has only unzipped his pants.

It doesn't seem like an act of two people in love, but something vile that makes my stomach churn.

Without looking at them again, I head to the door, forgetting about my bag and thinking about disappearing as quickly as I can. However, when I turn the handle, it won't open.

I twist the latch and manage to unlock it, but I quickly realize that someone outside is preventing me from leaving.

My hands become sweaty from fear, and when I look back, they're both watching me, smiling.

"Party time," the disgusting man says. "You can stop playing the saint, girl. I know you were on the upper deck without permission, and guess what? A diamond necklace belonging to one of the guests has gone missing tonight. You have two options: kneel down and use that pretty mouth of yours to satisfy me, or be accused of theft in a foreign country."

I'm terrified, but I'd rather be arrested than obey him. They'll have to kill me first.

I run to the bathroom and lock the door, thinking of the only person who could help me.

Xander Megalos.

I search for his name in my phonebook, my heart pounding in my ears.

I almost faint when he answers on the second ring.

"Xander?"

"*Who's calling?*"

"It's me, Zoe."

"*Zoe?*"

"Yes. I need help. I'm locked in the bathroom of my cabin... they... the captain and my roommate... they won't let me out."

Chapter 9

Christos

From the moment she called me, about an hour after we parted ways, until I stepped onto the ship, it took no more than twenty-five minutes.

On the way, I contacted Frank to authorize my entry, as I wouldn't be going through check-in since I'm not a passenger.

Eager to close the deal as it stands, he didn't question why I wanted to come here.

He informed me that an employee would be waiting for me.

The young man was confused when I told him to take me to the cabin Zoe had given me, trying to explain that it was the crew's quarters.

Patience is not my strong suit, especially when it comes to giving explanations, but right now, her safety was at stake.

I still don't quite understand what the hell is going on because the story seems so absurd it's hard to believe.

How is she locked in the bathroom? If it's what I'm thinking, my meeting with the captain won't be pretty. If he touched her, he can kiss his career goodbye.

While we were on the phone, I tried to get her to explain what happened, but she sounded too nervous and was rambling. Something about a necklace disappearing last night and them blackmailing her.

However, everything starts to make sense when, upon arriving with my security at the cabin the crew member directed me to, I see a guy lounging, arms crossed, as if guarding the way.

"Get out." My voice is as thunderous as a storm.

"If you're a guest, this is the crew's area."

I grab him by the collar.

"Get out of my way."

This time he seems to understand and, looking scared, steps aside.

"Open the door," I say to the employee who brought me here.

"I'm not sure I can do that."

I pick up the phone and quickly complete the call.

"Frank, I want to enter one of the crew's cabins. This will influence my decision to close the deal. Any problem?"

"*I'm not understanding anything, Christos.*"

"Just yes or no, Frank."

"*Yes, of course.*"

"I'll pass the phone to your employee."

Before they can speak, however, the door opens and the son of a bitch of a captain comes out, adjusting his shirt into his pants.

I go wild. Several possible scenarios flash through my mind.

No matter how much money I have now. My spirit is still that of a Greek island boy, used to physical confrontations and defending my views with my fists.

"Where is she?" I ask, pinning him against the wall, my fingers clawing at his throat.

"Are you insane? Let me go. Who?"

The man turns purple, the cynical smile he had when he opened the door disappearing.

"Zoe Turner."

The recognition in his face shows me she was telling the truth.

"Don't let him leave," I instruct my bodyguards, already heading for the room.

"You can't keep me here. I'm the highest authority on this ship."

"And at this moment, I've become your employer," I say, making a decision. "But you can also call me God."

As I see my men positioning themselves to prevent him from escaping, I enter the cabin.

There's a half-naked woman lying on the bed, but no sign of Zoe. When she sees me, she tries to cover herself.

"Zoe, it's me," I call out.

"Xander?"

Maybe it's time to correct the misunderstanding and tell her that everyone knows me as Christos and no one calls me by my second name, but somehow, I hold back the information. Even with the madness of the situation, I like the idea that she doesn't know who I am for now.

"Yes, it's me. Open the door. You're safe now."

Seconds later, I hear the sound of the latch being undone, but I wasn't prepared for what happens next.

A Zoe with a tear-streaked face throws herself into my arms as if I were her safe harbor, and something entirely unknown spreads within me.

Forgetting everyone around us, I hold her, touching her soft hair.

"Let's get out of here."

"The ship will be leaving soon."

"No, it won't, because I'll call the police. But that doesn't matter. It won't continue its voyage. If you want to go home, fine. But come with me. There's no way I'm leaving you unprotected here."

She pulls back a little to look at me, and I wait for her decision.

Seconds later, comes the response I was hoping for.

"Okay."

Barcelona — Spain

Two Hours Later

SHE'S RESTING IN THE suite of my apartment. After I had a doctor come to examine her and made sure my maid would take care of what she needed, I contacted my lawyers to handle the legal matters.

I decided to keep the fleet of ships — which was what I wanted anyway — but I will reformulate all the rules about relationships between crew members because, according to what my lawyers explained, it's not uncommon for such harassment from senior officers towards the crew.

I wanted to be present when they questioned that Tamara, and from what she said, she was having a consensual relationship with the captain. Up to that point, it wasn't my problem, but what she revealed next was.

She said that since dinner yesterday, when I first saw Zoe, there had been a plan by Bentley Williams to seduce her, which is why she was called to serve as a waitress in his cabin. But since I showed up and asked to tour the ship, the bastard didn't have a chance to keep her there any longer.

They went to the room to have sex knowing that Zoe had already returned and with the intention of persuading her to the *party*, but when she opened the door and caught them, she was so shocked that she locked herself in the bathroom.

She also revealed that the captain tried to blackmail her about a supposedly stolen necklace, which was a lie because there was no missing jewelry. He counted on Zoe being inexperienced and in a foreign country. He thought that if she felt afraid, she would give in.

When he didn't get results even with the threats, he wanted to force open the bathroom door, but with a shred of conscience, she convinced him not to, promising to reward him for the absence of her friend.

Friend, my ass! Friends don't conspire or betray.

According to her account, it wouldn't be the first time the man used more aggressive methods to convince someone in the crew to have sex with him. When verbal threats weren't enough, he resorted to physical coercion, and at least on one occasion, used the *Goodnight Cinderella* method.

These are serious allegations, but without proof beyond what happened today, they remain rumors, the lawyers said.

I had to use all my self-control not to kill the bastard. I don't like to think about what could have happened if the situation had been different and it had just been him and Zoe in the room.

I instructed my lawyers to dig into the man's life and punish him as much as possible. I will also make sure he never works in this position again.

I'm entering my apartment after nearly four hours at the police station when, as I turn after closing the door, I come face-to-face with the woman who, without fear of being wrong, became the only one in my life in the blink of an eye. From someone I felt insanely attracted to, Zoe has become the one I needed to protect.

I've never walked this road before, so instead of planning, as I do with everything in my universe, I decide to let life show me the next step.

Chapter 10

Christos

For the first time in my life, I don't know how to act.

Initially, I was so mesmerized by her beauty, the perfect body and angelic face, that I didn't even consider our age difference, but now, dressed in a huge robe for her delicate body, her hair wet from the bath and without any makeup, I realize that Zoe is just a girl.

I don't need to think for long, though, because without any indication of what she would do next, just like on the ship, she comes to me.

There is no hesitation. She wraps her arms around my neck, pressing our bodies together.

The woman has the power to trigger a side of me that has never surfaced with anyone I've been sexually involved with: the protective instinct.

"Thank you."

I don't want to speak. Not yet. I prefer to smell her freshly bathed body. The feminine curves molded to me and the way her fingers caress my neck.

I'm tense with desire because she awakens an animalistic longing in me, but I know that's not what she needs right now.

"Did you manage to sleep?"

She pulls away, finally seeming to become aware of what she's done.

"Yes, and I'm sorry for attacking you. I'm not usually so forward, but..."

I place my fingers over her lips.

"You had a hellish day and I'm the only familiar face."

"It's not that, but if I explain, you'll think I'm immature."

Despite all the shit we went through today, I smile.

"Try me."

"I usually like hugs and hate being alone. When I saw you, I did what I felt like."

"Hugging me?"

"Yes," she says, looking at the floor.

There is a submissiveness in her that excites me immensely because I know it's part of her temperament, but at the same time, she knows how to stand her ground when necessary, as she did when she refused me earlier.

"Are you hungry?" I ask, trying with all my might to focus on something neutral.

"Yes."

"Do you want to go out for dinner?"

"First, tell me what happened with the police."

I quickly explain what happened, not hiding the worst details, including Tamara's report that he had even drugged a crew member.

When I finish speaking, she is so pale that I think she might faint.

"Sit down."

She looks around, seeming lost.

I pick her up and place her on the sofa. When I look down, the robe has opened slightly, exposing a bit of her thigh. I step back to avoid giving in to the temptation to touch her. I'm not a boy. If all goes as I plan, I'll have plenty of time to get to know every inch of her delicious body.

"I can't believe they planned something like this for me. How could Tamara betray me like this?"

God, she's too innocent for this world.

"Was I naive?" she asks, as if she could read my thoughts.

"No. I think anyone in your place would be shocked. I'm an experienced guy and never imagined a situation like this."

"I need to call my mother. Can I use your phone? Oh my God! And my suitcase?"

"I had it brought. You were probably asleep when it arrived."

"I don't even know how to take the next step. I mean, I'll need to buy a plane ticket to go back home, but they haven't paid my salary for this week. I have to find a way to get it."

Her cheeks are burning, and I quickly understand that she has no means to return to the United States without receiving the payment from the ship.

"That won't be a problem."

"How can it not be? Oh, Jesus, I need to talk to Mom."

"Use the phone if you want. I can also arrange for your return to the United States, but first, I have a proposal for you."

"A proposal?" she asks, suddenly looking alert.

I know I'm probably racking up more time in hell for what I'm about to say, but she is irresistible.

"Yes. Spend some time with me in Europe. I won't be returning to the United States before the end of the summer, so let's get to know each other better."

I've never gone this far with a woman. What I'm proposing to Zoe is being tied to the same person for over a month.

She opens her mouth and closes it again, as if she's deciding, but finally says:

"We don't know anything about each other."

"We'll have time for that, but for now, no promises or expectations."

"Was that what I did earlier? Did I expect something from you?"

"No, actually you argued, and I respect you for that."

"What you wanted from me when you invited me to lunch this morning wasn't to get to know me better," I say.

"No. I wanted you, and that was all."

Once again, her beautiful mouth opens in a look of astonishment.

"You are brutally honest."

"Yes. Does that scare you?"

"I'm not sure, but I think I prefer honesty. If I say I'll stay with you, what does that imply?"

"Whatever we both want."

She may be young, but she's not so naive and understands perfectly what I'm not saying.

She looks at the floor.

"If I say yes, I need to let my mother know anyway and give her your address too."

"That won't be a problem, but I plan to leave on my boat. I don't want to stay in the city."

"Why not?"

"A lot of people know me. I want privacy with you."

"First, I'll accept your invitation for dinner. Then I'll decide about your proposal. I need to think, but either way" she stands up, moves close to the armchair where I'm sitting, and extends her hand "I want to thank you again."

I part my legs and pull her between them.

Still holding my hand, with the other she plays with the tie of her robe. She follows the movement, her breath quickening, but doesn't try to pull away.

"I want you. To taste every inch of you, Zoe, but the decision about staying with me is in your hands. If you want to go home, all you need to do is tell me."

"I've never done anything like this before."

"I figured as much."

"And you still want me?"

I stand up and hold her face with both hands, my thumbs caressing her cheeks.

I lower myself to speak near her ear, letting my lips brush against her earlobe.

"I don't usually repeat myself, but maybe you need a sample."

I nip, let my tongue run over the soft flesh, and she shivers against me, but I don't go too far. She needs to have the courage to decide, so I force myself to pull away.

"Go get changed. We'll leave in half an hour."

Chapter 11

Zoe

That Night

"Don't you ever eat a meal around other people?" I ask.

We're once again in a private area of the restaurant, although when we entered and walked between the tables, I saw several heads turning to watch us.

I know it wasn't because of me, so it must be because of him. Who is the man I'm with? I mean, I know his name and that he's very wealthy, but I now think he's famous too.

It might sound crazy, but even without knowing much about him besides his name, I feel safe with Xander. He conveys honesty and character.

Self-confidence and arrogance too, of course. But mainly, something that's crucial in my world: he makes me feel valued — or rather, desired.

Before we came to dinner, I called my mom. I didn't go into detail about what happened on the ship, just that I couldn't continue the trip because I wasn't feeling well inside. I said I'd be staying another week in Europe, even though I haven't fully decided on his proposal yet. It took a good fifteen minutes to convince her not to worry, although I didn't tell her I'd be with a man.

How could I, when I don't even know exactly what we are?

"In public places, if I can avoid it, no," he finally answers.

"Why not?"

"I don't like noise or having to shout to hear the person I'm talking to."

"Especially me, right? I mean, everyone says my voice is just a whisper."

He leans back in his restaurant chair, as if needing a bit more space to watch me.

"Out of shyness?" he asks, not denying it.

"I think so. Or maybe because, like you, I also dislike shouting. I've had too much of it in my life."

I see his forehead crease in confusion and immediately regret talking too much. Talking about my past is definitely not a good way to start whatever we're doing here.

"Why was there shouting in your past?"

"It's not a pleasant conversation to have over dinner."

"Life isn't always pleasant, Zoe, but I can handle it."

"I'm adopted. I lost my parents when I was young. I was taken in and rejected... um... several times. Most homes weren't made up of people who truly wanted a child, but the idea of having a child, of being parents. Children are a lot of work, and I think after a while, they decided I wasn't worth it."

As usual, I can't look at him while I tell this.

"How many times were you returned?"

I play with the fabric napkin.

"After a while, you lose count, but that's in the past" I lie, because only God knows how much it hurt every time I saw the pity in the social worker's face when they took me back. "I was adopted permanently at eleven, and since then I've had wonderful parents."

When I look back at him, his face is serious and his jaw clenched.

"What happened to your biological parents?"

"They both died. A few years apart. I don't even remember my father anymore, to be honest. I remember Mom, but it gets harder every day to recall our time together."

"How old are you?"

For the first time since this conversation started, I breathe a sigh of relief.

"Eighteen and a half. Too young?"

One of his fingers plays with his lower lip, and it's a bit hypnotic.

"Mm-hmm. I thought you were at least in your twenties."

"And you?"

"Thirty-five. Is that a problem?" he mimics my question.

"No. What you made me feel when you kissed me is much more important than our age difference."

After what I say, something changes in his face. I don't know enough about men, but I think it's desire. His gaze sends shivers down my spine.

Until now, he seemed to be studying me, giving no hint of what he thought about me, but now, I feel in every drop of blood in my body that he wants me.

Yes, I know he's already said that, but the fact is I don't believe much in words or promises. I've had a bunch of them in my life, and all of them were broken.

Now, however, I feel his wanting, and it makes me eager to experience more of whatever he has to teach me.

"Are we done?"

"Yes, we're done. Are we going home?"

"Not yet. I had something different in mind. Do you like to dance?"

"I love it, why?"

"There's a nightclub owned by a friend of mine a few minutes from here."

"I thought you didn't like crowds."

"This one has a private floor. We'll have privacy."

"Are you doing this for me?"

"Yes. After what you went through today, you deserve a bit of fun."

Hazard Nightclub

Barcelona

"YOU WEREN'T KIDDING when you said you liked to dance," he says, whispering in my ear as he moves very close to me.

We're in a *lounge* that seems to be the *VIP* section of the nightclub. This is only the second club I've been to, the other one being with high school friends.

There's no comparison to my first experience, though. Everything is so chic. Even the mirrors and chairs look luxurious.

There are no people around us, and I notice that even here, Xander's bodyguards are nearby, preventing anyone from approaching.

"I usually dance alone at home. Music makes me travel."

His hands are on my hips and my heartbeat is racing. He's not just drop-dead gorgeous but also incredibly *sexy*.

The way he looks at me makes me want to press my body against his, to be bold, but where does shyness allow that?

As if reading my desire, he moves closer, pulling me nearer.

"And what else makes you travel, beautiful Zoe?"

I lift my face to meet his gaze.

"I don't know yet, but I want to learn. Can you teach me?"

Before I can even take a breath, our mouths meet. At first, it's a kiss that seems more like mutual exploration. Lips touching, tongues, teeth.

Soon, however, I feel the firmness of his muscular body taking over me completely. Making me wish to be naked, melting in his arms.

Wanting more, I move my hips, undulating against his body, inviting him.

"I want to teach you everything, but not here. Shall we go?"

I know he's not just talking about going home, and if I had any brain cells functioning properly, I'd probably say no. But I'm not sure how long we'll be together, and despite my fear of living — and consequently suffering — I desire him too much to resist.

"Yes. I'm ready."

Chapter 12

Christos

This wasn't what I had planned; it was meant to be a slow conquest.

Although my motto is not to waste time, I know Zoe is special. Very young as well, which, for the first time, made me consider an alternative route, not diving straight into sex.

To keep her with me for a while and get to know each other, because she makes me want more than I've ever wanted with anyone else, even before we've slept together, and that's unprecedented for me.

These were good plans and intentions, but the fiery chemistry between us has its own rules.

Even in the car, while the driver drove through the streets of Barcelona, our mouths didn't part. Hands seeking each other, eager for touch, pure, violent, and uncontrollable electricity.

Zoe's curiosity, her raw desire, sent my plans straight to hell. I feel like a teenager, crazy to taste his first girlfriend in the backseat, when, in fact, I'm an experienced man with a sexual past close to debauchery.

I barely realized we had arrived home, and when I stepped out of the private elevator, I already had her in my arms. Like a caveman, I went straight to the bedroom without even thinking of slowing down or taking it easy.

The number of women who've been in my bed would make an average man blush. I like sex, and although I've never met anyone who sparked my desire with such fury before, I'm more than accustomed to carnal attraction.

There's something about her, however, that transcends the physical.

The primitive need to have her naked beneath me, an urgency bordering on madness.

I set her down after we enter the bedroom and open the door, bringing her out onto the rooftop terrace.

Her breathing is shallow as she watches me in the dim light.

I don't touch her. I keep my distance, but inside I'm racing, desire impossible to contain.

Ravenous lust, wanting to lose myself in her beautiful body.

I take a step closer.

"I've never..."

"I know, beautiful Zoe."

I run my finger along the strap of her dress, playing with lowering it.

"Every time you touch me, my whole body tingles."

"Physical attraction," I say, trying to convince both of us.

She doesn't respond, just looks at me with those eyes that seem like precious stones.

I turn on the central sound system with my phone, and a slow song begins to play.

"Shall we dance?" I smile, shyly.

"Why not?" I offer my hand and she comes closer.

Before taking her into my arms, I remove my blazer and leave it on a chair.

When I finally have her close, she seems impatient and hugs me.

"Is it right to feel so secure and intimate with someone I barely know?"

"Explain yourself better. I want to hear you. Tell me what you're thinking right now," I whisper in her ear.

"Being close to you makes me shiver and tremble. I don't know the script in a situation like this, but I want everything."

I nibble her ear lightly, and she moans.

I reach for the zipper on her back and unzip the short, simple dress, the blue of her eyes.

"I'm not embarrassed by you, and that's strange."

"Maybe our bodies recognize each other."

"Do you believe in that? Destiny?"

She's in lingerie and heels now. I step back to look at her.

She tries to cover her breasts and the front of her panties, looking very embarrassed.

"No, I want to see you."

She moves her hands away and looks at me. The innocence in her face touches something deep inside me.

"You're beautiful, Zoe Turner. And to answer your question, I don't know if I believe in destiny, but the universe aligns to make things happen. One minute more or less — I say, coming closer and placing my hands on her slim waist — would have been enough for us to never meet, but here we are.

Everything in me pulses, throbs, burns for her. Like a fire that can't be contained.

The desire for Zoe is like a storm, overwhelming in its force.

I tell myself there's no reason to rush; she's here, and at this moment, she's mine. But a feverish lust dominates my body and mind.

She seems to sense my need, and her fingers play with the buttons of my shirt.

"Open up," I command.

One by one, she frees them from their housings, focused on the task.

When she finishes, I release the cuffs of my shirt, and she slides it off my shoulders. Her action shows me that she's also caught in the same web of desire as I am because she doesn't seem to be the type who takes the initiative.

She looks at my bare chest and licks her lips, embarrassed but also covetous.

The combination of shyness with boldness ignites me, turning my blood into lava.

"You will look at me the entire time, Zoe. I've never wanted a woman as much as I want you, but I won't do anything without being certain you're with me all the way."

"Where? Where are we going?"

"Into each other."

She now looks at me openly, lust surpassing her naturally gentle demeanor.

I move my hand between us and touch her breast covered by the lingerie. Zoe shivers, and her reaction only confirms what I already suspected: she's sensitive, and when we make love, it will be delicious.

Maintaining any barrier is unacceptable, so I move my hand to her back and undo the clasp of her bra.

I feel, before I see, her hard nipples brushing against me. She shifts, perhaps unconsciously, and moans from the friction of her nipples against my chest.

I kiss her mouth, her neck, tracing a descending path to her cleavage. I lift my head to look at her while letting my tongue touch the rigid mound. She gasps and her legs buckle.

I pick her up because a moonlit seduction for a virgin might be more than she can handle.

Back in the bedroom, I try to lay her down on the bed, but she sits up.

"Are you going to get naked too?"

Incredibly, she no longer seems shy but rather curious.

"Is that what you want?" I ask, hand on the belt buckle.
A nod is my answer.

Chapter 13

Christos

I remove my pants, but not the boxers yet. I move to where she is and grip the inside of her thighs with both hands, feeling them against my fingers. She spreads them willingly, reclining on the bed, supported on her elbows.

I replace my hands with my lips, and Zoe moans softly.

Damn, she's a turn-on.

"I'm going to undress you for myself."

I pull down her panties, and she follows every movement. When I see her pussy with its short, light-colored hair for the first time, my mouth waters.

I tease her nipples, either caressing them with my thumb or pinching them with my index and middle fingers.

She moans and whimpers. She sits up on the bed.

"Learn to touch yourself. Have you ever done that?"

"No."

I take her hand and suck on her fingertips, then place it on her right breast.

"Like this, move it and find out what you like."

When she does as I instructed, I growl, wild with desire, and suck on her left breast, enjoying every moment.

Hungry, I cup both breasts with my hands, sucking them simultaneously.

She grabs my hair, pulling me closer.

Zoe melts with pleasure in my mouth, and I've barely started.

My fingers trace a path to the apex of her thighs.

I bite her nipple at the exact moment my thumb grazes her clitoris, and she almost lifts off the bed.

The force of my desire makes me want to take her all at once, hard and deep, but although I don't know much about virgins, since my partners are always experienced, I know this first time will be important to her.

I alternate between sucking and biting her breasts, recording her moans in my memory.

She's watching me, her eyes clouded with passion but also vulnerable, and it stirs something deep within me.

Zoe is a unique blend of devastating beauty, almost indecent sexuality, and a purity that unsettles me.

I spread her thighs, letting my hand explore the soaked pussy, feeling the warm softness.

She writhes against my fingers, instinctively chasing her pleasure.

When she moans and closes her eyes, a frightening feeling hits me, along with a voice echoing: *mine*.

I silence her, pushing her away, forcing myself to remain focused solely on the sexual pleasure.

I watch the outline of her lips swollen from my kisses. Her skin is warm with excitement, her breathing heavy.

She watches intently, but when I separate my lips from her pussy and suck on her clitoris, she goes wild.

I lick her sex with my mouth open, my tongue tasting her untouched interior for the first time.

I indulge in her body, not missing a single curve or indentation, not allowing myself to stop until every part of her has been tasted. When she orgasms, filling my mouth, I drink it all, sucking and swallowing, and it's not enough.

We're completely lost in the purest desire. Entangled with each other, forgotten about the world outside.

At this moment, all I want is to be inside her. There's nothing beyond this need.

Here, with me, Zoe is air and food.

I rise, and she looks confused.

Without stopping to look at her, I lower my boxers.

Her eyes widen. My cock is hard, thick, heavy, and I masturbate it slowly, gathering a bit of pre-cum from the tip.

I move closer and press my thumb against her lips.

"Suck it. Taste me."

She opens her mouth slightly, and I rub the liquid on her lower lip. Her tongue touches it, and she closes her eyes, savoring.

"Later today, I'll teach you to take me all the way in your mouth, but not now."

When she looks at me again, there's no fear, only need.

I position myself over her body, our mouths joining in an almost violent clamor.

The kiss isn't gentle but as hard and impetuous as my desire.

I hold her left breast, nibbling it lightly, and she screams, whimpering that she wants more.

I let a finger penetrate her halfway, massaging her inside, preparing her for me.

I watch in fascination as the shy girl transforms into a demanding, wild cat.

My cock is pure steel, and when she orgasms for the second time, I can't wait any longer.

I stand up to grab a condom and put it on in record time.

I position myself over her body again and test a light touch, moving only a few centimeters.

"Will it hurt?"

"A little, I think, but don't focus on that, think about the pleasure I'll give you afterward."

She bites her lip.

"I shouldn't, but I trust you."

I push just enough to make her feel the head of my cock, but she writhes, as if she knows what I need.

Damn, she's naturally sensual, even without knowing much about sex.

I move my hips, taking her in more.

I lick her nipple, and she grips my shoulders tightly. The intensity of her desire destroys any remaining restraint, and I penetrate her in one long thrust.

"Ahhhhh... it hurts."

"Just a little, beautiful. Don't move, it'll pass."

I kiss her mouth, playing with my tongue in her warmth. I rotate my hips so she can feel me, but also to help her relax for me.

"You're so tight, Zoe. You have a delicious pussy."

She moans and bites my chest.

"I like it when you say dirty things. Keep going."

She tries to move too, and I begin a slow rhythm, preparing her for what's to come.

"Oh, God!"

She pulses around my erection, and the restraint to not fuck her hard is killing me. When one of her legs lifts to wrap around my waist, I lose control.

I thrust a few more times in this position, and when she starts moaning loudly and scratching me, I alternate between deeper thrusts with long strokes.

Her hips rise, as if she can't wait to get more.

"Has the pain passed?"

"It still hurts, but I need all of you inside me."

Damn, she's so fucking delicious!

I brace myself on my elbows, thrusting at a steady rhythm, and reach down to her hard clitoris.

I massage the pleasure point until her breathing shows me she's about to climax. I don't stop until her last spasm subsides, and only then do I kneel on the bed, bringing both her thighs to my shoulders.

Her eyes are shining, glazed with desire.

I pull almost all the way out and slide back in slowly so she can get used to it.

In this position, she's going to feel me very deep.

"Show me everything, I want you," she begs.

I penetrate her to the base, the hair brushing. She closes around me like a tight glove, her inner walls convulsing.

Zoe is small, and my cock is very thick. I don't want to hurt her, but when she moves, moaning, I give her what she's asking for.

She's almost bent in half, her knees touching her chest, and the position has me on the edge, very close to climax.

Our mouths devour each other as the rhythm of our fucking speeds up, our bodies sweating.

I increase the speed, and it's like being hit by an electric shock. Each time my cock enters and exits her virgin body, I reach nirvana.

I maintain a relentless pounding, in and out, and she starts to deliriously plead for more and warns me she's about to climax.

The thrusts inside her are deep, and I know I'm close to my own orgasm as well.

I bite her nipples, but when I reach to touch her clitoris so she can come with me, she delivers another orgasm in an endless moan, her back arched, her pussy squeezing me even tighter.

I silence her passionate laments, filling her completely. My cock in her pussy, my tongue in her mouth.

For a long time, the dance of our bodies dominates the stillness of the early morning, the rhythm of our sex like an erotic music.

I suck her breasts, determined to make her come again, and when her hips start to move in circles, trying to reach her own climax, I pinch her clitoris.

"Now, Zoe."

It's like flipping a switch. She becomes even wilder, locking her legs around me, and we reach paradise almost simultaneously.

She's still with her eyes closed, lost in the ecstasy of our act, but I can't stop watching her.

Beautiful, naked, surrendered, and now, a woman.

And at this moment, I make a decision.

Zoe will be mine for an indefinite time.

Chapter 14

Zoe

I wake up not wanting to open my eyes.

I've always liked dreaming, but today reality is better.

The heat and scent of his body are still on me, embedded in my skin and senses, and I love this feeling.

I know he's already gotten up.

I moved around a lot during the night and I'm sprawled across the bed. There's no way he could have been here without me feeling it.

God, I can't believe I did that.

I lost my virginity to a stranger, a man whose only name I know.

No— I correct myself quickly— I know much more about him than just his name. Xander saved me, helped me when I needed it.

Despite what he did, choosing to stay with him—and yes, I'm already decided to stay until the end of the summer—has nothing to do with him being my hero yesterday, but because he makes me feel complete.

How crazy is that? Without knowing each other well, I feel more whole next to him than I have my entire life.

Despite the attraction he stirred in me, I didn't know what to expect, but certainly not what happened all through the night. To be honest, I was a bit afraid of sex. Not the act itself, but being naked in front of someone or allowing my body to be touched intimately.

However, since that kiss at his car door, when I thought we'd never see each other again, it felt like we'd been doing this forever.

Sighing, I surrender to the fact that I need to get up and go look for my phone to check the time.

I find it strange not to see my clothes scattered on the floor but neatly folded on an armchair. He must be organized, which is exactly the opposite of me.

As I'm about to enter the bathroom, I notice a note on top of my dress.

"Sleep as long as you want. My housekeeper will serve you breakfast as soon as you wake up. I had to leave."

The words are a cold shower and make my stomach clench.

Casual, dry, direct.

Without calling me by name or signing off with his.

I guess in his world, what happened between us was common, but not in mine. Of course, I wasn't expecting a marriage proposal, but at least that he'd be in the apartment when I woke up.

God, where did I get myself into?

How should I act? Is this note some kind of sign, meaning now that he's gotten what he wanted from me, I should leave? That he's changed his mind?

I shake my head. I need a shower and a cup of coffee. I can't think clearly yet.

HALF AN HOUR LATER, after my shower, I feel more lost than ever, and it doesn't get any better when, upon entering the kitchen, a woman looks me up and down as if I shouldn't be here.

Maybe part of this feeling comes from my natural insecurity, but people usually smile when they meet someone, even if just out of politeness. Instead, she simply asks me to sit so she can serve my breakfast.

I barely eat, nervous and desperate to leave, because that's who I am.

After a few sips of coffee, within minutes, I'm already on my feet, thinking of getting out of here quickly, when she intercepts my path and hands me an envelope.

The handwriting was the same as the note, so I assume it must be from Xander, and just to confirm, I ask her:

"Mr. Christos, you mean."

"No. Xander Megalos, your employer, right?"

"No one calls him that, although it is his full name: Christos Xander Megalos Lykaios. The whole world only knows him as Christos Lykaios," she says, frowning and looking at me with even more disdain, probably because I don't even know the name of the man I slept with.

But I'm no longer concerned with what she thinks of me, only with the discovery.

"Christos Lykaios. Christos Lykaios. Christos Lykaios..." — I repeat over and over as I leave the kitchen.

It can't be, my God! Life wouldn't be that cruel.

I walk to the bedroom, too horrified to believe it's true, and to distract myself from the panic I'm in, I open the envelope. Inside, there's money and another note.

"I thought you might need this."

I start to shake. He's paying me for the night of sex?

This only confirms that what I've discovered is true. I slept with the same despicable person who destroyed Pauline's life.

Stunned, I search for the name Christos Lykaios on *Google*.

Yes, it's him. Christos Lykaios, graduated from *Massachusetts College*, the same place near where the accident happened. He's the one who ruined my best friend's future.

A cruel man enough to offer me payment for a night of sex, even knowing I was a virgin before we slept together.

I throw my things haphazardly into my suitcase and leave the apartment without even bothering to say goodbye to the woman, Soraia.

I left a note on the bed, not because I think he deserves it, but to make sure he knows I never want to see him again.

A few words, but easily understood.

"Do not contact me. What happened was a mistake I will regret for the rest of my days."

Just like him, I did not say goodbye.

He doesn't deserve any consideration. He deserves nothing.

An hour and a half later

I'M IN LINE WAITING to board the plane when I notice a woman staring at me intently.

Even though I'm shy, I have a friendly nature, and if people start a conversation, I usually join in. Today, however, I just want to be alone.

I haven't cried yet, but my heart is shattered. Guilt is eating away at me like acid from the inside.

So, when she takes a few steps closer, I seriously consider dodging her, but I'm not rude.

"Hi, how are you?" she greets, and my first thought is that she must be confusing me with someone else.

"Hi," I reply, forcing myself to engage in the conversation.

"Are you a model?"

"What?" Of all the things I expected her to say, this wasn't one of them.

"I'm asking if you've ever worked as a model," she says, smiling, but then shakes her head. "Sorry, I'm being rude. My name is Bia Ramos, I'm a scout from an agency, and out of habit, I'm always looking for new faces. You're perfect."

"Forgive me for being honest, but this sounds crazy."

"I know, my approach wasn't the best, but I noticed you're about to board, and I didn't want to miss the opportunity. What's your name?"

"Zoe Turner."

She extends her hand, and I hesitate, but finally, I shake it.

"Nice to meet you, Zoe. How about this? I'll leave you my card, and you can look me up on the *internet* to make sure I'm not a *serial killer*."

She's smiling as she says this, and I end up relaxing a little.

I take the card she offers.

"What do you expect from me?"

"A test in front of the cameras, although I have no doubts that I'll hire you."

"Look, I'm flattered by what you're saying, but I'm having the worst day of my life, and believe me when I say that's a big deal because I've had several bad days, so I'll take your card and we can talk later, but today I really want to be alone."

"That's fine, Zoe. Just promise me you'll call."

"You have my word."

Chapter 15

Christos

The last thing I wanted was to leave the house before she woke up, but my plans went off the rails the moment my phone buzzed early in the morning with a message from the lawyers.

We needed to decide on the type of publicity we would give regarding the ship issue, as if everything comes to light, the acquisition of the fleet will become a mistake. The stock prices will plummet.

I ordered a thorough investigation to be conducted and the culprits brought to light. In this case, I think transparency would be the best solution, although I'm not too enthusiastic about involving Zoe's name in a scandal. Besides being very young, if what I intend to happen — staying with her without a defined end — becomes reality, the press won't give her peace.

My intention was to have breakfast together and clear up the confusion about my name. After yesterday, there was no reason not to come clean.

I think about the blonde goddess tangled in my sheets when I got up. She was a bit dazed, exhausted, and I wonder if I might have pushed too hard for our first night together. But then I remember that the second and third times, it was she who sought me out while I was trying to keep myself under control, fearing I might hurt her.

Zoe, despite her inexperience, is a sexual whirlwind, and soon she'll know everything about her own body. I want to be the one to teach her how to discover herself.

I've never made plans beyond a weekend with my girlfriends, but I find myself wondering if there would be room for her in my life when we return to the United States, since that's where my primary residence is.

She told me, in our conversation at the restaurant, that she lives in Boston but dreams of living in a rural property — which doesn't seem to fit at all with the stunning woman she is.

The kind of life she aspires to couldn't be further from mine. I have no connection to the countryside; I'm a man of the world, not so much by choice, but because of my business.

Anyway, I'd like to explore this intense sexual attraction further. It's only been a little over three hours since I left her, and I already feel eager to return to the apartment and lose myself in her *sexy* body.

Before leaving, I left a note saying that Soraia, my housekeeper, would be available to serve her breakfast. Shy as she is, I don't doubt she would have been hungry until I arrived, and I have no idea what time that will be.

I also left my housekeeper an envelope with more than double the payment she would receive from the ship. I don't want her to feel financially dependent on my side, although the amount that represents her salary is, to me, equivalent to the cost of a cup of coffee.

"Are you sure you want to close the deal?" my analyst asks, referring to the ships.

"Yes, I'm not going back on my word. How much longer will this meeting last?"

"Half an hour."

I run my hand through my hair, irritated, my thoughts completely focused on the beautiful woman waiting for me.

I slept beside her, which is a novelty because I never stay the whole night with a girlfriend. Sharing sleep with someone can lead to unrealistic expectations, and my life is always black and white, with any other colors excluded. But when she lay on top of me and I felt the warmth of her body, her soft breath, and her hands in my hair, any chance of me getting up disappeared.

The need for her is a kind of addiction, a compulsion that only grows the longer I stay by her side.

Along with that, the complete lack of desire to leave, was the fact that she went through too much crap yesterday.

I'm normally not a sensitive guy, but Zoe is in a foreign country, and I'm the only person she knows.

"Not a minute more," I determine to the men seated in front of me. "Time is already ticking. Make it count."

I CAN'T REMEMBER THE last time I felt this anxious to see a woman again. *Never...* would be a good guess.

As I enter the elevator to my penthouse, it's as if electricity is coursing through my body.

I plan to take her to the yacht later today, but right now, all I want is to be with her again.

I enter the code to unlock the door, and before I can open it, someone inside does it for me, but it's not Zoe, it's Soraia.

Strange. She should have left by now.

"Dr. Lykaios, I waited for you to arrive so I could inform you personally."

Her words trigger my concern immediately. Something must have happened to Zoe.

Damn it, I shouldn't have left her alone.

I walk into the apartment without looking at my staff member, heading straight for the bedroom.

"Dr. Lykaios..." the woman continues to call me, and I stop at the top of the stairs.

"Not now, Soraia. I need to speak with my... guest."

"But that's exactly what I'm trying to tell you. She's gone. About three hours ago, she left without saying goodbye."

"What do you mean *gone*?"

"She ate very little at breakfast. So, I handed her the envelope as you instructed. About fifteen minutes later, I heard the front door slam. When I checked the security camera, she was already at the lobby."

"Are you sure she left with her suitcase?"

She might have needed to buy something.

"Yes, with her suitcase," she says, and it may be crazy, but she seems satisfied.

Soraia is a staff member who is sent to my residences in Europe whenever I spend an extended period somewhere, although her fixed location is my apartment in London. She doesn't stay at any of my properties while I am there, though. Even though she's an excellent employee, sometimes I feel like she oversteps her duties.

"You can leave now."

"Do you need anything else, Dr. Lykaios?"

"I've said you can leave, Soraia."

She turns her back.

"Just one more thing. Why didn't you call me to let me know Zoe had left?"

"I didn't think it was important."

"Let's clear something up: I decide what's important in my life. Your job is to report any unusual occurrences in my properties. Am I clear?"

"Yes, sir."

I turn my back and head for the suite, still hoping that this could all be a misunderstanding.

Of course, I barely know her, but from what she's shown, Zoe doesn't seem like the type of girl who would run away without a word.

When I arrive at the bedroom, the first thing I see is a sheet of paper on the bed.

I'm not one to hesitate about anything, but I find myself slowing my steps before reaching it.

I'm angry with myself for acting this way and grab the piece of paper.

"Don't look for me. What happened was a mistake that I will regret for the rest of my days."

I read it three times to make sure my eyes aren't deceiving me.

A mistake?

She called last night *a mistake?*

Who are you really, Zoe Turner? Not the same beautiful girl who captivated me. She wouldn't be so cold in a farewell.

I replay and replay everything that happened between us from the moment I first saw her.

Yes, I wasn't very subtle in my approach, but I didn't force her. I even asked her yesterday if that's what I was doing.

The urge to grab my phone and clear everything up is immense, but I'd be dead before I allow anyone to crush my pride.

I'm Greek, and I don't bow my head to man or woman.

From this minute on, Zoe Turner is a thing of the past.

Chapter 16

Zoe

Boston

One Week Later

The cemetery is empty, almost as empty as my heart.

Nothing went as I expected when I got home. The guilt still consumes me, but it competes with the longing I feel for him, and I hate myself for it.

How can I be so stupid?

Aside from who he is, he treated me like a prostitute by handing over money for that woman to give me.

God, how embarrassing!

Is she used to this? Disposing of his affairs?

I push those thoughts away. It doesn't matter. It's not my concern.

"Hi, friend. I didn't do so well on our first trip. The ship was fun, even though I didn't meet that many people, as I'm still the same: shy and antisocial."

I sit on the ground, near the gravestone, and gather some dried leaves.

"Anyway, I took several photos with you, and they turned out beautiful, but I haven't had the courage to print them yet. I haven't felt like doing anything lately, and I think I might be depressed. I didn't tell Mom Macy about what happened on my first job or later in Barcelona, not wanting to worry her. Her health isn't very good, and Dad is afraid the cancer might have returned, but I'm so sad, Pauline."

I wipe a tear that runs down my cheek.

"I've been back for a week and should have come to visit you, but I was... still am, dying of embarrassment. I did something very bad, and before anything else, I need your forgiveness. I read somewhere that friends forgive each other, no matter what. Would you be able to do that for me?"

Someone passes by holding a little girl's hand, and I'm momentarily distracted.

Does the little girl, like I did at her age, have a lost loved one?

A bird sings in the distance, as if urging me to refocus on what I came to do.

"I know you're with me all the time, watching over me from heaven, Pauline, but even so, I felt the need to ask for your forgiveness in person, even though I've already done so in my prayers. He introduced himself as Xander Megalos, and I have no idea why. Only after..."—I take a breath because I'm suffocating—"only after we slept together did I find out he's the same man who hurt you in that accident. I was so angry with myself in Barcelona, but our minds are strange things. When I landed in Boston, I wanted it all to be a mistake, friend, because I fell in love with him. The night we... no, you don't need to hear that. I'm getting lost in what I need to say. I just want you to forgive me."

I can almost hear your voice, as if you were still alive, saying yes, you forgive me because Pauline was the best person who ever existed. I only got to see you again just before your passing, when Mom Macy adopted me. It was the first request I made: that she take me to visit my friend, but by then, it was too late.

"I went to see your mother the day before yesterday. I wasn't able to eat or sleep properly because I needed confirmation. I wanted it not to be true, but she showed me a photograph, and even though it happened many years ago, Xander's... Christos's face is unmistakable."

I pull tissues from my bag to dry my eyes.

"I wish I could tell you that I hate him, Pauline, but I can't. I can only guarantee that I hate myself for not being able to hate him. I'll make a confession and then a promise. When you asked me as a child to become a model and travel the world as if I were you, I only agreed because I wanted to see you happy. I loved seeing you smile, but I never wanted that for myself. Strutting in front of people and traveling everywhere is not my dream. I want a house in the countryside. Someone who loves me and whom I am passionate about—and even now, in front of my friend's grave, it's his face that comes to mind when I say this—and many children. A home from which no one can send me away."

I blow away some flower petals that insist on staying on your gravestone.

"But I'll make a deal: I'll first fulfill your dreams, then mine. I met a woman, as you might know, on the way back from the Barcelona trip. She's a kind of model scout, Pauline, and invited me to a test. Yesterday I called her, and she will send a ticket for me to go to New York to do this test in front of the cameras. I can't guarantee that it will work out or that they'll hire me, but at least I'm trying to fulfill your dream."

I stand up, ready to say goodbye. It's starting to get dark.

"I love you, Pauline. We didn't talk much after I grew up, but you and your plans, as well as the desire to make them come true to make you happy, were what often kept me from giving up every time I was rejected by my adoptive parents. I couldn't give up because I had made our pact. And I declare, even as sad as I feel now: I won't throw in the towel, as I'm reinforcing the promise. I'll do whatever it takes to become famous and travel the world with you."

Boston General Hospital

One Year and Two Months Later

"ARE YOU SURE YOU WANT to stay here, Zoe? I can book a hotel near the hospital. I don't want to be insensitive, but there's a fashion show in a few days, and you can't afford to show up with dark circles."

I take a deep breath, trying to calm down. I know she's not speaking out of malice, but because it's her job.

After the test I did in New York and got accepted, Bia Ramos, who I later found out is Brazilian, became a good friend. No matter where I am in the world, if I need to talk, she always answers with a comforting word.

Like now, when, after my mother's condition worsened, she came from Oceania to support me.

"I'll be fine, I just want to be close to her a bit longer. Once she falls asleep, I'll find a hotel. I can't leave my father alone."

"Alright, love, but promise you'll call me if you need anything?"

"I will. And also, there's a friend of my mother's from childhood, who is a professor at Massachusetts College, arriving to visit her, and Dad asked me to welcome him."

"You're unbelievable, Zoe Turner," she says, brushing her hand against my cheek. "Currently one of the most recognizable faces in the world, someone whom men would give an arm to take to dinner, but also the sweet girl who greets a family friend at the hospital like any ordinary person."

I look down at the floor.

"I'm ordinary, Bia. Don't be fooled. All the productions that dress me up or the clothes they put on me have nothing to do with the real Zoe."

"Then why all this?"

"Because I made a promise to someone very special. Now, I thank God for entering this world, because it's what allows me to cover my mother's hospital expenses."

"And if it depends on me, you'll earn even more."

"What are you talking about?"

Bia, along with Miguel, her right-hand man, became my agent. She doesn't offer this service to any other model, but as soon as I entered the profession, I was swindled by a dishonest agent who pocketed far more than he should from my payments.

"It's not the right time to talk about this, but we have a seven-figure contract in sight. They want exclusivity."

"So, I won't be modeling for other brands?"

"No, and not photographing either, but believe me, you won't need to. For now, enjoy your time with the lovely Macy and your dad. We'll talk in detail later. You know if they want to buy your beautiful face, I'll try to squeeze every last penny from them. Now, I have to go."

Half an Hour Later

I'M SITTING IN THE hospital corridor, checking my work messages, when a shadow falls over me.

I look up and see a very handsome man watching me.

Not wanting to sound conceited, it's not unusual, my face is quite well-known these days.

"Good evening, you must be Zoe."

I tilt my head, wondering how he might know my name, but then I remember the visitor my father was expecting.

"That's me. And you must be Mr. Mike Howard?"

"Just Mike, please. My students already call me that."

"I didn't mean to offend you," I say awkwardly.

"I'm not offended, Zoe. I just don't want to seem so old."

"You're not," I say sincerely. "Oh, my God. I think I'm making things worse. I'm terrible at social interactions."

"Don't apologize. You can always be yourself with me."

He smiles, and I believed this and many more lies he would tell me, until it was too late.

Chapter 17

Christos

New York

Seven Months Later

"Gorgeous, isn't she?" Yuri, my assistant for almost a decade, asks from behind my chair, in the headquarters of my offices.

I'm not a man who usually gives away what he's thinking, but I was so overwhelmed by the sight of her that I couldn't pretend. He must have noticed from my face that I couldn't take my eyes off the perfection in female form in the portfolio photos in front of me.

"Very," I say, as if I didn't know her, as if the girl wasn't embedded in every cell of my body for almost two years, as if I didn't fight my desire for her with military discipline.

I've followed her career and, of course, her rise. I had no doubt, from the first time I saw her, that Zoe Turner would be perfect for the runways and cameras.

Many times I was tempted to force a meeting, to look into her eyes to understand what the hell went wrong that night, but I've never humiliated myself for anyone, nor do I intend to, so instead, I stayed in the shadows, watching her from afar, desiring her in silence.

I was deciding what to do because I was sure that the end hadn't come for us yet.

I planned the logical path: to trap her in a contract with one of my brands. To keep her close until my obsession passed.

I had already made the offer when, surprising the entire world, about six months ago, she got married.

I was a hidden stalker, but attentive enough to make sure she wasn't even dating, so when the news of a sudden and secret wedding, just at the registry office, appeared in the papers, I was shocked.

A lump of iron lodges in my stomach as I remember that she is now committed to another man, because one word hammers relentlessly in my brain since that night in Barcelona.

Mine.

Mike Howard is the name of the bastard. A professor twenty years older.

"I can't believe we finally closed the deal with her. Zoe Turner was being courted by several brands, and now being exclusive to our group, she'll reach even greater heights. It was an excellent deal for both parties."

I know what he's talking about. Yuri has as much knowledge in the fashion world as I do. In no time, Zoe has become a phenomenon and, now, one of the highest-paid models in the world, as she signed a million-dollar contract with me.

No, she has no idea that my companies are behind it because I made one of my smaller brands — and most people are unaware that it belongs to me — the contracting party. I'll keep the surprise — and the shock, I'd say — until she sees me again, now that she's signed.

There's even a meeting scheduled for a few days from now.

"And do you know what's even more incredible?" he asks, with no idea where my thoughts are heading. "Despite her success, she's as sweet as a jar of honey. Kind, polite, shy. Incredibly, she hasn't been tainted with the arrogance that people with her kind of beauty usually have."

I think about what he's saying and can't disagree. Even after the way she left me, without a face-to-face conversation, Zoe has a unique quality in her personality that made her admired in the industry: she doesn't have tantrums, and it's said she's very easy to work with.

The only thing no one suspects is that she has a block of ice where her heart should be.

"Can I ask you something?"

"No, but I know you'll do it anyway."

"Why did you offer her so much? I mean, I'm not saying she doesn't deserve it, but..."

"I wanted her. I never enter into a negotiation to lose."

I know I wasn't rational, that I let myself be completely carried away by desire, whether for her or for revenge, but the fact is I want her within my reach.

He falls silent, and despite his reluctance, I shift my gaze from the photographs and look at him.

I'm not the most patient man in the world.

"Hmm... I'm not sure how to say what I'm thinking without being indiscreet."

"That would be a novelty, Yuri. You've never been known for being discreet, to begin with."

"When you said you want her... is it figuratively, as your employee, or literally?"

"As an employee," I say quickly, not giving him room for more questions, but then I mess everything up when the words slip out of my mouth. "What matters is that from now on, she's mine."

"Yours..." he echoes, but doesn't elaborate further, though I suspect he understands what I didn't say.

It's the result of years of familiarity, I suppose. He knows me well. I've never interfered in the hiring of a model, but with Zoe, I followed every step, even offering more when her agent asked and agreeing to the clause banning nudity — which I would have excluded anyway.

The truth is that no matter how much I tried to fight it, I knew that my story with Zoe was just waiting to happen. What happened in Spain was just an appetizer. We didn't have a real ending, and I don't leave anything open in my life. But once I found out she got married, I changed my plans.

I'm not going after another man's wife, so I kept observing her, and I must confess that I took petty satisfaction in discovering that Zoe isn't happy.

The goddess almost never smiles, and that made me sure she isn't living her fairy tale.

Twice we almost crossed paths at events, but I veered off course. I don't know if I could control my desire.

I also investigated the husband, and I didn't like what I found.

He's a conceited and vain little man who considers himself the epitome of wisdom.

I've met many professors like that when I studied at the same university where he works as an assistant professor. Individuals who needed to belittle young people to feel better about themselves.

Moreover, there are rumors of his involvement with current and former students, even after the marriage.

What kind of asshole would cheat on his wife a few months after marrying?

That's not your problem — reason tells me, but it's not in charge when it comes to the model.

"Given your interest in her, I assume you'll attend the meeting next week?"

"Yes, why?"

"Nothing much, just thinking about some rumors I've heard."

"I don't like gossip."

"It's not gossip, but it might be something that piques your interest."

"Spit it out, Yuri."

"There's a story circulating behind the scenes that her marriage has come to an end."

"What?"

"Yes, it seems that just six months after marrying, the dream is over. Soon, Zoe Turner will be free."

After dumping that on me, he leaves.

I get up and walk to the window, trying to pretend the information is indifferent to me.

But the only conclusion I reach is that since Zoe Turner entered my life, I've become an expert at lying to myself.

Chapter 18

Zoe

Boston

Days Later

I look at the people sitting at the table, straining to keep my emotions in check, but all I can think about is running away. The urge is so strong it makes me nauseous.

I'm sweating cold, with a damp forehead and palms, and I even started to think I caught that flu that's been spreading across the planet at an alarming rate. Several people have already died, but no one knows for sure what the main mode of transmission is yet.

I draw in a breath, and it doesn't come.

This isn't the first time I've felt like this. It's been recurring since I married Mike six months ago.

Yes, I was stupid and needy enough to believe that someone like him — handsome, kind, older, and even known to my family — would make me forget Christos Xander, when I always knew that, at least for me, there would never be another. I thought maybe I could have a fresh start, since my love life had been frozen since I left Barcelona.

Dreaming for the rest of my days about someone I wouldn't allow myself to be with, even if he wanted me, was quite a step towards insanity.

I was so miserable in the first few months that my mother sought out a free psychologist, who diagnosed me with depression.

The talks with him helped me get back on my feet and forgive myself. Following his advice, I did more research on the accident involving Christos and Pauline, but found almost nothing except an occurrence report with no details. The reports don't even explain who was at fault for the accident.

What her mother told me was that, since the Lykaios family is very wealthy, they demanded a private, confidential settlement. With no other option, she accepted it.

However, the money wasn't nearly enough to cover a decent life for Pauline, but the alternative was to fight the powerful Greek family in court for years, risking that they would still use their influence to render the case fruitless.

I researched his name more thoroughly only once: a Greek billionaire who immigrated with his family to the United States as a child, always surrounded by beautiful women, and as far as I could see, never maintained a long-term relationship.

To my surprise, I also discovered that his main business focuses are in the fashion world, and I was stunned to see that the most famous brands on the planet belong to his group.

Still, at all the fashion shows and events I've attended, we've never crossed paths, so I suppose he must have many people managing his wealth, since I remember well when he said he would buy the cruise ship fleet I worked on.

God, that feels like it happened in another life!

I've changed so much since then. If the situation were now, I would never have locked myself in the ship's bathroom out of fear of the captain and the traitor Tamara but would have caused a scene loud enough for first class to hear. I'm still shy, but I've never let anyone walk all over me again. Now I play by the rule of *an eye for an eye*.

The people at the table keep talking loudly and laughing.

I feel sharp pains in my head because I'm exhausted. I just want to go home and settle my issues with Mike once and for all.

The day after tomorrow, I'll need to go to New York to meet my new employer.

A few months ago, Bia came to me with a proposal for a million-dollar contract. An amount so unbelievable that it would be impossible to refuse. I signed without a second thought because the expenses for my mom's health are very high. Since she didn't have health insurance before she got sick, when I tried to get one, they claimed it was a pre-existing condition, which was true. The fact is, no matter how much I work, my bank account is always nearly empty. All I have left in savings are some stocks I invested in on Bia and Miguel's advice.

So, it's not like I could afford to turn down such a significant amount.

I'm going to New York just to finalize the details, but everything is already legally agreed upon, and that's one of the main reasons I want to file for separation today. Starting a new chapter without feeling like I'm in constant war within my own home will be a win. I rarely stay in Boston for long, but when I do, I want peace, and I haven't known the meaning of that word since I got married.

I'm incredibly nervous about this meeting with the new employer — yes, employer, because they paid to have my face and body in their campaigns for the next five years.

I'm no longer as fragile as I used to be and credit that to therapy, but I haven't become the bravest person in the world either. Debuts scare me. Interactions with strangers do too, and there will be a bit of both in New York.

I hear Mike's laughter and become even more irritated.

God, everything was wrong from the start.

The way I gave in, which I now see was cheap and very rehearsed charm... Trying to make my mother happy because she liked the idea of me being in a relationship, but mainly, believing that a prince could rescue me from loneliness.

I only managed to add more disappointment to the many I've already had in my past.

The only time we went to dinner at my parents' house, during one of my mother's flare-ups, Mike was arrogant and disparaged my family. We had been married for a month, but I was already thinking about leaving him since the wedding night.

When I told my father my intention, he talked to me and asked me to wait a little longer so I wouldn't be hasty.

"Marriage and the coexistence that comes with it can be very difficult," he said.

Difficult how? I'm twenty years old and feel more mature than Mike at forty, who behaves as if the world should pay him homage just like his students do.

"Have you read that book we're talking about, Zoe?" a very beautiful brunette asks me.

I know she is one of the students in my husband's course.

I rarely stay in the United States due to work travels, but I've attended two or three dinners with Mike's friends. At each of them, they looked at me as if, just because I'm a model, I had a pea for a brain.

"Just one more day, Zoe," I promise myself.

I waited and tried, as my father asked me to, but I can't even stand to hear my husband's voice. I'm getting sick again because he makes me feel like I should be on my knees thanking him for marrying me, when in reality, he's a toxic and immoral human being.

"Zoe?" I hear his voice, but I don't turn to look at him, focusing on the brunette.

"I don't think my young wife's idea of fun involves reading something so complex," he says before I can open my mouth, and I feel my face flush as everyone starts laughing.

My therapist told me the other day that Mike is triggering my anxiety, but at this moment, it's more of an anger trigger.

I look at his friends.

People who have belittled me since the first time we met. Professors and students half their age, just like me and Mike, except the women present are respected while I'm always the target of ridicule.

After glaring at each one, I turn to my husband, trying to strip away the colors with which I painted him before we married to fit my dreams.

Tonight, all I can see is a petty, small man who needs to humiliate his own wife to feel better.

I get up from the table and grab my purse.

"You're right. My pea-brained model self can't mingle with such brilliant minds. So, I'll leave you to your average citizen salaries while I go home to review the seven-figure contract I just signed."

Chapter 19

Zoe

My legs are trembling as I leave the restaurant. I don't want to go back to our apartment, but my bags are there, and I see no alternative.

Jesus, I've never openly confronted a single person in my entire life, and today I did it with six at once.

I'm not rude, but I'm too patient, yet my patience overflowed when I saw that cynical smile on his face.

Who do they think they are to judge me? I read a lot, but even if I didn't, that doesn't make me stupid. As my mother says, a diploma doesn't take the ass out of someone.

I ask a valet for a taxi, and as I'm getting in, I see Mike leaving the restaurant. He calls me, but I ignore him because, with the anger I'm feeling, I'm capable of causing a scene, and I wouldn't be surprised if someone took a photo and splashed it across the newspapers.

I want to end my marriage exactly as it began: quietly.

I have no doubt that he will follow me, because even though we've never reached this point before, our life has been hell since the wedding night, with frequent fights.

It's as if, by putting a ring on my finger, he thought he had a free pass to do whatever he wanted with me.

No more.

I'M FINISHING PACKING my suitcase when I hear the sound of the apartment alarm being turned off.

"What the hell got into you today?" is the first thing he asks as he enters the room.

I don't turn to face him, and I know he fell silent because he saw me closing the suitcase.

I just got back from a trip and, theoretically, should stay in Boston until the day after tomorrow before heading to New York for the meeting with my new employer. I'm not leaving the city today, but there's no chance I'll stay another minute beside him.

"Zoe, I asked you a question."

I turn to him.

"There's no point in answering it anymore. It doesn't matter, Mike. You know perfectly well what I'm doing: leaving," I say, keeping my voice firm and silently thanking therapy, which has taught me to love and respect myself.

I was rejected during my years in the orphanage, but I don't need to keep allowing it to happen to me as an adult.

From his look, I think he understands that I'm not just talking about the next trip, but forever.

Still, he pretends we're just having another one of our many arguments in our short marriage.

"You were very rude to my friends."

"More than they are with me?" I start, but then regret it. There's no point in prolonging this discussion when, in my mind, the decision is already made. "It's over, Mike. We both know that."

His face transforms into pure hatred. It's not the first time, but it's still terrifying. All the polish of a refined and intellectual man disappears.

"Because you didn't do anything to improve it. You never did anything for our marriage, Zoe."

"If doing something about our marriage means indulging in your fetishes, then yes, I didn't do anything for our marriage. I thought I was joining someone normal, not a man who needed... I don't even have the courage to put it into words... but someone with your preferences to get excited."

He moves so quickly that I don't anticipate the motion. In the next instant, a hard slap hits my face; I fall and hit my head against the nightstand.

Even dazed and terrified by that violent act, I reach for my phone on the bed and run to the bathroom. It feels like a replay of that day on the ship, but this time, I'm going to call the only man I trust in the world.

"Zoe?"

"Dad, I need you to come pick me up from home. Mike just hit me. I want to leave, but he's outside the room."

"Zoe, my God! Do you want me to call the police?"

"No, please, it would be a scandal. I'll think carefully about what to do later, but for now, I just want to get out of here."

"I'm on my way, honey."

"ZOE, IT'S DAD. YOU can come out now."

I look at my reflection in the mirror before opening the door. I haven't had the courage to do so until now. I knew it would be bad, as my entire face hurts.

The area where he hit me is sore, and I was afraid that seeing the evidence of his final disrespect toward me would make me fall apart.

Now, however, I see that imagination lost out to reality.

My entire left side is swollen, and my eye, which is naturally slanted, is even smaller in the area it was struck.

Oh God, there's no way I can leave here without someone seeing me. The last thing I want is for the end of my marriage to become a headline in celebrity magazines.

"Zoe?"

"I'm coming, Dad."

I unlock the door, and as soon as he sees me, his face turns beet red.

Instead of hugging me, he leaves the room, and I follow because I already imagine what will happen.

As I thought, my dad has Mike pinned against a wall, and his face is already turning somewhat purple.

"Dad, don't do this, I just want to get out of here."

"Never touch my daughter again, you bastard, or I'll kill you."

He opens the apartment door and waits for my husband to leave, but Mike still tries to approach me. My dad steps in his way.

"Zoe, forgive me. I lost my head."

I look at him and think that I should have left on our wedding night when he waited until we were married to tell me what he wanted from me.

"No. It's over. My lawyers will contact you with the divorce papers. The only thing I want from you now is to leave me alone."

He tries to approach again, but my dad stops him.

"I wasn't kidding, asshole. Touch my daughter again and I'll kill you."

This time, Dad doesn't wait for him to decide but pushes him out of the apartment and slams the door.

Then he opens his arms to me.

"Forgive me," he says.

"It wasn't your fault."

"It was. Early on, when you came to tell me the marriage wasn't going well, I should have listened to you, but I was fixated on the fact that you were very young and maybe just adjusting to married life. I had no idea he was abusive, sweetheart."

"It's the first time he's physically attacked me, if that's what you're talking about. But there are other forms of abuse that aren't physical. He was draining me, Dad, consuming my energy, which isn't much to begin with. Our marriage was a mistake."

"What do you mean by that?"

I think about what happened on our wedding night when he finally revealed himself. I didn't spend the night in the arms of the man I hoped to start a family with but crying alone in the next room.

"Nothing. It doesn't matter anymore," I say, because I don't have the courage to tell my dad about that. The only people who know are my therapist and Bia.

"Okay, but at least tell me what led him to attack you today."

"What makes a man hit a woman? Cowardice for knowing she is physically weaker? Seeing her as an object he can treat however he wants? I think it's a combination of all that, but mainly the lack of respect, Dad. We've never been okay, from the first day of marriage. He played a role until he was sure we were legally bound."

"And now, what are you going to do?"

"I'm going to ask Bia tomorrow to contact a divorce attorney."

"You could also go to the police station. He should pay for what he did to you."

"I know, but we can't afford to have my name in the headlines. With that contract I told you about, I'll be able to pay off your mortgage in full and give Mom more comfort as well, but if my name appears in a scandal, they might back out and cancel it."

"And will you travel a little less too? You always seem to be going back and forth, sweetheart."

"I don't know. In this new contract, they will have exclusivity over me."

"It's okay, my daughter. The last thing you need today is to be pressured. I just want you to know that I love you, Zoe. We both love you so much, and bringing you into our family was the best thing we've ever done."

He's crying, and it finally makes me fall apart.

"I love you too, Dad. I'm not good with words, and even less at showing emotions, but I love you both so much."

"We need to put ice on your face. How did that bastard have the nerve?"

"It's over, Dad. That's what matters. I was already determined to end it, and there have even been some rumors about it in the press. That's why I don't want to go to the police station. I'll ask Bia to hire an attorney. When she knows what Mike did, I'm sure she'll be able to keep him away from me."

"You're very strong, Zoe. People who see you from the outside, beautiful and delicate-looking, are mistaken. You're made of steel, kid."

"Not yet, but I'm learning."

Chapter 20

Christos

Two Days Later

"What the hell are you talking about, Yuri?"

"To be honest, I didn't quite understand, Christos. All I know is that her agent, Bia Ramos, requested as few people as possible at the meeting. And that it should be held in a discreet place."

"I've heard that part already, what I'm asking is why."

"It seems that... *um*... Zoe had an accident."

"What? When? And if that's the case, why hasn't it been reported?"

"I don't think it was that kind of accident, but a domestic one."

"A fall?"

"I really have no idea. Her agent shields her from the world, like a mother would, but we'll find out soon enough. I took the liberty of scheduling our meeting on the thirteenth floor because it's empty. Is that a problem?"

"Of course not. I just want to find out what kind of accident it was. Record this: from the moment she signed the contract, Zoe belongs to me, just like her life. I want to be informed even if she wakes up on a bad day."

He looks at me strangely, but I don't care. The control freak inside me needs to know what's going on, and it won't stop until it finds out.

I IMAGINED OUR REUNION many times in my head because I knew it would happen sooner or later.

Almost two years without seeing her in person.

A time during which I tried to convince myself that Zoe Turner wasn't as much as my memory made me believe.

That her skin wasn't as soft or that her moans and cries of pleasure every time I entered her body were like any other woman I'd been with. But now, with only a few minutes until our reunion, I can barely contain my desire.

You know the saying: be careful what you wish for, because you might get it? It's very true, because only at this moment do I realize that being around — even occasionally — with Zoe will be a hell of a difficulty.

While she's married, she's off-limits to me.

"Married," I repeat as a warning to my brain.

I'm not a liar; I want her, but I would never play the role of a third wheel in a relationship. Infidelity is a word that doesn't exist in my vocabulary.

Unacceptable. Unforgivable.

I don't invade another man's territory, even one as pathetic as Mike Howard.

I twirl the pen in my hand as a sort of exercise to slow myself down.

The secretary we brought to this floor has just announced that Zoe and her agent are coming up, and I try to convince myself that the reason my blood is pumping heavily through my body isn't the anxiety of seeing her again, but because there's so much resentment inside me from the way she left. What we had was the best night of my life in terms of sex.

I've been standing since I arrived because there's so much energy inside me that I could run a marathon.

When the door opens and a small woman enters, I tense up with anticipation.

And then, the platinum curtain appears. We are finally face to face.

I drink in every inch of her, starting from her feet, as I did the first time, but now in sophisticated *pumps*, not the cheap ones from the ship.

She wears fitted jeans that leave little to the imagination of the observer, and a white sleeveless shirt completes the simple yet elegant ensemble.

It's like taking a *tour* along a road you've longed to travel, but in my case, I've memorized every curve.

And then, I finally reach her beautiful face.

One second.

That's the exact amount of time it takes to know what happened.

I've been in many street fights when I was a kid in Greece.

Zoe was attacked. That's why she requested a discreet place.

I don't think. No brain cell of mine functions at the moment. When I realize, I'm already on her.

"Who did this?" I ask, standing in front of her.

She hadn't seen me yet, distracted, greeting Yuri, who formed a sort of barrier between us. But now her beautiful face rises, partially shielded by large sunglasses. The mouth I've kissed and taught to take me, now open in a look of surprise.

"You?"

"Everyone out," I command, because it's with her I want to speak.

Out of the corner of my eye, I see what I believe to be her agent trying to protest, and I also notice when Yuri says something to her, but still, she asks Zoe if she wants to be alone with me.

"It's okay, Bia," Zoe says, looking at me.

It's the first change I notice. In the past, she would have looked at the floor, embarrassed.

I don't move, even when I hear the door close.

"I must assume, Mr. Lykaios, that you are my new employer." Her voice is still soft but shows confidence. "If you're worried about how much money you'll lose because of the damage to my face, don't worry. I've already seen a surgeon and nothing was broken. Only my skin is..."

"Who did this, Zoe?"

I take a step forward, but before I do anything foolish, I put my hands in my pants pockets. She is a married woman.

What the hell is happening to me?

"I don't think it's a contractual clause to detail every aspect of my life."

Unable to control myself, I get close enough to almost feel the warmth of her breath.

But it's not desire that dominates me at the moment, but anger at seeing her hurt.

Angry with myself and with her because nothing I planned went as expected, I lash out.

"Do you really believe that? You should read the contract more carefully, because for the next five years, you belong to me, Zoe Turner."

Chapter 21

Zoe

I hope I'm a good actress. I'm trying to pretend that his proximity isn't affecting me when, in reality, my heart is pounding almost painfully against my chest.

It's not the memories of why we shouldn't be together, or even the way he dismissed me by sending that woman to hand me the envelope with the money, that's coming back to me now, but everything we shared in our one night together.

His kisses and the way his body moved over mine. His thick thighs demanding space between mine. Powerful muscles pressing against my softness.

The look of dark blue searching for me in the dim light of that shared night.

"I didn't sell myself to you when I signed the contract," I force myself to say, and I see he's focused on my mouth. "If I had known you were the contractor, I wouldn't have accepted."

"I doubt that. No one would give up such a large sum."

Damn it. He knows I'm bluffing. Even if I had known it was him my employer, I couldn't refuse the deal. My parents' house has been mortgaged twice already, and the amount of money I spend on the private room and nurses to be with her twenty-four hours a day is obscene.

I'm not complaining. No sacrifice is too great for her and Dad, but this meant that from the beginning, I had to accept almost every job that came my way, traveling nonstop.

He's staring at me and I don't back down, but admiring his beauty makes me aware of how I must look. As if he can read my thoughts, he asks:

"What happened to your face, Zoe?"

"Domestic accident." There's no way I'm telling him it was the result of the end of my marriage.

No one needs to know the level of disrespect my ex-husband reached.

Yesterday I went to a divorce specialist, and after recounting the entire story of my brief marriage, he advised me, despite what happened two days ago, to try for an amicable end if I really want to avoid scandal, which means I will still have to meet with Mike to settle the details.

I'll be staying a few more days in Boston, so with my dad and Bia present, along with the lawyer, of course, we'll have what I hope to be our final discussion before we sign the papers. Dr. Robin tried to schedule a meeting at his office, but Mike claimed he couldn't go because of work.

Mom is also at home, in *home care* this month, since whenever she improves, the doctor allows it as a way to make her feel like she's living as normally as possible.

"Does your domestic accident have a name?"

I notice his lips form a thin line, as if he's struggling to contain his anger.

"Is my personal life your business, Mr. Lykaios? Or should I call you Xander Megalos?"

He looks startled for a moment.

"Those are my middle names."

"Now I know. With the hasty dismissal the next day, it makes perfect sense not to want to give the full name."

Seconds after letting that slip, I'm already regretting it. Damn, the last thing I need is to show vulnerability in front of him. Besides, if I'm honest, when I discovered his true identity that day, I would have left anyway.

"It doesn't matter, it's in the past. Now I think we should let the people outside come in."

"Take off the glasses, Zoe."

I should tell him, along with his authoritarian attitude, to go to hell, but instead, I find myself obeying.

I do it, looking into his eyes. I'm not ashamed of what happened, and I won't be embarrassed for having been with a coward like Mike.

I know my appearance isn't as bad as on the first day, but you can still see shades of purple and yellow from the bruise that formed, which no makeup can hide.

The slap he gave me was so hard that only by a miracle did it not break a bone, according to the surgeon.

"Did your husband do this to you?"

I could deny it, but I'm tired of this game. I just want to know what will come of this meeting and then go back to Boston.

"Ex-husband. I started the divorce process."

No, I don't know why I said that or what he's thinking, because now his face has turned neutral.

"Answer me. Did he hit you?"

I nod, but without looking at him this time.

"But as I said before, the surgeon assured me..."

He comes closer and my heartbeat goes wild. I can't find air for my lungs.

"Free?" he asks.

My back is almost pressed against the door and I know I should stop him, but I can't. I don't want to.

"Yes."

The strength and intensity of Christos is something primal, raw, meeting all my feminine needs.

How could I think I could find a substitute for this man? Regardless of what he did and how we can never be together, I am his.

"At this moment, do you consider yourself free, Zoe?" His voice sounds husky.

I move my head up and down, and then my forbidden dreams, the ones I wouldn't allow myself to have while awake, come true.

His hand touches my waist as if testing, as if I were something precious. Reflexively, I spread my hands on his chest. His grip tightens and there's no distance between us when his mouth takes mine without warning, going against the gentle care of his hands.

His tongue is demanding and enters me without giving a chance for retreat. I respond with the same eagerness, taking everything from him as well.

I lose track of time, of where we are. I just know I want more.

"Why did you leave when, with just a touch from me, you melt into my arms, Zoe? When your body, even after all this time, still recognizes and responds to my caresses?"

I moan against his mouth, hungry and delighted, pressing myself against him, but suddenly he pulls away, making me feel lost and empty.

The way he looks at me is cold and brings me back to reality.

God, what have I done? How could I forget who he is?

"It doesn't matter anymore. You had a choice in the past and made a decision. Let's handle business. That's why you're here, Zoe."

Chapter 22

Zoe

The rest of the meeting passed in a blur for me.

I shouldn't have, but I was focused on him the entire time, to the point where Bia had to call my attention two or three times for ignoring a question she asked.

The time apart made my mind play with an image of a cruel, unscrupulous man, who, even knowing he destroyed a girl's life through his own irresponsibility, fled from his duty, offering a paltry sum to ease his conscience.

When I found out in Barcelona who he was, I knew nothing about Christos Lykaios beyond the insane desire he awakened in me. But now, trying to analyze him impartially, what Ernestine, Pauline's mother, told me, makes no sense.

Of course, people change. I'm not the same naïve and fearful girl he met on the ship, but that's not what I'm talking about.

Character is something you can't alter, and Christos doesn't show — now I realize — anything like someone who would shirk a responsibility.

I look at his hard face, with a shadow of stubble already appearing.

He doesn't seem to acknowledge my presence.

While I'm unable to get my neurons functioning properly, Christos remains impassive, not even glancing in my direction.

I hear the conversation, but I'm completely inattentive. I know that some new clauses have been added, and when Bia asked if I agreed, I nodded, but as far as I'm concerned, I could be negotiating my kidney on the black market because I wouldn't be able to say what it was about, even to save my own life.

"So, the first rehearsal will be in Greece, on Dr. Lykaios's private island."

Wait. What?

I look at Bia, confused, but she seems completely calm, so I'll save my freak-out for later.

That can't mean much. For photo shoots or commercial recordings, there are always many people around.

It's not like we'll be alone, and it doesn't even mean he'll be there.

"I think that wraps things up," the other man, whom I know to be Yuri, declares, and only then do my eyes meet those of my first *everything* again.

It lasts only a few seconds. Shortly after, he gets up.

"Good afternoon, ladies. Our meeting is over," he says.

He turns his back and leaves the room, leaving me confused and lost.

He seems angry with me.

Why did you leave when, with just a touch from me, you melt into my arms, Zoe? When your body, even after all this time, still recognizes and responds to my caresses?

How can he have asked me something like that after treating me like a nobody?

The pieces don't fit, and not just regarding us.

The honor Christos displays is at odds with everything Ernestine told me about him.

I rub my temple, with a headache, but determined to look into that story again.

Minutes Later

"WHAT HAPPENED IN THERE, Zoe?"

"In relation to what?"

"I could start with the fact that you seemed completely detached from reality during the entire meeting, but that's not what I'm talking about. I'm referring to before. It was obvious to everyone that you two already knew each other. The sexual energy between you could light up a country."

Bia has become my best friend and also my confidante, the one who knows everything about my marriage, even the sordid details of the wedding night. She hates Mike with all her heart, and it was her advice, much more than therapy, that led me to decide to separate.

Regardless of what happened, with that brunette trying to humiliate me and Mike laughing at me, I had already intended to end everything.

But what she's talking about now has nothing to do with my ex-husband. I never told her my story with Christos, and I think it's time I did.

"Yes, we have a past. And I think I need you to help me understand it."

Christos's assistant approaches in the hallway again and informs us that the Greek's private plane will take us back to Boston. I agree automatically, still overwhelmed by our encounter.

An hour and a half later, already inside the aircraft, Bia looks at me in shock.

"I don't even know where to start, but I'll try to organize my thoughts. The first thing to say is that I'm now sure your hiring wasn't a coincidence. He still wants you."

I had reached that conclusion as well. Not that he wants me, because despite the desire he showed, there was a lot of anger involved, but that my hiring wasn't the work of fate.

"Did you run from him because of your friend? Look, I'm sorry, Zoe, but Christos Lykaios is a very well-known figure not only in the fashion world but also as a billionaire philanthropist. I've dealt with rich people for years and have never seen his name among rumors of illegal activities. I'm talking mainly about drugs. Look at him. Does he look like someone who takes drugs to escape reality and then gets into a car accident and shirks responsibility?"

"No. He doesn't look like that."

"On the contrary, the man is a dominator. He shows a desire to have the world in the palm of his hand."

"I know, and even when I was younger, I went after that, to check out that story, but as Ernestine said, the agreement they made was behind closed doors. I'm so confused..."

"You were very young. What you experienced was a surreal situation, but I promise I will dig deep. Where did you say the accident happened?"

"In Boston itself. According to Ernestine, he was a college student and Pauline was very small."

"I have an ex-boyfriend who is a police detective and has contacts within the prosecutor's office. I promise I will find out the truth. Now, about the money in the envelope. Okay, it wasn't nice waking up and him not being there, but I attribute much of what you felt again to your youth because, honestly, I'll play devil's advocate here, but Lykaios doesn't need to offend a woman to get rid of her."

"And not pay her?"

"With that appearance? Darling, I bet that even if he were a beggar, he'd have fans following him. With all due respect, but the man's beauty is enough to make the Earth spin in the opposite direction."

"There's no need to apologize, he's nothing to me."

"If you say so... the fact is that I have many more years of experience than you, Zoe, and I say without fear of being wrong that that man wants you. And judging by the state you were in, it's mutual."

"There's still the issue of Pauline."

"Yes, there is, and I promised I would investigate it for you. But what if it was all just a lie from that woman? For God's sake, she sent you back to the orphanage when you were a little girl."

"She and several other families. It's more common than you think, Bia. And I swear I'm not trying to defend her, but saying this because it's a fact. In her case, there was never an intention to adopt me, I just didn't expect to be returned so quickly because I loved Pauline. I still love her."

"The purest friendship in the world: between two children. Innocent hearts."

"She was beautiful and so happy. Pauline is my best memory of my entire childhood. Even after she left, I continued talking to her in my thoughts, celebrating each achievement. That's why I was so horrified when I found out who Christos was."

"I will investigate this, Zoe, but even without any solid basis, I can assure you that whatever happened, it wasn't like that Ernestine told you."

Chapter 23

Christos

One Hour Later

I plan everything.

Except for Zoe — how we met and my invitation for her to spend the summer with me. I'm not an impulsive guy; my life is practically a file, each folder labeled and in its place.

Attack the enemy at his weak point. Don't let him prepare or anticipate the blow, and make the punishment as painful as possible: that's who I am. At this moment, however, I want to go after Mike Howard and snap his neck for having hurt her. To feel the pleasure of hearing him crack under my hands.

I grab my phone and call the only person who wouldn't judge me.

"*What's up, buddy?*" he says when he answers. "*I know when you call me, it's because* you *see no other way out. You're the hero, I'm the villain.*"

"There's nothing heroic about me, and we both know that."

"*But you're not the rotten apple, like me.*"

"I need you to find out everything you can about Mike Howard. He's a professor at *Massachusetts College*."

"*Her ex-husband*" he says, because the man just seems to know everything.

I've never mentioned Zoe to him, but I wouldn't be surprised if he knows all the details of our story, and perhaps even my obsession with her.

Yes, because what other name can I give to my attachment to her, even after she left me with nothing more than a note referring to what happened between us as a mistake two years ago? Today I had proof that nothing has changed. I still desire her with every drop of my blood.

"Ex-husband. He hit her," I say.

"*What happened?*" His relaxed tone shifts to tense, and I know the reason. Violence against women is his Achilles' heel. Having witnessed his adoptive father do this to his mother many times during childhood, Beau doesn't tolerate such cowardice.

"She didn't go into details, but her face is bruised."

"*Son of a bitch. What do you want?*"

"Whatever you can find out. I've investigated him through normal means. I want to go further now, though."

"*Give me two hours and I'll tell you even when his first baby tooth fell out.*"

I LOOK AT THE REPORT in front of me.

I don't know how he managed it, but just over two hours after I called him, my secretary informed me that a courier had arrived with a file that could only be delivered to me. I had no doubt it was from Beau.

Before I can open it, however, my phone lights up with a message.

Zoe.

Yes, her number is still saved in my contacts, and apparently, she has kept mine as well, since nothing in the agreements we made involves personal information.

Zoe: *"I'd like to ask a question."*

What power does this woman have over me that just reading a damn message with no significant content is enough to make my blood boil?

I press the button to complete the call.

"And why should I answer you?"

"Forget it, Christos."

Shit! This would be my cue to end the call and keep everything between us on a professional basis, but how can I do that when I can still taste her tongue in my mouth?

"What do you want to know?"

"The money in the envelope you left me in Barcelona, was it a dismissal? A coded message for me to leave your apartment?"

"What the hell are you talking about?"

"I thought it might be some sort of payment for..."

"Don't finish that sentence, Zoe. Don't insult us both like that."

"Okay. That's all. Thanks."

"There's no way you're hanging up like that. We're not done yet."

"What do you want?"

You naked, under me. Your silky thighs on my shoulders while I eat your pussy. Hearing your screams begging me to go deeper into your tight body.

"Have dinner with me."

"Doesn't the contract forbid it?"

"Fuck the contract, Zoe. You're the one who reached out to me, and now I'm not stopping. I'm heading to Boston."

"But I... we... it will be impossible today. Besides, it's not a good idea for us to be seen together."

"You told me you're already in the process of divorcing."

"Yes, I am, but nothing has been announced in the press. It would be madness for us to meet. We are both too well-known."

"I'll send someone to pick you up tomorrow for lunch, then."

"That's not why I wrote to you. I wasn't expecting a meeting."

"You met me two years ago, Zoe Turner, and you know perfectly well that subtlety is not my strength. If we're going to clear up the past, it won't be through a message or even a damn phone call. Be ready at noon."

"You plan to come to Boston today?"

"At this very moment, I'm heading to the elevator. Noon sharp. Don't be late."

After I hang up, I send a message to Yuri to check if my plane is ready to take me to Boston, as it should have returned from there just a few hours ago.

I also carry the file that Beau had delivered to me. I plan to read the report on Mike Howard inside the plane.

BEAU HAS CONTACTS THAT can uncover even the most well-kept secrets, but even though my opinion of her ex-husband was the worst possible, I didn't expect this.

It's not just about betrayals, but sexual orgies with students regardless of gender. He and a group of professors, apparently, participated in these parties where there was partner swapping or everyone at once.

I can't believe she's involved in that, so the only conclusion I reach is that he cheated on her indiscriminately, putting her health at risk.

Son of a bitch!

I don't consider myself a moralist. I've done many crazy things when it comes to sexual satisfaction, but always with one partner at a time, and if I had to bet all my fortune on something, it would be that Zoe doesn't fit into his lifestyle.

I push the thought away because just thinking about another man touching her already makes me want to kill someone, let alone imagining her being passed around.

I turn the page to the section about recurring assaults on ex-girlfriends.

How is it possible he's avoided an accusation? At least half a dozen women claim to have been beaten by the bastard.

As I read on, my hatred grows. As if it weren't enough that he hurt her, he stole from her.

Zoe doesn't know yet, but all her investments are gone.

Apparently, he's been robbing her for months, but yesterday there was a large transfer of what was left, as well as the sale of her shares.

At this very moment, her checking account contains enough to barely cover her mother's medication. Now, more than ever, she'll need the contract we signed.

I pick up the phone to address the first issue: destroying the world Mike Howard knows. But that doesn't even come close to what I have planned for him. He will suffer in life until I bring his existence to an end.

Ten minutes and one phone call. That's all it took to make his universe crumble. Tomorrow, he'll be dismissed from his position as a teaching assistant because I demanded it.

As a former student and one of the university's most generous patrons, I only needed to play the card of potentially suspending my contribution if my request wasn't met. The bastard was out.

Welcome to the first of your last days on this fucking planet, Mike.

I can't wait to meet you in person.

"TWO PHONE CALLS IN one day. That means you've read the report."

"I have, and I want you to recommend someone to keep an eye on her. Watch her from a distance, just in case he tries to approach. Men to secure her parents' house while Zoe is in town."

"Okay. I can arrange that by tomorrow morning. But what about him? Will you put an end to it once and for all?"

"You know me. What do you think?"

"Something discreet?"

I know he's talking about the death of Commander Bentley Williams, which many attributed to suicide, but which we both know wasn't the case.

"Yes," I reply without elaborating further.

"So you've made up your mind? She's yours from now on?"

She's always been mine.

"Nothing is set in stone."

"But you want to protect her anyway," he asserts.

"Zoe has just signed a contract with me. It's in my interest to ensure her safety."

He says nothing, and I understand because even to my own ears, it sounds like a shitty excuse.

"You know how my men operate in case of danger, Christos."

"I do, and that's exactly why I'm asking you. At the first sign of risk to her, there can be no hesitation."

"Don't worry, it will be done. Starting tomorrow, Zoe will have someone watching her twenty-four hours a day. Her... contractor? Do you prefer that term? She will be protected."

Chapter 24

Zoe

Boston

That Night

"How are you feeling, Mom?" She seems cheerful today, and my heart always feels lighter when I see her smile. Watching a loved one lose their strength gradually is not beautiful; cancer is the worst disease of all.

There are moments of hope for all three of us, as well as those that border on despair.

I've been praying a lot for her to get better, but if it's to avoid suffering, otherwise, I'd prefer it to be God's will.

It's a drop of hope in an ocean of certainty.

The doctors don't have the answers I need. She improves and worsens, and because of this, they increasingly allow her to come home.

Thank God I'm able to pay for a room set up like a hospital, as well as a nurse. I don't care how much time she has left; I want her to enjoy every comfort I can provide.

"I'm fine, dear, but very sad too."

I look at my hands. I don't need to ask why. I know it's because of the assault I suffered from Mike.

"Don't think about it, Mom. Everything will be resolved this week."

"Your father told me you asked him for help days after the wedding. I'm so embarrassed he told you to try a little longer."

"And I regret listening. I thought there was something wrong with me, Mom. I always think there's something wrong with me since I don't have many people who love me."

"It's their loss, dear. There's nothing wrong with you. You're a beautiful girl inside and out."

"How do we know when we love someone, Mom?"

"Are you talking about Mike?"

"No. Even before what he did, I could never love him. If I'm being completely honest, I didn't even like him. I think what happened was that I was so afraid of losing you. You and Dad are my only stability in life. He appeared and seemed like a caring, understanding older shoulder to lean on. I confused everything. I'm not saying I gave him a reason or excusing what he did to me, because there's much more I'm not willing to share at the moment, but I'm saying I also made a mistake marrying someone I had only known for a month."

"If it wasn't Mike you were referring to when you asked me about love, then who?"

"Someone from the past."

"The man from Barcelona?"

"Why are you asking me this?"

"Zoe, you came back from there almost dead. I would never invade your privacy when you didn't seem willing to tell me, but I knew something serious had happened. Then came your depression, and I focused on helping you recover. Nothing else mattered."

"It's that man, yes. I found him again. I think I love him. That I've always loved him, but..."

"But what?"

"He might have done something very bad in the past."

"Did you talk about it?"

"No. I've only been with him today after the time in Barcelona. We're having lunch together tomorrow."

"Aren't you rushing things? I mean, you just got out of a relationship."

"And if I miss this chance? And if I lose him forever?"

"But what about what you said he might have done wrong?"

"I'm not sure, Mom. In my immaturity, I judged and condemned him without even giving him a chance to defend himself."

"Follow your intuition. You're a sensible girl; you've never caused me trouble, but about this lunch, I'd prefer you didn't go to a restaurant. The doctors are constantly talking on the *tv* about the rise in cases of this new flu. They're predicting something of global reach. Your father even bought masks about two weeks ago. Now it seems they're completely sold out, along with hand sanitizer."

I stay silent, looking at her with sadness.

"What's wrong, dear?"

"I can't stop working. If this new flu thing is serious, I'll need to talk to you only via video call. The risk of me getting infected at some airport is high, and I wouldn't forgive myself if I caused you harm in any way."

She holds my hand, and my heart sinks when I see how thin she's become.

I bring her fingers to my lips and kiss them.

"Let's not suffer in advance. For now, just take care of yourself. I'd prefer if you wore a mask when you go outside."

"That would be great. Especially with my face like this."

"How can you joke about something like this?"

"I can't, Mom, but I see you're blaming yourself for what Mike did, and that's not fair. No one should be held responsible for that cowardice except him."

"Neither your father nor I had any idea he was like that, or we would have never allowed him near you. Mike was a good guy when he was younger; I don't know what happened."

A short while later, she starts to doze off.

I walk to the window, but I'm not paying attention to the night outside, instead, I'm caught up in memories of my marriage.

A dream that turned into a nightmare.

Me, the silly girl who dreamed of a love for a lifetime, ended up with a depraved man who hid his other face until it was too late.

I think about what my mother said about Mike being a good guy. I doubt it. He probably hid his true personality from everyone, as he did with me. No one goes to bed honest and wakes up a liar and pervert. It must take years of practice to learn to pretend so well.

God, if she knew what I went through. The only thing that kept me going for so long was that we barely saw each other.

With my travels around the world, we might not have spent a total of thirty days together in six months, probably less, and when we did, it usually ended in a fight, like the night he assaulted me.

What would my parents and friends say if I told them that the golden man, assistant professor at one of the country's top universities, bluntly told me on our wedding night that he only got pleasure from group sex? That he could never get aroused in a regular relationship? That he expected me to sleep with his friends so he could watch, because he couldn't get excited any other way with a woman?

Girls tell wonders about their wedding nights. Mine had no sex, no affection, nothing. I was locked in the suite next to his, vomiting from nerves and crying.

We wouldn't have gone on a honeymoon anyway because I had work commitments, so the next morning, I ran to ask my father for help.

That's when he told me that married life is hard.

Even without experience, I knew that had nothing to do with adjustment; it was a distortion within Mike that couldn't be corrected.

I spent the first month away, and when I returned, he was once again the kind man I knew, though he didn't try to touch me. I think he believed I'd become curious about sex and eventually give in, which only proves he didn't know anything about me. I began to feel disgusted by him.

Our relationship was never based on physical attraction but, from my side, on friendship. So, regarding the fact that he gave no indication of wanting to have sex with me, I'm not ashamed to admit it was a relief.

During the three days I stayed in Boston, we talked like we used to, even though he slept in the room next door.

To be honest, I got used to the situation because it was only after we were married that I realized I didn't want another man touching me.

The calm lasted until I returned home a month and a half later.

Again, after a disastrous dinner with his friends, he blamed me for our marriage not working and brought up the group sex story again.

I decided to leave home and stay with my parents, determined to, the next day, tell Bia everything and ask her to help me with the divorce process.

That same night, Mom took a turn for the worse, and we thought we were going to lose her. The doctor suggested an expensive and alternative chemotherapy, a new method. I had to focus on earning money to cover the hospital bills, because I'd never forgive myself if she died because we couldn't afford her treatment.

Life was a carousel of bad emotions during this period. I traveled, fearing a phone call from my father saying she had passed away, so I lived in tension, sleeping little and eating poorly.

Overwhelmed, I told Bia everything, and she said she would support me one hundred percent in trying for a discreet divorce. It was with this intention that I returned home this week. Regardless of what happened that night, I was going to end our union. His assault was the final nail in the coffin of our relationship.

What relationship, Lord? There was no relationship, only a deception. We were never even friends, now I see.

I remember Christos's phone call.

Did I make a mistake sending that message? Should I have waited for Bia to clear everything up with her ex before talking to him?

I don't regret taking the initiative, finally accepting that it could have been a horrible misunderstanding.

God, he wanted to see me today! There must be some significance in him dropping everything to come see me, especially after how things ended between us.

I knew I hadn't forgotten him, that I would never forget him, but I didn't expect to feel him so strongly in my heart after all this time.

It was as if he had touched me yesterday. As if I were still the insecure girl who gave herself to her dark hero one night in Barcelona.

I need to hear his side of the story, even if only to move on.

However, right now, still unsure about Pauline's accident, I know that whatever the outcome, there will never be another for me.

Chapter 25

Zoe

One Hour Later

"Where are you going?" Bia asks, nearly giving me a heart attack as I pass through the hallway.

"I was going to borrow your car. Mine is out of gas, and I want to buy ice cream."

"Excited?"

I nod, indicating yes.

"You can take it, but first, listen to what I have to say. I just spoke with my detective friend, and..."

"I thought you said he was an ex-boyfriend."

"If I tell you what I actually call him, you won't like it. I'm afraid you might faint."

Despite the craziness of these past few days, I start laughing because Bia has a mouth as dirty as a sailor's, even though she looks like a Victorian lady.

"Speak. I've shown plenty of times that I'm a grown-up. I can handle a swear word or two."

"Pimp friend."

"Oh Jesus!"

"I warned you."

"And what does that mean?"

"The relationship is strong enough for me to consider him a friend, but not enough for me to want him as a boyfriend. Cops are too uptight for my taste."

"Said the bad girl," I tease.

"I wouldn't go that far, but I do like men who break the rules."

"A lawbreaker is your ideal type?"

"Who knows? I've never tried it, but I won't lie and pretend that a wilder sex doesn't excite me."

"Too much information, miss," I say, covering my ears. "Now tell me what your friend said."

I haven't told her yet about my meeting with Christos tomorrow. I'll need the courage from sugar before making confessions.

"He said that by tomorrow he will be able to access what we need and that it's common for very wealthy people involved in civil actions to settle confidentially about the amount of compensation. But it doesn't make much sense to demand such a clause if the amount was negligible, like Ernestine told you. Furthermore, he did a quick search and didn't find any criminal actions against Lykaios. Usually, in such cases, both run parallel."

"I'm not sure I understand."

"Which part?"

"The part about the amount."

"He explained that when confidentiality is required in an agreement, the amount is usually astronomical."

"That's impossible, Bia. They lived in poverty. I was small, but I knew well that they lacked everything in that house. When my biological mother was still alive, we weren't even close to being rich, but there was fruit and cookies for me. In Ernestine's house, it was almost a case of need. She controlled every spoonful of rice we ate."

"And what if she spent the money?"

"But you said it would have been an astronomical amount."

"Yes, but even large amounts, if poorly managed, can run out. There are many cases of people who win the lottery and end up in poverty."

"That's true. I even watched a documentary once about these former rich people."

"Well, for now, it's all speculation, but we'll find out, Zoe. I promise."

I walk over to her and give her a hug.

"You're the best friend I could ask for."

"I'm more like a mother, right? Given my age."

"Well, I'll pray to look as good as you do when I'm forty-five."

She smiles awkwardly. Like me, she doesn't handle compliments very well.

"Did you mention going to buy ice cream?" She changes the subject.

"Yes, I'm treating myself. After everything that happened today, I'm allowed to break the diet."

I literally starve myself to stay within the limits of the contracts I sign, but every now and then I let myself indulge, even though I'll probably have to run ten kilometers tomorrow to make up for it.

"Do you think you can keep up this lifestyle for long? I mean, currently, a modeling career is quite promising, and you can model and photograph until you're almost my age because the fashion industry has finally realized that modern women have money to pay their own bills from thirty onward, not from twelve."

"I don't think I can. It was never what I wanted for myself. I planned to stay for a couple of years, just to fulfill the promise I made to Pauline."

"And you did it perfectly, because with the contract you just signed with Lykaios, you've become one of the top five highest-paid models on the planet. No offense, but he didn't need to offer so much. It would have taken you at least another three years to reach that level. This man has feelings for you, Zoe."

"I so want to be wrong, Bia. When I saw him today, it was as if I had never left."

"I want you to be wrong too, but please, take it slow. I'll always be rooting for your happiness, but this time you two might want to slow down a bit. The meeting you had in the past, from what you told me, was explosive."

I look at her, not knowing what to say. She's probably right, of course, but on the other hand, considering what happens when Christos and I are close, slowing down seems like a utopia.

"We'll figure out the story about your friend's accident. I have faith in God, but now tell me, what flavor of ice cream are you going to buy?"

"Don't you want to come with me?"

"Forgive me, but no. I'm dead tired, but I would have some ice cream," she says, winking.

"Lazy. Luckily for you, I like you enough to share my treats."

I TAKE LONGER THAN I intended at the supermarket because, apparently, everyone decided to shop at eleven o'clock at night.

If it were in another neighborhood, I wouldn't go out alone at this hour, but here it's quite calm. Besides, dressed as a boy, as Bia called my three-size-too-large sweatpants, loose jacket, and hooded sweatshirt with my hair hidden, no one would believe it's me.

Oh, and following my mom's recommendation, I decided to wear a mask. I felt ridiculous leaving the house, but to my surprise, when I arrived at the supermarket, the attendant was not only wearing one but explained that the governor would make it mandatory starting next Saturday. So, as I walked through the aisles, several people were also *masked*.

How crazy! I need to read more about this virus. My life is so hectic that when I get a break, I'm usually exhausted. People think modeling is super easy, but no one has any idea what it's like to stand for ten or twelve hours filming a commercial in freezing cold while wearing a tiny bikini.

I pass by a refrigerator and smile when I see my reflection.

In my profession, I can never neglect my appearance because a *paparazzo* could appear at any moment, but Bia told me that coming *disguised* was a good idea because it would help hide my bruised face.

So, while I browse the freezers for the flavor I want—strawberry with chocolate flakes—I feel like a secret agent.

Of course, there's only one tub of my favorite flavor, and the lid is slightly open.

Ugh!

Damn, I'll have to choose another one. Who knows if some crazy person messed with the ice cream and put something nasty inside.

There's no way I'll have the courage to eat something that isn't sealed.

"Can I help you?" an employee asks.

I don't look at him, afraid he might recognize me, but then I start laughing behind my mask. How could he?

"I wanted the strawberry with chocolate flakes, but the only tub is open."

"Ah, those neighborhood kids! They've been coming here and doing this lately. But if you're not in a hurry, I can go inside and see if I can find some sealed tubs."

"Would you do that?"
"Definitely. Strawberry with chocolate flakes is the best flavor."
"Isn't it? And I've been craving it for over a month."
"Wait a minute, my dear, and I'll see if I can find some."

Chapter 26

Mike

Minutes Later

Finally, that meddlesome Bia Ramos has left. I was losing hope, thinking she would spend the night at the old folks' house, but now that she's gone with the car, I can put my plan into action.

I look around before stepping out of the van, just to make sure there's no one on the street, and when I confirm it's deserted, I grab my equipment. From what I researched on the *internet*, I'll need only ten minutes for everything to be finished.

And *finished* is a good choice of word because when everything comes to an end, there won't be a beam left standing.

I wasn't planning to go back to her anyway. After seven months together, six married, during which I was patient and loving, I realized that the ice princess would never yield or adapt to my lifestyle.

Making Zoe my wife wasn't a matter of chance.

One fine morning, my mother was showing me in the newspaper a photograph of a friend's adopted daughter, and I had to admit she was beautiful. However, what caught my attention wasn't that but what she told me about the girl.

A model of only twenty years with a rising career. A pocket full of money that, unfortunately, was being wasted on old Macy, who didn't have the decency to die and get off her daughter's back.

I had been looking for a stable partner for my sexual preferences for a long time. And who better to be molded than an orphan, a needy girl rejected by several families?

Yes, I had my mother tell me everything about her. Being adopted by Macy and her husband was something of a last resort. Zoe was already quite old for anyone else to want her, so she was very lucky that the couple chose her. Maybe that's why she's grateful and keeps spending money on the two useless old folks.

She was such an easy target that I didn't need much effort. A shoulder to cry on for a needy woman is irresistible.

I didn't worry that she didn't open up to sex because sleeping with just one woman doesn't excite me. I even tried those little blue pills, but I still felt like I was eating a dish without salt or pepper. That's why my secret relationship with a Mexican woman didn't work out. A few years ago, I vacationed in that country and made the foolish mistake of marrying the woman in front of the authorities. It lasted a month. I returned to the United States, abandoning her without a word, and never thought about it again. Since I didn't recognize the marriage in any local registry office, no one has any idea of my mistake.

I think about my current wife, the ice queen—or would it be more accurate to say my "second wife"?

The idea of being married to two women without either knowing about the other excites me so much. I feel like a sultan.

I worked all my charm so that, after our marriage, she would understand how things would work, but that's when the saintly one surprised me by being horrified.

For God's sake, what century does she live in? Doesn't she understand how lucky she was for me to choose her? An acclaimed professor, who could have any student with a snap of my fingers, deigning to be with a reject?

She cried and locked herself in the room on our wedding night. Then she went to her parents' house, and only then did I realize I had been hasty. Yes, I dreamed of Zoe naked, being shared between me and my sex partners, but I also wanted the thousands of dollars in her bank account. Sooner or later, the old woman would die, and then I could enjoy what was rightfully mine.

I admit her fussiness was already irritating me, and to punish her for not yielding, I started playing games with my friends when I took her to our dinners, usually discussing a topic she was unfamiliar with, showing how she was stupid and inferior and should feel lucky to have the honor of being seen with me in public.

She never reacted, until our last dinner at the restaurant, where she seemed possessed when she disrespected my friends and humiliated me in front of everyone.

But of course, I knew I had just signed a million-dollar contract and couldn't simply let her go. I went after her at our house, but I'm not very good at making up, and because of the bitch, I ended up hitting her.

There. That was enough for the princess to call daddy and start World War III.

This week, we were supposed to meet to discuss the divorce, but for her misfortune and my luck, I will probably attend the funeral of my beloved wife.

I took out a life insurance policy for her worth three million dollars. With that amount, I'll be set for life, working only for fun.

The money from the stocks I sold, as well as the cleanout I did on our joint checking account, only served to pay my debts.

But now, it's over. I'm saying goodbye to a life of sacrifices and a middle-class salary, as the little whore threw in my face that day.

Mike Howard is about to become a millionaire.

Chapter 27

Zoe

Happiness exists and has a name and surname: strawberry ice cream.

The nice guy managed to get not just one, but two tubs, and now I'm completely committed to eating one all by myself. Bia usually likes to share, both the ice cream and the guilt of giving in to temptation, but today I'm going to go wild and finish off my half-liter tub alone.

I also bought some things for breakfast because dad lately doesn't have time for anything else, poor thing.

He's been so tired that I'm afraid he might end up falling ill too.

I turn the corner to enter my parents' street, and a little creature, which I believe is a skunk, chooses that exact moment to cross, nearly giving me a heart attack. I brake for a moment and watch until the little rascal walks away calmly, as if it has no worries in the world, while my soul has left my body and come back about ten times.

I start driving again and hear the announcer talking about the flu. Jesus, I'm starting to get terrified.

I can't just think about myself, but also about my elderly parents.

With the amount of traveling I do, I wouldn't be surprised if I end up getting infected, and if that happens, I won't be able to see mom. Her immunity is very low due to cancer and she can't even think of exposing herself to something like this.

Bia even said she believes that if the situation worsens, they'll soon declare a *lockdown* here in the United States, even closing the borders.

It sounds like science fiction and I hope it's all just alarmism because I can't afford to stop working. My family, and especially my mother's health, depends on me.

Now I estimate it's about two minutes until I get home. The night is dark, a starless sky, so when I see a bright flash, it's strange.

At first, I think it might be fireworks, but that doesn't make any sense since it's not the Fourth of July.

The closer I get, the more the sense of dread spreads inside me, and when I finally arrive, I scream in horror.

My parents' house is in flames.

I leave everything behind and, while running, call *911*.

"My parents' house is on fire. My mom has cancer, please send the fire department!"

"*Ma'am, what's your name?*"

"Zoe Turner. Did you hear what I said? My parents' house is in flames."

"*Please calm down.*"

"I'll be damned if I calm down! The address is 1014, Peanut Drive."

I throw the phone to the ground and run to the door just as it opens and my father comes out with mom in his arms. The nurse follows, shouting behind him.

Thank God!

But then I remember Bia.

"Where's Bia, Dad?"

"I don't know if she managed to get out, my daughter."

"Oh my Jesus!"

I run back inside but can't get past the living room. The heat is unbearable and I start having trouble breathing.

"Bia!"
"Zoe?"
"Come here, I'm here!"
"I can't make it, Zoe..."
"For God's sake, don't say that. Of course you can."
"Get out of the house, Zoe. Protect yourself!"
"No. I'm not leaving without you. There's no way I'm leaving without you."
"I trapped him, Zoe. I managed to trap the bastard in the room."
"Who? Who are you talking about?"
"Mike. He's the one who set the house on fire. He thought I was you."

I hear the fire truck siren in the distance but don't know if they'll arrive in time. I need to save my friend.

I grab a blanket from the only armchair that isn't on fire and, as I saw in a movie once, I make my way to where she is.

"You're crazy, Zoe! Get out of here! We're both going to die! Save yourself!"

"Not without you."

I feel the heat of the fire on my legs, but I don't stop until her hand grabs mine.

We're both crying.

"Crazy, Zoe! Why did you do this?"

"I would never leave you."

We start making our way to the exit and, despite feeling dizzy, in pain, and struggling to breathe, I can see movement outside and men approaching. But then, like in a nightmare, a heavy beam falls in front of us and everything turns red. The world is a ball of fire.

SCREAMS, CRYING, AND sirens reassure me that I'm still alive.

My eyelids are trembling as I try to open my eyes, but it feels like they're glued shut.

My legs are burning.

Voices drift in and out, and somehow, I know I'm outdoors.

I've never liked open spaces.

It's not exactly agoraphobia, but I prefer places where I feel protected.

They're moving me, and there's an oxygen mask over my face.

I try to recall the recent events, but it's all very confusing.

"She's reacting!" a voice says above me.

"Excellent! She's too pretty to die so young."

"Are you kidding? Pretty? The woman is beautiful! This is Zoe Turner, the *top model*!"

I feel a hand on my face, brushing away my hair.

"Jesus, it really is her! I didn't recognize her because of the soot. It's lucky her face wasn't damaged. It would be a crime if she hadn't managed to escape the fire."

At the mention of the word fire, my memory starts to return.

The fire, my parents. Bia telling me it was Mike who did it.

Where is my family? Nurse Ann? My friend?

I remember going into the house to try to save her and the beam falling in front of us. Then, before everything turned to darkness, the terrified look of the woman who had become one of my cornerstones.

If everyone is gone, it will be my fault, and as punishment, I'll be alone forever.

Chapter 28

Christos

Boston

That Same Night

I grew up hearing my mother say that phone calls in the middle of the night are never a good sign.

This concept of night is very relative to me. I've always slept only as much as necessary; I need only a few hours of sleep to feel complete, so it's not a problem that the phone rings almost at one in the morning, but who's calling is the issue.

Beau.

When he calls, no matter the time, it always brings with it the forewarning of something bad. He's a man of few words and never engages in social interactions without a purpose. Especially since we've talked twice today, which is a record for us both.

"What happened?"

"*Your girl, Zoe. There was a fire. She's alive, but she's been hospitalized.*"

It takes me less than a second to get up, my heart pounding irregularly.

"Send me the information on which hospital and everything else you can find out. I'm just going to change clothes and I'll be on my way."

As I get dressed, I don't let any other thoughts invade my mind, except for the fact that she's alive.

I'm used to suppressing my emotions. It's this self-imposed discipline that stopped me from going after her when she left me in Barcelona, but at this moment, none of my damn rules apply because nothing is stronger in me than sheer terror.

Minutes later, I leave the hotel room in Boston, at the same time sending a message to Yuri to inform him of what happened and passing on the name of the hospital Beau just sent me.

I'm not a relative, so to get to her, I'll have to use my influence. According to Beau, Zoe's parents were also at the house, which means there's no one else responsible for her because, as far as I know, they are all the family she has.

For the first time in years, I ignore any security protocols or plans; I just want to find her.

When I get to the elevator, my phone rings again.

"*I have a driver at your hotel door*," Beau informs me, and I don't even ask how he knows where I'm staying.

I'm not the type to rely on anyone, but at this moment, I'm relieved he has taken the initiative and arranged everything.

"Tell me what happened."

"*The house caught fire; they suspect arson, and if that's the case, I already suspect who is responsible.*"

"I'll kill him."

"*He's disappeared; I've already sent out a search. But that's not important right now. What matters is that everyone in the house survived.*"

"Everyone? How many were there?"

"*The parents and the agent, Bia Ramos.*"

"How did you find out about the fire?"

"*Because I trust my instincts. As we agreed, I was going to arrange protection for her starting tomorrow... today, but something told me to* get ahead of it. When my men arrived, however, they found the fire department already on site. There was nothing more to be done, so they did what they do best: investigate. They found a van parked outside, and before the police realized, they went looking for fingerprints. It belongs to or was at least used by Mike Howard."

"Do you think he found out we were checking him out and therefore took revenge?"

"No. He hadn't been informed of his dismissal from the university yet. I believe he would have tried something anyway. It's more likely he tried to kill her because he didn't want the divorce, but for now, it's all speculation, and I only deal with facts."

"How do you know he didn't die too? You said the *van* was parked in front of her parents' house."

"Because one of my men has already checked with someone from the fire department. It seems Zoe mentioned her husband's name while she was being rescued. The paramedics thought she was calling for him, but if you want a guess, I think she was trying to warn that it was him. Anyway, after they put out the flames, they did a search, and no other bodies were found at the scene. If he was there, he fled."

"I want him, Beau. Find him, but don't do anything. I'll handle this matter."

"*As for Zoe, we'll only know her real condition when we speak to someone in person. From what we know so far, she didn't suffer any serious burns, they were second-degree.*"

I close my eyes for a moment. Imagining her hurt is like having a razor cutting through my chest. The real sensation of something tearing me apart.

"It doesn't matter. She's alive. Everything else is secondary. The only thing I couldn't give back to her would be her life. As for the medical care she needs, she will have it available, even if I have to buy a hospital for it."

I hang up the phone and get into the car that, as he informed, was already waiting for me.

I barely close the door when my phone rings.

"*Christos, it's me,*" my assistant says. "*Your entry into the hospital has been cleared. Just say you're her boyfriend, but there's something you need to know. It's very serious. I have information from inside the government. The flu is spreading worldwide, and there are suspected cases in people hospitalized in the same hospital where Zoe is with her parents and her agent.*"

"And the level of contamination of this virus is very high," I say, since I've researched the subject. I think up to now the world hasn't been paying attention to the severity of the problem, but I'm always two steps ahead and had already anticipated, based on what experts were saying, that it wouldn't be just a common flu.

"*Yes, very high. Deadly, actually, especially for people the age of her parents. What I'm trying to say is that the government will shut everything down: businesses and any non-essential activities. Zoe's parents will be discharged later today because they didn't suffer anything serious. They were the first to leave, but as you should know, her mother has cancer. She will likely need to return to medical care soon. I thought about setting up a clinic with everything she would need, but outside a hospital environment. If it's true that the isolation will happen and she's hospitalized, they won't let her husband get close.*"

I think of my parents, who have been together for over forty years. If what Yuri is saying is true and they had to be separated, I don't think they would survive.

"Do whatever it takes. Hire doctors and nurses exclusively for her and make them available."

"*And about Zoe?*"

"I'm arriving at the hospital."

"*Her condition is not severe, although she's been sedated, but Bia Ramos is in a coma. Even if we arrange for Zoe to be moved to a safe place, her agent will have to remain hospitalized. No doctor will discharge her."*

"One thing at a time, Yuri. Take care of her parents. I'll handle the rest."

Chapter 29

Christos

Dawn

Getting into the hospital and obtaining information about her was relatively easy. There's almost nothing that money or influence can't buy, and I have plenty of both.

Her parents, along with the trusted nurse, will be moved by midday today to a clinic set up specifically to care for Zoe's mother.

When I arrived, I learned that I couldn't see her yet because she was being treated, so I went to them and introduced myself as her daughter's new employer.

What else could I say? That I'm the man who's obsessed with their daughter?

Macy and Scott are simple, kind people, and her mother reminds me a lot of mine: someone capable of smiling even in the greatest adversities.

She appears physically fragile, which contrasts with her personality. Clear-headed, she asked me about the details of the fire.

I didn't have many answers to give for now, but I intend to find out everything.

Besides trying to kill Zoe, the bastard set the house on fire with two elderly people inside. I hope what Beau discovered is true and that Mike is still alive, because I want to personally rid the planet of that vermin.

Neither of them, nor the nurse, could tell me what happened, only that they woke up to Bia's screams telling them to run out of the house.

They didn't mention Mike Howard's name, so I assumed they have no idea he's involved.

What was interesting was that when I explained the need to move them to a private clinic, her father didn't show surprise but said it would be the best solution, as he, like me, believed much more in the lethality of the new virus than the average person.

People inside the hospital, especially the staff, are already wearing masks — which only shows that many people in high places knew this virus was more contagious than was being reported. You can't take such rapid measures unless a security protocol was already being orchestrated behind the scenes.

I asked for written authorization to take charge of Zoe's care, and then her mother asked me a question that left me disoriented.

She asked if I was the *man from Barcelona*.

Her father looked at us, confused, so I understood she had shared about us with her mother.

I answered yes, even though I had no idea if that was a good thing.

Before I said goodbye, they wanted to speak with the doctor who treated their daughter. I stayed in the room.

The doctor explained to us, as Beau had already informed me, that the agent, who apparently is also a friend since she was staying at her parents' house, is in a coma, while Zoe is sedated due to the pain.

Neither of them suffered severe burns, they were second-degree and not deep, but we were told that they are somewhat painful and that the full recovery time could be one to three weeks. Even so, there may be scarring.

I will need to speak with the doctor alone later. If Zoe's situation isn't so grave, just like with her parents, I'll have her moved from the hospital as soon as possible. I won't risk her being contaminated by the virus.

As for the agent, there's nothing to be done. I don't believe they would authorize me to move someone in her condition.

From what I understood, what concerned the medical team was that both were exposed to smoke. Additionally, Bia Ramos took a severe blow to the head, which is why she is in a coma.

I mentally filed the information as I always do, committed to taking the necessary steps to ensure the agent receives the best possible care, but my thoughts now are all for Zoe.

I've rarely felt so lost.

It's as if life is forcing me to remove the blindfold of pride I've been wearing; it's like receiving a call for a wake-up.

For two years, I've been spinning in circles, keeping my distance, a true abyss, when I always knew there was no chance of burying what happened between us in the past.

I decide that the game is over.

I could have lost her today. The only woman who has misaligned my world, who in a short time made me feel and want more.

I don't know what will happen from here on out, but I will no longer keep my distance.

"Christos, I'd like to speak with you alone," her mother asks. After the doctor and Zoe's father left for the hallway, I was preparing to leave as well.

"Of course."

She points to the armchair near her bed. As soon as I arrived, I arranged for them to be transferred to a private room.

"Please, sit down. I want to talk about Zoe."

"About what you asked regarding me being the man from Barcelona?" I repeat the expression she used.

"Also, but for now, let me tell you about my girl. First of all, keep in mind that I am very old, but I am lucid. Yesterday, I had a conversation with my daughter, and now that you're here, I just had to put two and two together."

"I'm not sure I'm understanding."

"I believe you want to see Zoe right now. So do I, but according to the doctor, she is still sedated, so we have time. I'll start from the beginning. I always wanted to have children, but for some reason, God decided I wouldn't have my own biological ones. When my husband and I decided to adopt, we thought and weighed everything carefully. We were never rich, just lower-middle-class, both working from Monday to Friday, salaried. However, we believed we had what was essential for someone to be called a parent: an abundance of love to give."

"When we met in Barcelona, Zoe told me she had been rejected by several homes."

I speak to her, but in reality, that memory serves more for me.

I don't know if I had forgotten these details. More likely, I pushed them to the back of my mind, as a sort of defense mechanism against the woman who, now I have the courage to admit, not only hurt my pride but my feelings as well.

"Yes, we took her in during her pre-teen years, and I swear by everything sacred that I had never seen a sadder look in a child. She was always beautiful, but it wasn't that which made me certain I wanted her, but the hopelessness in her face. I won't go back and recount everything in detail because I don't feel emotionally strong enough for that. It was a difficult time for all three of us until we managed to convince her that we would never abandon her."

Now I am fully attentive to the conversation. Hearing Macy's words is like watching a film of Zoe's childhood and adolescence. She tells me how the girl was afraid to show her desires, always fearful that, by not pleasing them, she could be returned.

"Why were they rejecting her?"

"Who knows? Probably because they realized that being a parent was a twenty-four-hour-a-day, seven-days-a-week job. You don't turn off a child when you're tired of playing with her. It requires attention, love. It demands commitment. But I'm telling you this to get to the point about meeting you in Barcelona. I don't know what happened there in Spain. She didn't tell me what happened on the ship or that she had met someone, but when she returned, she fell into a deep depression. Even the prospect of the new career, which started soon after her return, didn't improve her. She went on trips, but when she came back, she locked herself in her room and hardly spoke."

"Do you think it was me who caused that?" I ask, utterly confused. "Zoe left me with only a note."

It's uncomfortable to share our brief relationship. I'm not one for confessions, but since the cards are on the table, so be it.

I recall what she asked me about whether the money in the envelope was a kind of payment.

Could it be? Was that the reason she left? Did she think I paid for the sex we had?

No, there has to be more to it than that. I might have been determined to win her over with a heavy hand, but at no point did I treat her like an escort.

"Keep in mind that she was only eighteen. She was always mature for her age, but still very young." There's no recrimination in her tone. "If you are here after so long, it's because what existed between you hasn't ended."

"As far as I'm concerned, it hasn't."

She nods her head.

"I can't say if the depression she had was related to what happened in Spain, and I don't want to meddle in your relationship, but I'm telling you all this to ask you, Mr. Lykaios, that if what you want with my daughter is just a fling, then leave right now."

I open my mouth, but she gestures with her hand, stopping me.

"Zoe is much stronger now than she was a few years ago, but she has already suffered too many losses. You are a rich and generous man. I thank you with all my heart for what you are doing for me, but do not hurt my daughter, or I will curse you for the rest of my days on Earth."

Chapter 30

Christos

Hours Later

It's already three in the afternoon, and Zoe's parents have been transferred to the clinic set up exclusively for their needs.

I also asked Yuri to arrange a property for them in case they wish to return to a *home,* and to assist them in obtaining new documentation.

I transferred a large sum of money to Scott's bank account. With the fire, they lost everything, including bank and credit cards.

I checked with the medical team, and there is no change in Bia Ramos's condition, and as I suspected, her removal to a private clinic is out of the question.

Now I am heading to Zoe's room. I've finally been authorized to see her, even though she is still sedated.

After the revealing conversation with Macy, my mind is boiling with information, and I can't come to any conclusions.

Yes, she was... *is* very young, but it couldn't have been just the confusion about the money that made her run away from me.

So what, then?

The truth is, it doesn't matter anymore. Everything pales in comparison to what happened, to the possibility that, at this moment, she could be dead.

I know that when I cross the threshold of the door, there won't be any more masks.

I reach for the doorknob, but before I can enter, the head doctor of the team caring for Zoe and Bia approaches.

"Mr. Lykaios, we need to speak urgently."

"Now?"

"Yes. Three patients who passed away yesterday tested positive for the new virus. If you have the means, I advise you to move Miss Turner as far away from here as possible, as quickly as possible."

"But she hasn't woken up yet."

"Yes, I know. But just as you arranged a private clinic for her parents, I believe you can do the same for Miss Turner. Her burns were not severe, although she might need corrective surgery on her hand in the near future, but none of that is as important as getting her out of here. She can recover at home. I'm sure you can set up home care in record time."

"Will she remain sedated?"

"For another day or two, at most, but you should take her away today."

I watch him walk away and think that, once again, all my plans with Zoe have gone off track. What matters now, however, is ensuring she stays alive.

Three Hours Later

I WENT OUT TO ARRANGE everything necessary for her transfer to a house that Yuri rented.

A team is now in place, and the doctor advised me to leave as soon as possible.

Once again, I'm standing in front of Zoe's room. Any moment now, the staff who will assist in her transport will arrive, so I take a few stolen minutes to check on her without any witnesses.

I open the door and, before approaching, I observe her from a distance. Knowing that she survived the fire and seeing that proof before my eyes are two completely different things.

The burning in my chest becomes unbearable, making it hard for me to breathe.

Fear. I was afraid of losing her.

Some might question this feeling, because until a few days ago, Zoe was still married to someone else, but what is a damn piece of paper compared to the certainty within me that she has always belonged to me? And always will.

"She could have died," the voice repeats in my mind, *"and then all that would remain are the memories of that night."*

Since she is still asleep, I have time to examine her without hurry.

The bed is raised at a thirty-degree angle, and the doctors informed me that it is necessary to keep it this way, as even though her nasal passages have been cleared, this is the standard procedure in cases of smoke inhalation.

Her face has not a single scratch, her right hand sticking out from under the sheet is bandaged, as well as the lower part of her legs, but nothing will be able to destroy her perfection for me.

When I first met her, I thought what attracted me to Zoe was her beauty; now I realize that there is no way to define what she evokes in me.

It's the feeling of being pulled by a magnet, a recognition of souls that she herself pointed out on the night we were together. It's as if everything between us *was meant to be*. No explanations or rules. We just are.

The bed seems too large for the delicacy of her body. Zoe shouldn't be in a hospital room, injured and defenseless.

A crazy urge to make her wake up, to prove that she's okay, overtakes me.

Once again, I silently swear that I will take revenge on Howard. There will be no mercy.

Beau is conducting a parallel investigation to the police's. I'm sure it's much deeper and more efficient, and at some point, we will catch him.

With the increasing number of deaths worldwide, as well as the rise in virus cases in our country, the new disease is already being treated as a pandemic, and the newspapers and *news sites* are only talking about it.

This has relegated what happened to Zoe's parents' house to a secondary issue.

Of course, I also used my influence to try to downplay the incident as much as possible, but if the fire had happened at another time, it would have been reported in the newspapers for months, since even though they don't know the whereabouts of Zoe's ex-husband, the police already suspects his involvement.

They questioned her parents, and both reported that their daughter was in the process of separation. Added to that is the fact that the police have been unable to locate Howard anywhere, which has solidified the suspicions about him.

What the investigators don't know is that they will never lay their hands on the bastard. There is no way to judge and condemn a dead man. Because that's what Mike Howard already is.

Zoe coughs, her face turning a deep, reddish color, but she soon returns to normal breathing.

Even in the period after her departure, when I refused to admit that I still desired her, there wasn't a day when, even for a brief moment, the blonde goddess didn't occupy my mind.

I brush the back of my hand over her face, and it feels like receiving pure, renewed oxygen in my lungs. In denial during these past two years, I didn't accept how much I wanted her. I preferred to work through that feeling as if it were resentment.

I'm not used to losing anything, and Zoe's departure in Barcelona took me by surprise.

All the theories I had created about her before dissolved when we reunited in my office in New York.

She is not frivolous, nor did she simply leave because she changed her mind.

Nor was what happened between us a figment of my imagination or a one-sided attraction. Every kiss and moan given by both of us that night were real and full of desire.

And now, after almost losing her, I've decided that I am no longer willing to deny myself anything.

I want everything, and it will be with her.

As if my will emitted a call, her eyes open and she looks at me.

"Christos, what happened?"

But then she seems to remember, letting out a scream of pure terror.

Chapter 31

Zoe

Days Later

They sedated me again. I know this because, through the haze of sleep, I heard a man talking to Christos.

I haven't spent the last few days completely unconscious, although I couldn't understand what people were saying.

I was terrified when I saw him in the hospital. My confused mind believed that no one but me had survived the fire, but now I remember seeing my parents leave, as well as Nurse Ann.

And what about Bia? Where is my friend?

I open my eyes and struggle to sit up. I brace my hand on the bed and let out a cry of pain. My skin pulls and burns. It's no longer bandaged, and when I see what's happened to the back of my hand, I start to feel dizzy.

I pull back the sheets and look at my legs. There are no more bandages, just a few scars from burns smaller than those on my hand, and they're painless.

Suddenly, something crosses my mind. I raise my hand to touch my face, but stop and get out of bed to try and see myself in the mirror.

Jesus Christ, please don't let me have been injured. I need my image to cover my mother's medical expenses.

My God!

When I step onto the floor, however, my legs give way and collapse.

A nurse appears, and when she sees me on the floor, she rushes to help me.

I immediately realize that although she is dressed in white, we are not in a hospital but in a house.

"My dear, I only stepped out for a moment. I'm so sorry."

"It wasn't your fault. I shouldn't have tried to get up." I struggle to speak, but my voice comes out raspy, and I end up in a coughing fit.

The woman is very strong, as she lifts me with ease and, after helping me back into bed, asks how I'm feeling.

I don't know how to answer that, so instead, I ask where I am.

"In Dr. Lykaios's house. I mean, I don't know if it belongs to him, but he was the one who brought us here. We arrived four days ago."

"Four days? And he... um... Mr. Lykaios stayed as well?"

"Yes. In fact, for the last forty-eight hours, no one has been allowed to leave. It has been officially declared that the world is in a pandemic, and the governor, in addition to imposing a curfew after five in the afternoon, has asked that no one leaves their homes except for essential workers."

"What? A curfew? Not leaving the house?"

I start to feel anxious again.

"Where are my parents?"

"Safe, in a clinic. Even before the *lockdown* was declared, there were already rumors of a huge increase in cases, and it seems that Dr. Lykaios anticipated it. That's why you're here too. It was advised by the team that treated you. No one should remain hospitalized unless absolutely necessary, as the risk of contamination is extremely high. Now, please try to stay calm. Are you in pain?"

"No," I reply, looking at my hand again. "Did I injure my face?"

"No, my dear. I don't know exactly what happened to you, but what's being said is that your house was destroyed by the fire. You were very lucky. You only have this mark on your hand, which a good surgeon will be able to fix."

"I'm not worried about vanity, but because I need my face to live. My family depends on me."

"Oh!" She seems startled. "I know who you are, of course, but I didn't know you worked to help your family. In any case, rest assured. Nothing more serious has happened."

I muster the courage to ask what I need, but the fear of the answer makes me feel nauseous.

"When I fainted during the fire, there was a woman with me. She's my agent and also my best friend, Bia Ramos. Do you know where she is?"

"Not in detail. Only that she remains hospitalized."

"Please, can you help me change clothes? I need to find a phone and find out where my friend is."

"I'm not sure if I should. It's better to speak with the doctor first."

"Christos... is Dr. Lykaios here in this house too?"

"Yes, I believe he's in the office, on the first floor."

"I need to speak with him, but first I want to take a shower."

"We'll wash you as best as we can and protect the wounds. Believe me when I say that the sensation of the water hitting them will be very painful."

AFTER MUCH DIFFICULTY and with the nurse's help, I took a bath with my legs out of the tub.

She washed my hair because my burned hand, at least for now, has become useless.

It's the only physical pain I'm feeling; in fact, it's more of a burning sensation. But nothing compares to the weight that's pressing on my chest.

Bia alone in the hospital? Why didn't he bring her too?

"Do you need help getting down?"

"Yes, please. Take me to Mr. Lykaios."

My steps are unsteady because I feel weak, and coupled with that is the fear of having to rest my injured hand on the railing and hurting myself further.

The staircase seems endless, and it takes us about five minutes to descend. When we finally reach the bottom, a very angry-faced Christos is staring at me.

"Zoe, what the hell do you think you're doing?"

Due to my timid nature, at first, I forget the entire situation and, accustomed to retreating when confronted, I step back, almost causing myself to fall.

To prevent the fall, I brace my injured hand and let out a cry of distress. The pain is so intense that tears stream down my face.

Seconds later, arms lift me up. Without a word, he walks me into a room and closes the door.

"Put me down," I ask, trying to salvage some dignity.

"No."

"I don't want to argue."

"I'm not arguing with you, just preventing you from killing yourself."

Damn controlling man!

Knowing that I have no chance of winning this battle, I allow myself to be carried in silence until he settles me on a comfortable sofa. But he doesn't move away. He sits on the edge — which is almost impossible, given his size — and examines my injured hand.

I flinch at his touch.

He notices but doesn't let go.

"Don't do that again," he says. "You could have fallen down the stairs."

"I needed to come down to talk to you." I don't look at him because, even with the pain, his proximity sets my body on fire. "Nurse Beth couldn't tell me what happened to Bia. I know my parents are fine, and I'm very grateful for what you did for them, but now I want to hear about everything else."

"Calm down."

"I can't. I need to know where Bia is, Christos. Please, tell me the truth."

"In a coma."

Chapter 32

Christos

Damn it! This wasn't how I planned to reveal everything to her, but I'm not known for sugar-coating things.

"Tell me everything."

I was expecting tears, so I'm fucking surprised when Zoe looks at me with a serene expression. She's definitely not the woman I knew in Spain, and yet, she's just as fascinating.

In our reunion and later, in the hospital, I assumed, perhaps based on past experiences, that she would need to be taken care of. Now, it only took me two seconds to realize that she doesn't. Zoe is sensitive and may have gone through much more shit in her young life than most people, but she's not a delicate flower.

I get up and sit in the chair across from her because the urge to touch her is too strong, and this is not the right time for that.

"I'll tell you everything, but first tell me how you're feeling."

"I'm not in pain, just the injury on my hand is a bit bothersome."

"From what I've discussed with the doctors, both of you passed out inside the burning room. A beam fell and hit your agent on the head."

"So it's serious?"

"I think any head injury warrants concern."

Again, no tears, but the hand that isn't injured clenches into a fist.

"It was Mike... my ex-husband."

I try not to show surprise at the confirmation. Zoe has no idea that I already know all about him.

"How are you sure?"

"Bia told me. I went out to buy ice cream. I was wearing loose clothing, had my hair hidden, and wore a mask because my mom asked me to."

"A mask?"

"Yes. The nurse told me we're locked down in this house because of the so-called virus. Mom told me that Dad had predicted this months ago. He's a Virgo with a Capricorn rising," she says, as if that makes any sense, "so he's always prepared for the worst."

"You shouldn't have gone out alone so late."

"I usually don't, but I was dying to... " her cheeks flush "maybe I shouldn't say this since you're my new employer, but the truth is I was treating myself to a half-liter tub of ice cream."

"Why did we meet? Was that what made you anxious?"

"That too, but mostly because of what happened that last week. As I told you, I asked for a divorce. I had already started the divorce process through a lawyer."

"I want to hear about that later."

She doesn't respond, and I don't press further.

"Continue telling me about the night of the fire. You'll need to give a statement to the police, but I spoke with my lawyers, and they will arrange for it to be done via video call."

"Is the situation that serious?"

"Worse than anyone would think. There were many infected people who didn't realize it. The virus spread rapidly, but there are laboratories worldwide in a real race against time to create a vaccine. Now, finish telling me about the night of the fire."

"I was gone for about half an hour. I took longer than I intended because I couldn't find the flavor... God, it seems so trivial now, compared to what happened."

"Continue."

"I stayed out longer than I expected. When I came back, I immediately knew something was wrong from the glow in the sky. I called emergency services and ran to my parents' house. They were already out on the porch. Dad struggling to walk with Mom in his arms. Ann, the nurse, was coming up behind them, but there was no sign of Bia."

I try to keep the tension and rage I've been holding back for days in check because I don't want her to know what I've planned for the bastard.

"I went into the house. It was very hot, and there was fire everywhere. Bia was screaming that it was Mike and that she had trapped him in the room. From what I understood, he mistook us both because I had left the house in my friend's car and was also wearing large clothes. Now she's in a coma because of me."

"No, Zoe, you couldn't have predicted that. How could you? Unless... wait. Had he threatened you before?"

"Threatened, no," she says, seeming uncomfortable.

"Then. No one could have suspected he would go to that extreme. I found out he was stalking you."

"He was?"

"Yes. A van was found almost directly in front of your parents' house. If he hadn't attacked then, he would have done it while everyone was asleep."

I feel my jaw tighten at the thought. The anger I feel is overwhelming.

"Oh, my God!"

She covers her face with her hands, and the sight of the injury makes me lose control. Lockdown or not, I'm going after the bastard.

"You shouldn't have gone into the house, Zoe."

"Bia couldn't get from the hallway to the exit. How could I leave her there, alone? Mimicking what I'd seen in a movie, I wrapped a blanket around my body and walked through the fire. I protected us both and we were almost out when the beam fell, I think. But I didn't realize it had hit her head."

"You said your ex-husband hadn't threatened you before," I say, trying to understand what drove the bastard to go so far. But the word *ex* scratches my throat like acid.

"Yes. What you saw on my face, the assault I suffered, was the first time it happened. That night, I told him our marriage was over."

Hearing her say that makes a whole mess of confused emotions rise within me.

She's free or, at least, no longer considers herself married.

But she *was* married.

Somehow, what happened between us wasn't strong enough because she moved on while I stayed frozen in time.

I get up and walk to the window, turning my back to her.

"It wasn't your fault. Neither the assault nor the fire. It wasn't something that could be predicted."

"But after he assaulted me, I should have stayed in a hotel. I ended up putting my family at risk."

"Regretting the past changes nothing," I say, turning back to face her.

This applies to both of us, of course. And I'm not only referring to the recent past.

I think she gets it because she opens her mouth, but before she can say anything, I continue:

"About your friend, she's not in danger of dying, but unfortunately, she can't be moved from there, so the primary concern right now is the virus. But as soon as the doctors clear her, I'll arrange for you to see her."

"You mean, she's coming here?"

"Or I can arrange a residence for both of you. I don't think it's advisable for you to stay with your parents because of Macy's health, but the final decision is yours."

"I thought no one could leave... I mean, I thought we'd stay here. That you'd stay."

"I can't put my life on hold. You're not a prisoner, but there's no set time for you to leave. I just ask that if you decide to do it again, this time, tell me face to face."

Chapter 33

Zoe

"Mom?"

"Zoe, my daughter, I can't believe you're awake! I've been calling every day."

"Ask Dad to join the video call. I want to see you both."

"I'm a mess. You'll be in for a shock."

Against all odds, I start laughing. Mom Macy has always been very vain, and even though cancer has taken almost half her weight, she makes sure her regrown hair is always neatly done. She also never skips her lipstick.

After Christos left me alone, the nurse came by with a box containing a cellphone. My line had been transferred to this new device. The man thinks of everything.

Being with him again is like riding a roller coaster. Exciting and a little scary. His mood swings confuse me. He argued with me when I arrived, then seemed like he wanted to stay by my side, only to minutes later suggest that if I wanted, I could move out.

The Zoe he knew would have run away without a second thought, but that's no longer how I face my problems.

We need to talk, but it's not the best time. However, I don't intend to go anywhere. When Bia is discharged—God willing, it will be soon—I'll ask him to bring her here. As for me, I won't budge until we've cleared up everything about the past.

I'm tired of being afraid to live.

I left Barcelona thinking he was involved in the incident with Pauline, but if I'm honest, I probably would have fled anyway upon receiving that money in the envelope.

No more. I almost died and lost my family and friend because of that sick man I married. It's time to face adversity as an adult.

"*Done,*" Mom says, and Dad appears behind her on the screen, waving.

"I love you both. I can't express how much. Forgive me for what happened."

They look so old... So fragile.

"*We only found out that Mike might have been the one who set our house on fire when the police came to question us at the hospital. You're not to blame for anything, my daughter. If Bia hadn't been so smart, it could have been much worse.*"

"I promise I'll work to get you another house, Mom."

The insurance should cover the damage caused by the fire, but since the house had already been mortgaged twice, for my parents, it won't make a difference. My goal is to pay off those debts and buy them a new home.

"*It doesn't matter, Zoe. We can replace material things, not lives. I'd like to hear news about Bia. I'm worried about leaving her alone in that hospital.*"

"I am too, Mom, especially since she has no family, only us. I plan to call Miguel later to confirm if that's true because if not, someone needs to be informed."

"*How are the burns?*"

"They were superficial. Maybe the one on my hand will leave scars, but I can fix it with surgery. And you?"

"*Ann and I only had smoke inhalation. Other than that, it's just worry about you and Bia.*"

"And your... *um...* other pains?"

I hate the word cancer.

"*I think I've gone through so many emotions these past few days that God spared me from everything else. I've hardly needed the medication.*"

"That's good! And Dad?"

"*I'm fine too, my daughter,*" he says, appearing on the screen again. "*Now, take care, okay? And let us know about Bia as soon as you hear any news.*"

I end the call and look up the hospital number where Beth said my friend is hospitalized on *Google*.

It takes a while for someone to answer, and when they do, it takes at least ten minutes before they tell me there has been no change in her condition.

I need to call Miguel later. He's probably somewhere around the world, but he'll want to know about our friend.

Three Days Later

I HAVEN'T SEEN HIM since. Yesterday, I had dinner alone in the room because the nurse told me Dr. Lykaios was locked in his office and didn't want to be disturbed.

I took that as: *keep your distance,* and being a good girl, I obeyed.

But today I decided I won't stay in the suite just so he won't see me.

If my presence bothers him, why did he bring me here?

He might not want to talk, but I do.

I woke up feeling better and no longer find it so difficult to hold things with my burned hand. The problem is when I bump the back of it against something. That really stings.

Besides the nurse, there was a doctor stationed on the first floor of the house, but he said yesterday that since I no longer need care, Beth is enough to stay with me. Apparently, hospitals need all the staff they can get as cases keep rising.

This morning I called my mom again and asked her what's going on with Mike's disappearance.

She doesn't know anything either and said that when she tried calling his mother, her friend, she refused to answer. Or rather, she answered but said she didn't want to speak to anyone from our family.

The police must have been looking for her, of course. It's the only reason for her to be angry since I've only seen her once. Not even at my wedding, at the courthouse, did she show up.

Today it finally hit me what happened that night of the fire.

Mike must have gone insane. Does he hate me so much that he would destroy his own life just to get revenge for me leaving him?

I never considered myself a violent person, but I don't think it would be safe for him to cross my path if I were holding a weapon.

I walk to the bedroom door, glad that my legs are more stable now. My plan is to walk around the garden of the house, which is huge.

I put on one of the dresses from the *closet* that fits me perfectly.

God, he thought of everything.

Why take care of me if, when we were together, he seemed to want to stay as far away as possible?

I shake my head, confused, with no idea what those mixed signals from him mean.

I barely set foot outside the room when my phone rings. I had forgotten it on the bedside table and go back to answer it.

"Hello?"

"*Zoe Turner?*"

"Yes. Who's speaking?"

"*My name is Nick Irving. I'm a police detective and a friend of Bia Ramos.*"

Chapter 34

Zoe

"*Ah, the damn guy.*" I think, feeling my cheeks heat up. "Yes, now I know who you are. If you're calling to ask about Bia..."

"No, I've already been to see her. I'm from the Miami Police, but when I heard what had happened, I flew to Boston."

"And they let you in?"

"*I used some persuasive methods,*" he says enigmatically.

"I'm so worried about her, Mr. Irving."

"*The worst is over, Miss...*"

"Just Zoe."

"*Alright, then you can call me Nick. The doctors told me she's in an induced coma now, Zoe,*" he says, as I sit on the bed, mentally thanking God. "*There was no serious damage. The swelling in her brain has gone down, too.*"

"Oh, Jesus!" I almost groan but regret it two seconds later. "I'm sorry, I'm just very sensitive about hospitalizations, especially with loved ones. Bia is my best friend."

"*She also speaks very highly of you.*"

"Thank you so much for calling me, Nick. I've been so anxious without news about her."

"*It's good to know you're feeling more at ease, but that's not why I called.*"

"It's not?"

"*Bia asked me to investigate a financial settlement related to an accident. Apparently, the party compensated claimed they didn't receive enough for the victim's treatment, in this case, a little girl named Pauline Lambert. Is that correct?*"

"Yes."

"*The agreed settlement was one million dollars.*"

"What? That's impossible. They lived in poverty. Ernestine... Pauline's mother still lives like that to this day."

"*Yes, I know. I'm a detective, Zoe. Almost a bloodhound. The moment I sense something off, I don't stop until I uncover everything. I know how she and her daughter lived, and there's a reason for that. Your friend's mother handed all the money she received to a boyfriend to invest, and the guy disappeared, leaving them without any resources.*"

"Jesus Christ! Why would she do something like that?"

"*If you want an honest answer, she never intended to use that money for her daughter's treatment. She thought the settlement was a sort of lottery ticket. And there's more: the Lykaios family didn't even need to provide any money. They weren't at fault in the accident. It was Ernestine's boyfriend who was on drugs, driving the vehicle that carried your friend and caused the accident. He died on the spot. Even the person Bia asked me to investigate, Christos, was injured. He broke a leg and was hospitalized with a suspected concussion.*"

I feel my stomach churn. I had suspected, after reuniting with him, that Christos wasn't the kind of person Ernestine had painted him to be and that the story hadn't happened as she said, but I didn't imagine it was something so sordid.

"I don't even know what to say. If the boyfriend died, then who ran off with the settlement money?"

"*Someone else. Apparently, the woman has a knack for choosing the wrong men.*" "*I don't know what this guy means to you, my dear, but if you had any doubts about his character, you can go ahead and find your happiness. He did much more for your friend than was required. Some would say he wasn't obligated at all."*

"If he wasn't at fault, why offer the settlement?"

"If I had to guess, first of all because both he and his parents are honorable people with money saved for several lifetimes. Moreover, even without any fault, it wouldn't be advantageous for the Lykaios family to have their name involved in an accident. In any case, they did far more than they needed to. If your friend ended up in need after the accident, the only person responsible for that is her mother."

"Thank you again, Nick. You have no idea what you've done."

"You could return the favor by keeping me updated on Bia's condition. I can't always leave everything here in Florida, so I don't know when I'll be able to see her again."

"Don't worry about that. I'll call you as soon as there's any news. Is this the number you used to call me?"

"Yes. Well, I'd better go. Take care, Zoe."

"You too."

"Just one more thing. When the police catch your... your ex-husband, right?"

"Yes."

"When the police catch him, I plan to keep a close eye on everything and make sure he never sees the light of day again."

After he hangs up, I can't bring myself to get out of bed. There's so much to process, especially concerning Pauline's suffering.

One million dollars!

Money more than enough for my friend to have a good quality of life.

But there's something else, something much more serious that I need to correct.

Christos.

I judged and condemned him without even giving him a chance to explain.

When I asked him if the money he left for me in Barcelona was payment for our night together, he told me not to insult us both by saying something like that. And now, with Nick's answer, I realize I wasted two years of our lives suffering and blaming him for something he didn't do.

Nothing would guarantee we'd still be together today, of course, but at least we would have enjoyed that summer.

I leave the room determined to clear up our story once and for all.

I want a second chance for both of us, and I'll do whatever it takes to get it.

THE OFFICE DOOR IS closed, as usual, but now I hear music coming from inside.

A saxophone.

He mentioned to me, during our one dinner in Spain, that he played the instrument and usually did so when he was stressed.

The soft melody fills the house, calming the anxious beats of my heart.

Somewhat in a trance, I walk towards the sound.

It's almost like a call.

The music gets louder as I get closer. I don't know if he wants to see me, but we've been apart for too long.

After today's revelations, free from guilt, I feel hungry for him.

I look at my feet, summoning the courage to turn the doorknob. I take a deep breath and slowly push the door open.

I lift my head, and he's playing, his back to me, seemingly lost in his own world.

I feel like an intruder and turn to leave.

"Don't go."

In my mind, it's like a replay of when we first met. As if life is giving us a chance to start over.

"I'm sorry to interrupt you," I say as I watch him place the saxophone on an armchair. "No, that's a lie. I don't regret coming in. I've stayed away for too long, Christos. I want you."

Chapter 35

Christos

I've waited a long time for this.

The moment I would have her as mine again.

I know that despite what she says, she's nervous but also excited. Her eyes are sparkling, and her cheeks have a deeper pink in the center.

I move closer, overwhelmed by her beauty.

"You're perfect."

Zoe shakes her head and lifts her hand with the burn.

"Not anymore."

"You will always be perfect to me."

"I don't usually believe in compliments. People seem to say what we want to hear, but I feel beautiful next to you."

We're close, but not touching.

"You said you wanted me. Show me."

"I don't know how to seduce."

"Just breathe, Zoe. Even your breath turns me on."

Encouraged, she presses our bodies together. She closes her eyes for a few seconds.

"Like last time."

"What?"

"The same tingling. The shivers. Being close to you is like touching the sun, Christos."

I can't resist moving my mouth down her silky skin. Soft and feminine. Fragrant.

She places her hand on my chest and, like me, inhales my scent. At that moment, we are two animals, male and female, recognizing each other.

Her uninjured hand comes to my face.

"I remember everything from that night. I wanted to forget, but I couldn't," she says.

"I won't let you forget. This time, I'll mark you so deeply inside that you won't be able to leave."

I take her mouth in a desperate kiss, even more urgent than the one we shared in my office.

Licks, sucks, kisses.

An erotic, lustful, immoral contact.

In no time, kisses are no longer enough. I want to feel her skin.

To look at and touch her breasts, pussy, and ass. To taste with my tongue and teeth. To earn moans. Cries for more.

I pick her up and carry her up the stairs straight to my room.

When I set her down on the floor, I take a step back, devouring with my eyes the *sexy* body covered by a light dress.

She doesn't seem willing to wait and comes towards me. She bites my chin and traces her finger along the collar of my shirt.

She opens a button and kisses the patch of skin underneath, then bites again.

My cock is hard as steel, and it's hard to let her explore.

"I missed you so much," she says.

Now uninhibited, she opens the rest of the buttons, but it takes her a while since she's using only one hand, so I take the chance to watch her.

"Look at me, Zoe."

"I dreamed of touching you," she says.

I rid myself of my shirt.

"I can't allow that today. I can't go easy or wait. I'm dying to feel that tight pussy holding me."

"Oh my God..."

I run a finger down the neckline of the dress and then lick the valley between her breasts.

"Too much fabric."

I pull the dress over her head, and she raises her arms to help me.

She's only in panties, her pointed nipples offering themselves, begging for my tongue.

I lean in and take one between my lips.

"Ahhhhhhhh..."

I suck harder, letting my teeth graze, and she leans on me.

"Bed. I don't want to hurt you."

I sit her on the edge, legs dangling. I pull down her panties and inhale her womanly scent.

She screams at the feel of my stubble on her sensitive clit, peeking out from between the slick lips of her arousal.

"I want that honey dripping on my chin."

I spread her thighs and lick her pussy.

I suck on her clit, preparing her for me, my middle finger playing in her warm, wet heat.

She tries to move away, restless and eager. I know she's close to climaxing. Delicious and sensitive.

Her hips move in circles. Soon, she tells me she's coming, but even when her pleasure fills my mouth, I don't stop.

It's not a choice. I can't stop. Her taste is the finest delicacy in the world.

I force myself to get up and remove the rest of my clothes. Zoe is still reeling from her climax, somewhat disconnected from the world.

Like the first time we had sex, a visceral desire drives me to possess her endlessly.

She opens her eyes and her gaze at my naked body makes it hard for me to keep my arousal at a safe level.

"I don't want to use a condom. I'm clean."

"So am I, but I'm not on the pill. There was no need."

"I'll be careful, but I want to feel your wet flesh on my cock. I want you to feel every vein of mine opening you up."

"You're going to kill me if you keep saying those things."

I move between her legs, spreading them wide.

I lick her clit once more because I can't resist, but I can't wait any longer to be inside her.

"I'm dying to feel you inside me."

I rub my cock against her pleasure spot, and she moans.

"Please."

I only place the head at her opening and, watching my erection part her pink flesh, I plunge all the way in.

We both scream. My body is tense; I pull out slowly to thrust back into her tight walls.

I thrust hard and she lifts her hips, all female, fiery, needy.

Zoe is on fire beneath me, feverish, begging, sucking my nipples, ordering me to go harder.

She holds me inside her, not just physically.

It's been like this since the first time. I was inside her; I've always been inside her.

I focus on our bodies, as I can't name what we are or feel.

I pound harder and feel her expand to accommodate me. She's too delicious, and her muscles pulsing around my flesh are driving me insane.

"I'm crazy about you, Zoe," I say, thrusting harder. "I haven't been with anyone else since you left because no one else would satisfy me. It's just this pussy, your moans of pleasure, and that beautiful face I want on me."

My words seem to trigger something in her. She becomes wild, her legs closing around my waist, pulling me into a harder fuck.

I quicken the pace and she asks for more.

The sensation of our slick bodies fitting together is incredibly erotic, driving me to an even greater state of madness.

I fuck her deeply and quickly, and she howls, coming in constant spasms.

She tightens and releases around my cock, and I'm delirious, out of control, licking wherever my tongue can reach, needing every bit of her.

I thrust a few more times, without restraint. I want to prolong this delicious torture forever, but as my cock thickens even more, heavy and eager to spill inside her, I know I've reached my limit.

I massage her clit, wanting to drag her with me.

"Come for me," I whisper, nibbling her earlobe, and she does, screaming my name.

I pull out of her and kneel between her legs. I jerk off my cock, and then my orgasm hits with the force of a wild gallop.

I watch my seed spill onto her breasts and abdomen.

I lower myself onto her body, bracing on my elbows.

She spreads her thighs further to accommodate me.

"You're mine, Zoe."

"I never doubted that, Christos. Since that first night, it's always been you. I love you."

Chapter 36

Christos

The next morning

"Tell me about yourself. This between us is madness. I feel like I know you deeply, and at the same time, I know nothing. At that dinner in Spain, you didn't give me much about yourself."

"Why did you leave? I know what happened between us was strong for you too."

"How could it not be? You were my first." She looks away. "You were my *only*."

"What?"

"I don't want to talk about it in detail right now, but Mike and I, we never... please, let's not ruin everything by bringing him into this. Just know that my marriage was never consummated."

I want her to tell me more about it, but I let it go. However, I wouldn't be myself if I didn't investigate what I need to know.

"I'll talk about myself, but if we're starting over, I need to understand why you left, Zoe. That's how my mind works: organize one room before moving to the next."

"I need to get dressed. It's a serious topic, and I don't want to discuss it naked."

I reach out and turn on the bedside lamp.

She holds the sheet against her body as she gets up. I watch her without looking away. We both know that after this night, I know every inch of her even better than before. Every curve and spot, because I've studied my goddess.

Looking embarrassed, yet paradoxically with a challenging gaze, she lets the fabric fall, allowing me to see her.

My cock reacts.

"Are you teasing me?"

"No," she replies, but I know she's lying because her nipples are hard.

"Do you want to talk or fuck?"

"You said you wanted to clarify..."

"The past can wait a little longer."

I stand up and her throat moves when she sees my arousal.

I move my hand over my cock and she watches intently.

"Kneel, Zoe. I want to taste your mouth."

Obediently, she does as I command, but surprises me when, after just licking the head of my cock, she takes me in deeply.

The sensation of her hot tongue, her soft, hungry mouth swallowing me, is so pleasurable that I fear I might not be able to stay on my feet.

I never relinquish control during sex, but seeing her brave enough to take the initiative is driving me insane with desire.

I push my hips and she chokes, but soon gets the hang of it.

"That's it. Take me all the way, Zoe. You suck so damn good."

I caress her face as I watch my woman, naked, sucking my cock. I grab her nipple, pinching it, and she intensifies her sucking.

I reach my limit.

"I'm about to come. Relax your throat. I want to see you drinking me, love. Swallow it all."

I hold her face and push deeper. One, two, three times, before spilling into the warmth of her mouth.

I close my eyes for a moment, the force of the orgasm knocking me off balance.

I lower myself and lift her into my arms.

"You're not going anywhere anymore, my Zoe. You should never have gone anywhere."

Two days later

IT'S MORNING NOW, AND I realize we were quite presumptuous to think we could have any serious conversations within the first forty-eight hours together.

We haven't left the room except to eat.

I took the opportunity to dismiss the nurse, since the doctor had already left.

Zoe went out to say goodbye to her, and her embarrassment at realizing what Beth would think made me see how she's still a girl.

Now, with the house to ourselves, I'm preparing a pasta dish while she sits on a stool at the island, watching me.

"Tell me why you left. The serious topic you said we needed to discuss."

"It wasn't because of the money you left in the envelope, although it crossed my mind... anyway..."

"I would never offend a woman like that."

"Now I know that, but I knew so little about you. I still don't know you, to be honest." She pushes a strand of hair away from her face. "What I'm trying to say is that yes, I was offended by the money, but I would have left anyway after what I discovered."

"Let's clarify the money issue. I was going to buy that fleet anyway, which made me, in a way, your employer. You never received payment for the time you worked there. You were in a foreign country, after all the shit you went through, and without a dime. I didn't want you to stay with me out of necessity, but out of choice. That money, although more than your payment on the ship, was security for you."

"I ended up using it anyway," she says, blushing. "There was no way I could leave without doing so. But I'm not sure I understood what you just said."

"I said you didn't know me well, Zoe. The opposite was also true. I imagined that everything that happened between us was reciprocal, but there might come a time when you wanted to leave and were too shy to tell me."

"Since you're clarifying some points, let me do the same, Christos. I was very young..."

"You're still young."

"Yes, but I knew what I wanted when I agreed to stay with you. I would never let a man touch me against my will. It didn't occur to me that the money represented security for me. I never had a serious boyfriend. Despite that, as I said before, it wasn't what made me leave but a misjudgment."

I put down the knife I was using to cut the tomatoes and move closer to her. It's not often that I'm surprised.

"Misjudgment about me?"

"You introduced yourself as Xander Megalos and, that morning, when I called you that for your maid, she corrected me, saying everyone knew you as Christos Lykaios. I had heard your name many times in one of the foster homes where I lived. I went through several, as I told you, but in one, in particular, there was a girl. She became quadriplegic when the car she was in had an accident and flipped over. Her name was Pauline Lambert."

Ice spreads in my chest. I know who she's talking about. How could I forget?

Tears are rolling down her cheeks and I want to comfort her, but I'm not sure if that's what she wants.

"Her mother, Ernestine, painted you as a demon. The man who, because he was high..."

"What?"

"Let me finish, please. She repeated every day that, because of you, my best friend, my only friend at that time, couldn't walk or sit. She said other horrible things I don't want to remember. I had lost my mother recently. It was already the third temporary home I was in, and Pauline and I had formed a very strong bond. I ran without wanting to, took rain and jumped on one foot because she couldn't do any of that. It was for her that I became a model. That was her dream. The last request she made of me when I left her home. Do you remember the day we met?"

"You were taking pictures."

"Yes, with a little doll in hand that represented her. I loved her with all my heart and, in return, hated you, the man who hurt my friend. But even when I discovered your name, I didn't want to believe it, so I went to Ernestine's house. She repeated the whole story she had told me when Pauline died."

"She died?"

"Yes, very young still. Soon after Mommy Macy adopted me."

I rub my face.

Damn it! I never imagined anything like this.

I step away to turn off the heat.

"If you're here with me, I assume you already know the whole truth."

"I do, and that's why I made a decision, Christos. When we were together for the first time and I discovered who you were, I thought fate was mocking me. Now I think differently. I believe we met because it was meant to be. I'm not asking for anything, especially since I'm not completely free yet, but this time, I'm not leaving. If it ends, you'll have to say goodbye to me."

Chapter 37

Christos

Hours later

Her words keep echoing in my head.
"*If it ends, you'll have to say goodbye to me.*"
Destiny. Choices.
Leaving everything to chance?
No, we're beyond that stage.
Decisions. That's the central issue now.

We've separated, spun the world around, and in the end, we've ended up the same way as two years ago. This time, I hope for a different outcome.

"I'm Greek, as you already know," I begin, giving her what she asked for.

Zoe is right. When we met, in my arrogance, I didn't share anything about myself because I thought we'd have time for that.

"Only child. My parents have been married for over forty years and moved to the United States when I was only three. I spent much of my life between London, New York, and California, working."

"I love California."

"I thought your dream was to be a farmer."

She lifts her head from my chest.

"You remember that?"

"I do."

She seems awkward and changes the subject.

"Which part of California?"

"My home?"

"Yes."

"The main one is in Sausalito, near San Francisco, but I have other places in the country as well. New York, Chicago. My work requires a lot of travel, and I don't like hotels."

That's something Beau and I have in common. We both own properties around the country so we don't have to stay in hotels.

"I understand. They're so impersonal." She smiles. "I miss my pillow."

"The pillow?" I only now realize how thirsty I am to learn every little thing about her. No newspaper or research could reveal what's part of her secret world.

She smiles again and nods.

"Yes. I have one shaped like a boomerang and I can't sleep properly without it. Besides fashion, what other fields are you involved in?"

"I'd need to get a notebook. Sometimes even I get lost. I have various companies, but most are related to fashion."

"Did you demand exclusivity because you wanted me back?" she asks point-blank.

"I don't know how to forgive, Zoe. To be honest, I told myself I wanted you around, but I didn't give myself a real reason. I just wanted you close."

"To get revenge."

"Maybe."

"Two years ago, when we met, I didn't know what you wanted from me. I wanted you, but I thought it would be impossible for a man like you to be with an inexperienced and unsophisticated girl like me. You captivated me, Christos, and I fell from fifty stories when I thought you were the one who hurt my friend."

"I wasn't to blame for the accident, Zoe, but I'm no saint."

"What does that mean?"

"That I'll go to hell, but I'll find Mike Howard. And then, I'll punish him for what he did."

"Punish how?"

"You don't want to know, baby. Just remember one thing: I never forget or forgive."

"You've forgiven me."

"There was nothing to forgive. What happened was a misunderstanding. You were wrong to leave without asking my side of the story first, but as your mother said when we talked, you were too young. I don't have that excuse. I credit my Greek pride for never having gone after you."

"My marriage was a mistake."

"Why didn't you love him?"

"I did, but mainly because I never forgot you. And I hated myself for that. Even though I thought he was responsible for Pauline's accident, I still wanted him."

"So why did you get married? I mean, dating I understand, but marriage is a very definitive step."

"I could blame my youth for that as well, but it happened less than a year ago, so that's not a good excuse. The truth is, I was vulnerable." She shakes her head from side to side. "If it were the other way around, it would break my heart."

"What?"

"Seeing you married to another woman."

"Why?"

"Because I knew I had married for all the wrong reasons, but not you. That's not part of who you are, Christos. On the day you marry a woman, I believe she will be yours forever."

"Yes, that's true."

I know that, like my parents, when I choose a woman, she will be the only one for me.

"Mike and I... we never had intimacy."

"Because he was promiscuous?"

"How do you know that?"

"I told you, Zoe. I'm no saint. I did a cursory investigation when I learned you were married, but when I saw his face that day, the way the bastard hurt you, I had a deeper investigation done."

"He wasn't just promiscuous; it was much worse. Our relationship was never based on physical attraction. We exchanged no more than half a dozen kisses in the month before the wedding, which was also the entire period we knew each other. Anyway, I barely signed my name at the registry office and knew I had made a mistake, but I only understood the extent of that mistake when, on our wedding night, he told me he would only be satisfied with group sex. I'm embarrassed to tell the rest. It's so infamous."

"It's not necessary; I know everything."

"I was so stupid to get involved with him, and my family almost paid the price. Bia could have died."

"Naive, impulsive, yes. Not stupid. He was a family friend."

"Yes, that's true."

"There's something I need to tell you. I told you I investigated Howard, but I didn't mention that I ended his career at the university. The same day you left New York, right after discovering he had assaulted you, I destroyed his professional life."

She looks surprised but not shocked.

"Is that what you meant by punishing him?"

"No, that was what I did for daring to hurt you, but for trying to kill you, there is no forgiveness."

"If I didn't say that this side of you scares me, I'd be lying."

"But it's who I am, Zoe. For better or for worse."

"And yet, even being so relentless, you wanted me back."

"It's not something I can control."

"And would you, if you could?"

"I don't know. This thing we have together, I've never lived it before. I've never been jealous of a woman or considered her mine, but I went crazy when I found out about your marriage. I wouldn't have hired you if I knew you were married."

"Would I be a terrible person if I said I'm glad you didn't find out until we closed the deal? Otherwise, I don't think we'd ever get close again."

"I don't believe that. Life always finds a way to align the pieces on the board. Our game wasn't over. We barely started, and you soon abandoned the game."

"And how much longer do you think it will take to reach the end? Until this feeling, this madness that takes over my body when you touch me, that makes me forget my own name, ends?"

"Maybe never."

I hope it never does.

But she's not ready to hear that yet.

Chapter 38

Christos

One Week Later

"Mom, you can't leave the house."

Jesus, I'm trying my best not to lose my patience, but I swear to God she drives me crazy with her nonchalance. I've lost count of how many times she's told me in the last few days that she won't give up the few years she has left — which I think is an exaggeration, given that the women in her family live past a hundred — being cooped up inside the house.

To anyone listening, it sounds like she's in a studio apartment, not a nine-bedroom mansion.

"Christos, I'm not saying I'm going to wander around aimlessly, but we don't know how long this phase the world is going through will last. We need to find a way to get together."

"The only safe way would be for me to drive to see you."

"That's seven hours of driving."

"Mom, even if I use my plane, there are still the flight attendants who've had contact with other people. I won't risk contaminating you."

I run my hand through my hair, frustrated. I'm very close to my parents. Although work doesn't allow us to get together often, when possible, we spend time together, including on my island in Greece.

"I want to meet her. You never told me about your girlfriends, but you've mentioned Zoe five times in the last few minutes."

Did I? I didn't even realize it.

"I'll talk to her, but I could introduce you via video call."

"Nothing replaces a hug. I know you, my son. You've spent more time than I'd like jumping from woman to woman, and if you're taking this girl as yours, there's much more behind it than just taking care of a model who just signed a contract with your companies and who suffered a horrible accident."

I haven't told her about already knowing Zoe from the past, because the story isn't just mine to share. However, Mom isn't naive and knows that just the fact that Zoe is staying in the same house as me means something.

"You're right, it's not the reason I kept her with me, but because what we have is special." I simplify and change the subject. "We'll keep in touch and also follow the news. I think the best solution would be for me to drive."

"It will be quite an event. With the number of bodyguards protecting you, the trip will look like a parade."

We talk for a few more minutes until she says goodbye, mentioning that my father is waiting for her to go for a walk around the property. They try to stay fit even with the lockdown, and that's the only exercise they've been getting.

Thank God the house I'm staying in has a full gym. I have too much energy inside me, and even with the recent sexual marathon, I still feel energized most of the time.

I think about what my mom said about me never bringing a woman so close.

It's not that I had the idea of a perfect relationship in my mind; I just never met anyone before Zoe who made me want something more permanent.

My parents have a relationship of total complicity. That kind of love that the world knows is forever. A love I never thought I'd experience, but now that Zoe and I have finally stopped resisting each other, I wonder if I didn't find it two years ago.

I'm a skeptic by nature. I believe in desire, in physical attraction, and somehow, I always separated that from love. From the outside, my parents seem more like friends than lovers, but maybe I was just approaching the issue from the wrong angle.

When I imagined my future, I thought I'd end my days with someone who roughly followed the family model I witnessed. Now, however, I'm beginning to understand that love doesn't have a mold that relationships must fit into, but rather each couple's story adapts love, making it unique to them.

As if she could read my thoughts, Zoe knocks on the door and, without waiting for a response, walks in.

Zoe has changed. She's more certain of what she wants, and although shyness is still an important part of her nature, she no longer bows her head to life.

"I'm not sure if you're working and didn't want to interrupt, but I just got a call from the hospital. Bia is awake."

"That's great news," I say, reaching out my hand for her to come closer.

I've set up an office very similar to the ones I have scattered around the world.

She walks over to the desk, seeming hesitant.

I don't think it's lingering embarrassment. It can't be, after what we've shared over the past week. I can say for certain that I've never known a woman's body as well as I know hers now.

Zoe is wild in bed. She keeps showing me what she likes, and I'm determined to learn everything about her, to discover what makes her moan for more or scream with pleasure.

My body reacts to the memories of what we've done in the past few days, and when I pull her to sit on my lap, she notices.

She looks at me, and I know she's excited too. We can't stay dressed around each other for long, but as much as I want to have her on my desk and enjoy her for breakfast, I don't want her to think that all I want with her is sex.

I made a fucked-up mess of our first round together in Barcelona. This time, I plan to change the script.

"Did they say when she'll be discharged?" I ask, brushing the hair from her neck and kissing the exact spot where a vein pulses.

"I can't concentrate with you doing that," she confesses, squirming on my lap. "It feels so good."

"I'm sorry," I say, not at all regretful.

She turns around and straddles me.

"For a ruthless CEO, you're a terrible liar, Mr. Lykaios."

"You already knew that. You once accused me of being brutally honest."

"I prefer it this way. I hate liars."

I know she's talking about her ex-husband, but I don't want to go down that road now. What I needed to say about the bastard, I've said. Now, the problem is between me and Mike Howard.

"I want to speak with Bia on the phone. Do you think they'll allow it?"

"If she's come out of the coma, they must have moved her to a private room as I instructed. She definitely has a phone there."

"Besides being eager to hear her voice, I want to tell her what happened because she must be confused. I also need to let her know that you arranged for documents for all of us."

I lean back in the chair a bit to observe her.

"Doesn't it bother you that I always take the lead?"

"You're helping me, not trying to override me. If that were the case, I would have already given you a shove."

Damn, why does everything that comes out of my witch's mouth have to be so exciting?

I clear my throat because it took me less than three minutes to forget my resolve not to lay her on my desk and take her from behind. Zoe stirs hunger and desire in me simply by coming close. No matter how many times we have sex, my desire doesn't wane.

"My mom wants to meet you."

She looks at me.

"What's wrong?"

"Do you want me to meet her?"

I don't need to think about it.

"I do."

"I'm not going to lie."

"About what?"

"About being in the process of divorce. I think she might not like to know that."

"My mom isn't like that, Zoe. She's Greek and can be quite conventional too, but above all, she believes in happiness."

"So I guess we have the right ingredients, Mr. Lykaios, or should I call you doctor, like the staff does?"

I give her a playful slap on the butt.

"Cheeky."

"Only with you." She smiles.

"Why do we have the right ingredients, Zoe?"

"Hmm?"

"When I said my mom believes in happiness, you countered that our relationship has the right ingredients."

"I can only speak for myself. You make me happy, Christos. If that's important, we already have a good start."

Chapter 39

Zoe

Five Days Later

"Zoe, we're really alive, right? I was so scared that something had happened to you. I woke up terrified. Thank Mr. Lykaios for arranging a private nurse for me. When I woke up, she gave me all the information I needed to calm my heart."

I can hardly believe it when I hear her voice.

"I didn't know he did that."

Christos is unbelievable. He told me he's not a saint, but anyway, I don't believe in saints or that people are good all the time.

Everyone has a dark side.

After what I went through in the years I was returned to the orphanage, I know life isn't all roses. What matters, though, is that he's good where it counts.

Dedicated to all those who... loves? Is that what he feels for me? He didn't say it back when I confessed the other day, but he still shows care for me in each of his actions.

I feel closer to him during the short time we've been together than I did in my marriage with Mike.

Maybe because, deep down, he was never really far away. He's always been in my heart, no matter how much I fought against it.

On the night I gave myself to him again, he told me that since we broke up, he hasn't slept with another woman. If it were anyone else saying that, I wouldn't take it seriously, but I believe him.

Christos isn't the type to sugarcoat things to please the recipient of the message, and staying two years without touching a woman because he only desired me has to mean something. So, I decided I don't need him to say the exact phrase. An "I love you" isn't as important as actions. I think they sometimes carry more weight than declarations of love.

Mike said he loved me before we got married, and I, like a foolish, needy person, believed him. If our toxic relationship served any purpose, it was to help me wake up to reality.

"You have no idea how much calmer I am hearing that. I prayed day and night. How are you feeling?"

"Like I've been hit by a truck. My whole body hurts, but the doctor thinks it's a consequence of all this time lying down. A nasty bonus for being over forty. When I start working out again, I'll have lost all my muscles."

Bia, unlike me, who considers running the only tolerable physical activity, loves working out and has a beautiful body full of curves.

"Does your head hurt?"

"No. And according to the doctors, everything is fine with it. What's scaring me is this virus. I'd like to get out of here as soon as possible, but the medical team told me that in addition to waiting a few more days for observation until they confirm that I'm okay to be discharged, I'll also need to take a test to see if I'm infected."

"Did they give a timeline?"

"In three days, I'll be officially discharged, but I can only leave the hospital once the test results are in."

"When they give the okay, I can ask Christos to send someone to pick you up. I've already talked to him. You can stay here with us."

"With us, huh? I'm glad to know you've worked things out. You deserve to be happy, Zoe."

"I was an idiot for not seeking the truth sooner."

"No. You were gullible, which unfortunately, in today's world, is a flaw. But now everything is resolved, right? Nick called me and said you talked."

"Yes, he's really nice. I think you should update your status to 'in a serious relationship' on social media. Friend with benefits isn't very flattering."

"Did you just swear, princess?" she teases.

"Maybe it's the influence of Christos. The man has such a dirty mouth it makes mine look like a nun's. But don't change the subject. Seriously now, why have you never been together for real?"

"Because we don't like each other that way. The sex is great, but outside of the bedroom, we don't make each other dream, you know? I want more, Zoe. I won't settle for anything less than the whole package. I'm not talking about getting married in a wedding dress, but having someone with me who..."

"Makes your body tingle?"

"Exactly. I think I'm waiting for my bad boy to show up."

"Here you go again with that story. Be careful. I really believe in that saying that when we wish for something, the universe conspires to make it happen. What if a mobster crosses your path?"

"Don't say that because just thinking about it makes my heart race."

I laugh.

"Yeah, now I know you're okay. Still the same crazy as always."

"Yes, the same. Changing the subject, I need to say something. That Ernestine deserved a few slaps in the face. Besides being a liar who messed up your love story, she made her daughter live in poverty by handing the money over to a man. How could she have been so stupid? First, she got involved with a man who drove high with a little girl in the back seat without a seatbelt, and then she handed the accident settlement to a thief."

"When all this is over, I'm going to look for her. It might not do any good, because I believe someone who does what she did to her own daughter doesn't have a shred of conscience. But at least I'll say everything I think about her face-to-face."

"We talked about everything and I didn't ask the most important thing. Were you hurt?"

"My hand has a scar. I might get plastic surgery, not because it bothers me, but because it could be a problem for future employers. Now, more than ever, I need to keep this contract with Christos. My parents lost everything, Bia. Not a single photograph from their wedding is left, nothing. I only didn't lose the ones of my biological mother because over a year ago I had them digitized, but other than that, my memories will rely on my memory."

"If I found Howard, I'd kill him with my own hands. Nick told me he's on the run."

"He is, and as for killing him, you'll have to get in line. I hate him."

"Did he show any signs of madness before this event? I'm not kidding, Zoe. The man isn't normal. What he did, trying to kill us all, destroyed his career."

"That would have happened anyway."

"How so?"

"Christos had already taken measures regarding this after he saw my bruised face."

"I'll tell you one thing, I was rooting for you two before, but now I can say without fear of being wrong that I'm a huge fan of your Greek."

"He's not mine... yet."

"Whoa. That's how you talk, girl. I'm liking this change."

"Almost dying opened my eyes, Bia. The thread of life is very fragile. On the day I went out to buy ice cream, I thought my world was relatively under control. I had signed a million-dollar contract, separated from Mike, and reunited with Christos. And then, less than half an hour later, my universe had disappeared. My parents' home no longer existed, and my best friend was in a coma."

"I understand what you're saying, and at least something good came out of that fucked-up situation. Now tell me about your plans."

"His parents want to meet me."

"Wow, so this is serious then."

"I don't know, I'm going to visit them next week. We'll take the test first to see if we're infected. I'd really like to see my mom, but her doctor said no because even the test could give a false negative."

"This whole situation is a shitshow."

"Did you wake up from the coma with a list of swear words from A to Z?"

"I'm training to get back to my old self."

"You didn't answer about coming here when you're finally discharged."

"I appreciate it from the bottom of my heart, Zoe, but I need to be alone for a while. As soon as the borders are reopened, I want to go on a vacation to the Caribbean, but for now, I'll stay quietly in my apartment."

"I won't force the issue, Bia, but any time you change your mind, just let me know."

"Of course I will. Any news about the fashion shows?"

"Yuri, Christos's assistant, is planning to do an online event. We'd present the new collection, but it would be streamed on his brand's channels. Nothing in person."

"I love the idea. Let me know if you need me."

"I love you, Bia. Take care. I hope we can see each other soon."

"I'm sure the vaccine will be ready soon and life will go back to normal."

Chapter 40

Christos

On the Same Day

I end the video call with Yuri. We spent over an hour discussing strategies for my haute couture brands during the global crisis.

The only pending issue was the cancellation of in-person fashion shows. We decided to stream them live, but until we have certainty about how the global health situation will evolve, I don't want crowds gathered or to bear the blame for a mass contamination.

The *lockdown* hasn't affected my profits at all. People are still buying, but if the situation persists, the fashion industry may be hit, of course. Why buy clothes if you don't need to leave the house? Even I, who hadn't worn jeans during the week for years, turned them, along with long-sleeve black shirts, into a sort of uniform.

Barefoot, though. Free from socks or shoes.

I have to admit that, after spending most of my adult life in suits or *blazers*, it's a relief to wear more casual clothes. I didn't even realize how much I missed it until I had to stay home by force.

Slowing down isn't my style because I'm my father's son. Work has always come first, but being cooped up with Zoe, since only a housekeeper who lives on the property now comes twice a week, has made me reconsider various aspects of my life.

Instead of dinners in fancy restaurants, sometimes we eat a sandwich or share a bucket of popcorn while watching movies.

Soaking in the hot tub, swimming naked in the pool at midnight, having sex in the middle of the day, talking.

Activities that, even with all the luxury I could afford in my adult life, I never enjoyed, or if I did, it was with a set end time because I was always chasing my next million.

More contracts, more money, and inside me, emptiness.

However, I have no doubt that this peace I feel is because I'm with her. I can't imagine being isolated with anyone else without it driving me crazy — not even with my parents —, but with Zoe, I savor every minute.

It was physical attraction that brought us together, but after we reunited, there's so much more involved. I want her. Not because of the past or in an attempt to give us a second chance. I want her for today.

For that, however, I need to eliminate a weed: Mike Howard.

Beau still hasn't managed to find out anything about his whereabouts, which is no small feat, as my friend has contacts in layers of society referred to as *outlaws*.

So, I have one last card to play. Someone I didn't want to involve.

My cousin, who ended up becoming a younger brother: Odin Lykaios.

The reckoning with Howard won't be *conventional*, so I didn't want the family involved. Especially since Odin has his own demons to fight, but I see no other solution. As certain as hell is hot, the bastard who tried to kill Zoe won't go unpunished after what he did.

And who else could locate him other than the man who owns the largest IT company in the country? In the twenty-first century, with cameras everywhere, you can't hide unless you're dead or locked up in some basement. Otherwise, you'll leave a trail.

We met as adults.

It was a mutual friend who pointed out that our last names were the same, which piqued my curiosity since even in Greece it's not very common.

What are the chances of two *CEOs* having Lykaios as a last name? Small, I'd say.

To make a long story short, we discovered that we are distant cousins.

Dad was thrilled to find a relative since when he came to the United States over thirty years ago, he lost touch with the rest of the Greek family.

However, our friendship wasn't easy at first.

Both of us were suspicious and wary of each other. I have no doubt that just as I investigated him, he did the same with me.

I search for his number in my contacts and press it on the screen.

"Christos, did something happen?" he asks as soon as he answers.

We share the fact that we act straightforwardly, without beating around the bush.

"Besides the end of the world seeming like a certainty?"

"The vaccine will appear soon. The speed with which it will be made will be record-breaking. But I'm sure you didn't call to talk about the future of the planet."

"No. I need you to find someone for me."

"The man who set fire to your girlfriend's house?"

"I don't even know why I'm calling you or Beau. We could save time and communicate telepathically."

"Beau?"

"Forget it, I said too much."

"You know I won't forget. I never forget anything."

"Seriously, Odin. He's not someone you should know."

"You're talking like an older brother. I'm a big boy already."

"Speaking of which, how's the negotiation to buy that Greek island going?"

"Technically, it's already mine, but I'll have to postpone my plans until this shitstorm is over."

"You mentioned the vaccine. Do you have any idea when it will be ready?"

"In a few months" he says with a confidence that reassures me. I have no doubt that he has access to privileged information. "When I have news about the son of a bitch, I'll let you know."

"Do you need any additional information about him?"

Odin gives one of his rare laughs.

"I'm the one who gifts the world with information, cousin. Not the one who seeks it."

One Hour Later

"SO, WE'LL HAVE TO GET tested before visiting your parents?"

"Yes, and they will too. I'm not sure if it's necessary since none of us four are going out, but the doctors said it's a safety protocol. Is that okay with you?"

"Sure, I'm not squeamish. I just wish I could see my family too."

"My cousin told me today that the vaccine won't take long."

"I hope not. Today I called the insurance to check on the situation with my parents' house. Not regarding the mortgages, of course. About that, there's nothing to be done. They don't owe us, but the bank, because the house belonged to the institution. Twice."

"Why did they need to mortgage it a second time?"

"Mom got sick again before I started making money from the fashion shows. Even though my career took off quickly, it wasn't enough."

"I can take care of it."

"No. You're already doing too much. I'll pay with..." She stops and her eyes widen. "Is the contract still valid? I'm asking because we won't be doing that shoot in Greece anytime soon."

"Yes, it's still valid. We'll find a way to photograph her," he says, looking at me strangely.

"What's wrong?"

"What's wrong with what?"

"It looks like you were about to say something and then stopped."

"You once accused me of being blunt, so here it goes. Greece was an excuse. I wanted some time alone with you. Isolated, where you couldn't run away."

"Even though you thought I was still married?"

"My assistant said there were rumors you were separating."

She nods, but the corner of her mouth lifts, hiding a smile.

"Why do I get the feeling you're smiling *at me* and not *for me*?"

She sits on my lap.

"Let's say both."

"Can I know why?"

"Nothing. I was just thinking. A powerful *CEO*, king of the world, making an excuse to take me to a deserted island..."

"It's not deserted, we have over a hundred staff there."

"Don't ruin my dream. As I was saying, a powerful *CEO*..."

I roll my eyes.

"Get to the point. I don't need an ego boost."

"Maybe you're not ready for what I'm going to say, Lykaios."

"I'm tough. Lay it on me."

"You were crazy about me. You just didn't admit it."

I pull her by the hips, settling her over my cock.

"Fifty percent right."

"What did I get wrong?"

"The verb tense. I'm *still* crazy about you, Zoe."

Chapter 41

Christos

On the Day of the Trip to Washington, DC

The security guards are loading Zoe's luggage into the car when my phone vibrates with the arrival of a message.
    Beau: *"I have news. Call me. It's urgent."*
I can't even finish the call, and my phone rings.
Odin.
What the hell? Both of them at the same time can only mean one thing: they've located Mike Howard.
"*I found him,*" my cousin says as soon as I answer.
"Yeah? And where is the son of a bitch?"
"*Dead. Car accident. Poetic justice or not, the car caught fire.*"
"Are you sure about that?"
"*I'm not a coroner, Christos, but the forensics say so, so why doubt it?*"
"Where did it happen?"
"*Mexico. He crossed the border. Probably trying to escape. An accident on a road, it seems. Lost control and fell into a ravine. End of the line.*"
"Too easy compared to what he deserved."
"*I know.*"

I'm sure the crime Howard committed by burning down Zoe's parents' house is a sensitive subject for my cousin, since he lost his entire family in a fire: his parents and younger sister.

"*I can keep checking. I'll try to find out through other means if it was really him.*"

"What other means?" Strange.

"*Again, playing the older brother.*"

"It's inevitable. Don't get into trouble because of me. I can verify if it was really Howard without you exposing yourself."

"*You know I'd never expose myself. Covering tracks is my specialty, but I don't want to interfere. If you really want to handle it alone...*"

"You've already done enough by bringing me this."

"*Alright. Take care, Christos.*"

He hangs up, and as I'm about to complete the call to Beau, since I'm now sure it was about Mike he wanted to talk about, Zoe comes out of the house.

She seems to notice something on my face because I was smiling, but a *little* furrow appears in the middle of her forehead.

"What happened? My parents?"

She looks terrified.

"No. They're fine, but we need to talk. Your ex-husband is dead."

"What?"

"A car accident in Mexico. The car caught fire."

"Are you sure it was him?"

No, I'm not, but I won't tell her that. If Howard is still on this planet, it won't be for long anyway.

Before I can answer, she adds:

"I don't regret it. I hope he suffered," she says, surprising me. "Because of what he did, my parents' lives were destroyed. Their stories and memories. He hurt Bia, thinking she was me."

"He almost killed you too," I growl, feeling the same hatred for the bastard that I felt when I saw her in that hospital room.

My phone rings, and I know it's Beau. Maybe he's calling to give the same news Odin did.

"I need to take this," I say, stepping away because I have no idea what the conversation will entail.

"*What part of urgent didn't you understand?*"

"I was talking to my cousin and then Zoe. He told me Mike Howard is dead."

"*What?*"

"Wait, wasn't that what you were going to tell me?"

"*No, but it seems your news is better than mine. Was it really him?*"

"I don't know, what do you think?"

"*I don't believe it, maybe because, like you, I'm naturally skeptical. But I'll know by tomorrow morning. Now, to the point. Whether he's dead or alive, your wife will get rid of the bastard much sooner than you think.*"

"I don't understand."

"*When he married your Zoe, the professor had already been married to someone else for over ten years. He's a bigamist, Christos, which means the second marriage, which is with your girl, is invalid.*"

"I thought nothing about him would surprise me anymore, but the bastard managed to outdo himself."

"*It's a win for both of you. Any good lawyer will be able to handle the annulment... I don't even know if that's the right term, after all, how do you annul what never existed? Anyway, any good lawyer will sort this out quickly.*"

"I'll contact my lawyers later today."

"*I'll give you some free advice. You said you're unsure if he's really dead. Let Zoe think he is. If Howard is still walking this vale of tears, it won't be for long.*"

"I'd already thought of that. I don't want to involve her in my plans."

"Exactly. When we find him, dying burned inside a car will sound like paradise."

An Hour Later

"YOU HAVE THAT LOOK again, like you want to say something and then change your mind halfway. Are you having second thoughts about the trip?"

"What? No."

"Look, if you've changed your mind about me meeting your family..."

"You should know by now that no one forces me to do what I don't want to, Zoe."

"Alright. So what's wrong, Christos? This guessing game is making me anxious. I'm already nervous about meeting your parents, and you looking at me like that isn't helping."

I take her hand, which was resting on her thigh, and bring it to my lips, leaving a light kiss.

"It has nothing to do with the trip. I still want you to meet my family."

"Then what's the problem?"

"I'm thinking about how to tell you something."

"Is it about Mike? If you're worried about how I feel about his death, don't be. I'm not going to lose five minutes of sleep over it. I don't know exactly what happened, Christos, but I've decided I'll save my tears for those who deserve them. Dead or alive, I'll never forgive him for what he did to my family. How could he have the audacity to set fire to the house with my parents inside, knowing my mother has cancer and how hard she's fought to survive? I mean, I understand that, in his twisted mind, he wanted to get revenge on me. But my parents? No, you won't see me mourning his death."

"It has nothing to do with the bastard's death."

I signal and take a turn off the road. I notice in the rearview mirror that the two cars with the bodyguards are doing the same.

I turn off the engine and face her.

"Your marriage to Mike is invalid."

"What?"

I wouldn't win any awards for diplomacy, so I lay it all out at once.

"I had them locate him. It's not in my nature to sit back and wait for the police to find him. My friend went after him as I asked, but instead of finding him..."

"Wasn't he the one who delivered the news of Mike's death?"

"No, that was my cousin. Anyway, my friend found out that Mike has a wife, which makes your marriage invalid. And there's more," I continue, as it makes no sense to hold back the rest of the information. "He shouldn't have tried to move his checking account, with all this crap going on lately, but he cleaned it out, as well as the investments you had."

Chapter 42

Christos

She unfastens her seatbelt and opens the car door. She steps out, her hands on her head.

I follow her. I knew she'd be pissed when she found out Howard had stolen from her, but I didn't anticipate such a desperate reaction.

"Oh my God!"

"Zoe."

"It's too much information, Christos. What have I done with my life? I'm relieved that our marriage was a sham. Not just the relationship itself, but also legally. What can you expect from a liar who waited to put a ring on my finger just to then decide to tell me about his lifestyle? His sexual deviations? That's not what's making me nervous right now, but the fact that he sold the stocks. They were my only investment. My mother's illness... it requires a lot of money."

"I can cover it."

"I know, but it's not your responsibility. That's not why I'm with you. I've always paid my own bills."

"Zoe, we closed a multimillion-dollar deal that's still in effect. You'll get your finances in order."

"It doesn't seem right to accept that money, and we don't even know when I'll be back to work..."

"But you will be. Don't worry about that. Now, let's get back to the car or my mother will give you a lecture when we arrive. She doesn't like dinner delays."

She comes closer and hugs me.

"I'm not being dramatic. I'm used to being alone, paying my bills and my family's. Not sharing worries."

"I'm not good at sharing either, but I'm the best when it comes to handling problems," I joke, since she still looks tense.

She lifts her head from my chest.

"Your confidence has always excited me. You're so arrogant, but in a *sexy* way."

"Everything about you excites me."

She stands on her tiptoes and wraps her arms around my neck for a kiss. I don't usually show public displays of affection, especially knowing that the bodyguards are likely watching us, but nothing with Zoe is about rules. I've made my peace with the fact that she's unique in my life.

It doesn't take long before we're both breathless, our skin burning with desire.

She takes the initiative to pull away, perhaps finally aware that we're not alone.

Still, she can't hide her excitement. Her lips are swollen from the kiss, and her porcelain skin is flushed. Gorgeous as hell!

"How do I sever any ties with him, Christos? I don't want anything more to do with that man."

"It's much easier since you didn't change your name when you *got married*."

Even knowing now that it was a sham marriage, the word still feels like acid going down my throat. Imagining her tied to someone for the rest of her life drives me crazy with jealousy.

"Imagining her tied to someone *other than you* drives you crazy with jealousy," a voice inside my head says what I haven't had the courage to admit until now.

I look at her and realize she's staring back. It's as if we're both trying to figure out what the other means in their world.

Yes, she said she loves me, but I don't think Zoe can understand us, just as I can't. The odds were against us and we had everything to fail. However, life brought us together. I'm not willing to waste this second chance.

I take her hand and, after opening the car door for her to get in, I settle behind the wheel.

"I'll contact my lawyers as soon as we arrive in D.C. It'll be quick. Soon you'll be free."

"I never even felt married."

"Does the idea appeal to you?"

"What?" She tries to hide it.

"Getting married. Starting a family."

Her face turns a darker shade of red.

"I've been abandoned for longer than I've had a home. In therapy, I learned that this will always be my weakness: living in search of what I didn't have. So yes, getting married and having my own family is a goal."

I still haven't started the engine, my mind overwhelmed by a certainty that has just revealed itself. I want her for myself. Not for a while, until we explore what I feel or what we are. I want Zoe as my *forever*.

"And the farm?" I ask.

"What?"

"Do you want a farm too? And I suppose... with many children...?"

"Yes, as many as God wants to give me," she says, looking out the car window.

I know she's uncomfortable, but I need to know more.

"And what about your career?"

"As you mentioned, I signed a multimillion-dollar contract with a Greek who's obsessed with me," she tries to joke, but fails. "I won't be able to finish this commitment anytime soon."

I know that's a sensitive point for her. Zoe feels awkward about our relationship involving money.

"It has nothing to do with the two of us. Yes, I chose you mainly because I wanted you back, but you're beautiful and will be a huge asset to my brands. You'll represent *Vanity*."

"What? But the contract was for a smaller brand. *Vanity* is synonymous with luxury worldwide. I waited over a year in a huge line to buy the purse of my dreams."

"You're the image I want for *Vanity*: beautiful, sophisticated, and young. I've wanted to rejuvenate this brand for a long time. To show it can be worn by all ages."

"I don't know what to say. Or rather, I do. Thank you. Modeling for a brand synonymous with luxury is every model's dream."

It doesn't take me long to read what she doesn't reveal.

"But not yours."

"I don't want to sound ungrateful, but as I've told you before, I started my career because of Pauline, and I continued out of necessity. Dieting for the rest of my life isn't my idea of fun."

I'd never looked at models' situations from this perspective. To me, it was just how they earned their living.

"And what's your idea of fun, pretty girl?"

She looks at her hands.

"I'm going to fulfill all my dreams, Christos. I made a mistake the first time, but when I marry again, it will be with someone who values me. Someone who wants to give, rather than just take. Someone with whom I'm not ashamed to be myself. Not always strong or brave. Not always put together or made up. The real Zoe."

"You're beautiful, no matter what you wear."

She looks out the window again.

"Is that all you see in me? Beauty?"

"No," I reply without hesitation. "What I saw first, maybe, but not anymore."

"What then?"

"The woman I want."

She doesn't look at me as I expected.

"You already have me, but I think this is only working between us because we're stuck at home. Soon your life will go back to normal."

"And what's my normal, Zoe?"

"Traveling, parties, *glamour*. And none of that is part of my world, Christos, except for work obligations. I've been thinking a lot these past few days. With the money from the contract we signed, I'm going to pay off all my parents' debts and buy them another house. Then, I'll go after my real dream. I won't sign any more contracts with any other brand. You will be my last."

In more ways than you can imagine, Zoe. You will be mine forever.

Chapter 43

Zoe

Washington — DC

"I can't believe I'm hugging you, my son," Christos's mother says, and I find myself smiling because the woman has no reservations about showing affection.

I watch his reaction. I thought he'd be embarrassed by his mother's extravagant display, even to the point of pinching his cheek as if he were still a little boy. But no. He holds her in an embrace and returns her kiss with a lingering one.

I feel my eyes well up with tears, thinking of my two mothers, my biological and my adoptive ones. I wish I could receive a hug like that too.

"Mom, this is Zoe."

As soon as Christos parked in front of the mansion, she ran out to greet us.

She's short, a little plump, with gray hair cut to shoulder length. She's not beautiful—yes, I have that flaw. Working among models who approach physical perfection makes me scrutinize everyone's appearance—but she is so full of life that she becomes stunning. You can almost touch her vital force.

She finally releases her son and comes over to me.

"My dear, what a pleasure to meet you. I'm so sorry for the tragedy you've been through. How are your parents?"

Contrary to what usually happens when I'm confronted with very direct people, I don't feel uncomfortable. She doesn't seem to be asking out of nosiness, but because she genuinely cares. She shows concern for my family.

"Nice to meet you, Mrs. Danae."

"Danae. I'm not that old."

"Right." I smile. "Nice to meet you, Danae. They're doing well, as well as can be expected."

"I can't imagine the nightmare you've been through, Zoe, but they're all alive, and that's what matters. Now let's go inside, Alekos is already complaining of hunger," she says, referring to her husband.

As if sensing we were talking about him, Christos's father appears. It's like seeing an older version of my boyfriend. The man must have been drop-dead gorgeous when he was younger. I wonder if Danae knows how to shoot. I would definitely sign up for a shooting course if I had to stay with her son for the rest of my life.

The thought spreads a warm feeling through my chest, but I push it away. I wish I had more time with him and I don't intend to leave his life, but I also don't want to delude myself into thinking we'll be together forever.

"Alekos, come meet your son's girlfriend."

He comes over, but first stops to kiss his wife on the forehead. Then I realize that, regardless of the man's looks, he's deeply in love with his wife. There's no physical attribute that can surpass that.

I look at Christos and see him watching me as his father hugs me and gives me a kiss on the cheek.

I smile awkwardly but am very happy with the warm welcome. Mike only had his mother alive, and she looked at me oddly the one time we met.

I have serious issues with rejection and may never fully overcome them. The reception from Christos's parents has calmed my heart, for now I have the courage to admit: I was terrified they would treat me coldly.

WE ATE SO MUCH AND I learned what a true Greek lunch is like. I tried *moussaka*, *dolmadakia*, and for dessert, *portokalopita*, which is an orange cake with cinnamon. It's fluffy and very delicious.

By the end, I felt like I was about to explode, but the three Greeks were chatting as if this were just a regular meal for them.

Christos is a chameleon. I've seen him in public both in Barcelona and at his office in New York, and I know how powerful and imposing he is in his daily life, but here, with his parents, he seems completely relaxed. I think it's because he's among those he truly considers his own.

Twice, when I called, Mom asked to speak with him, and they talked on the phone for about five minutes. In the end, my boyfriend wanted to speak with my dad as well, and it touched my heart.

Mike never made any effort to be kind to my parents. Even before the marriage, I never saw him paying attention to them.

"Zoe, we need to plan a trip to Greece once all this is over. My son's island is beautiful."

"She'll be doing a photo shoot there, so it will be sooner than you think."

"Great. Let's all go together," Alekos says, inviting himself, and I feel like laughing. "God knows we need a break from this chaos that the world has become. We can go on your plane, son."

"I'd love to, but first I want to visit my parents. I talk to Mom every day on the phone, but I want to see her. I don't know if you can understand."

"Of course we do, my dear," Danae says, holding my hand. "Nothing replaces being face-to-face."

"I was going to plan a surprise, but I don't want to make you anxious," Christos says.

"*Surprise?*"

"Yes. When we get back to Boston, we'll see your parents. I've already arranged everything with Macy. There just won't be any hugging, because the doctor is still firm on the restriction, but your dad will set up some chairs in the garden, and we can talk."

"I thought they were still at the clinic. I mean, they were until yesterday."

"Yes, but when I arranged the clinic, I asked Yuri to also rent a house in case they wanted to get out of the hospital environment if your mother was well enough for that."

I open and close my mouth, astonished.

"You went to the trouble of organizing all that?"

For the first time since we met, I get the impression that he's blushing.

"It was nothing. I..."

Before he finishes, I stand up and go over to him, and without stopping to think about what I'm doing, I give him a kiss on the cheek.

"Thank you."

I prepare to return to my seat, but he pulls out the chair, lifts me onto his lap, and kisses me on the mouth in front of his parents.

"Now I consider that a proper thank you."

I hear Alekos laughing and turn as red as a pepper.

I avoid looking at any of the three, but I feel the Lykaios family's eyes on me the entire time.

One Hour Later

TO MY COMPLETE SURPRISE, Alekos and his son said they would clean up after lunch. Like us in Boston, Christos' parents only have a housekeeper twice a week to avoid having people circulating inside the house and, thus, the risk of contamination.

Christos has done the dishes even at our home, and I've always admired that, as it reflects the upbringing he received. I can't stand people who sit around waiting to be served, and my boyfriend is a man of action in every aspect of his life.

However, I never imagined he would be like this in his parents' home too, nor that the elder Lykaios would be the one to take the initiative to send us out while they took care of everything.

"Are you feeling calmer now that you know you're going to see your mom?"

"I am. Life is so strange, right? I spent the last few years worried about her cancer, and then this damn virus comes and trips us up. My current anxiety is about the possibility of Mom deteriorating and needing to be admitted to a real hospital if the clinic Christos arranged isn't sufficient."

"Let's have faith, dear. I know we're all uncertain about the future, but we need to stay positive. Becoming mentally ill can be as dangerous as becoming physically ill."

"I know, but when I talk about anxiety, it's not like the way people usually experience it; it's something that paralyzes me. That's why I continue with therapy twice a week, *online.*

I look at her as I speak. I'm not going to pretend to be someone I'm not to win her sympathy. I had depression when I returned from Barcelona, and I thought it was an isolated incident due to everything I had experienced, but my therapist told me it could happen again.

"There's nothing wrong with seeking help. I don't know about your life, Zoe, but I'm sure you're a special girl."

She brought me into her flower greenhouse, and as we walk around, I think that I want one like this for myself in the future. I had never paid much attention to flowers, but Christos' mother told me she considers caring for her orchids a form of therapy.

"Why?" I ask, referring to what she just said.

"You'll hardly find someone more averse to relationships than Christos, and yet, here you are."

"It's not like your son had much choice, you know? I'm staying at his house."

"You're a smart girl, so answer me this: why is my Christos in Boston and not in New York, where his primary residence is?"

I remain silent, understanding what she means. With his fortune, Christos could be anywhere in the world during this crisis, and yet he chose to stay with me.

A glimmer of hope begins to stir in my heart.

"Our story is complicated."

"I have time and consider myself a good listener."

Their property is enormous, and as we walk, now in the sunlight, I explain everything to her. From the moment he caught me taking photos on the forbidden deck of the ship in Barcelona, through my return to the United States without saying goodbye, to the moment of our reunion.

"The accident you're talking about, besides injuring him physically, deeply affected my son's mind. Even without reason, he blamed himself for the little girl. The man driving the car was high—not just a little, but almost in overdose. He could have killed everyone."

"I only believed Ernestine's story because I didn't know him well. Anyone who spends ten minutes with Christos knows he's not the type to shirk responsibilities."

"You're in love with him, Zoe."

"I think I always have been. There was no choice. From the first exchange of words, he captivated me."

She looks at me as if she knows a secret I have no idea about, so I continue.

"I'm afraid of getting hurt, though. My fake marriage didn't manage to hurt me because I never loved him, but Christos could destroy me."

"I'm not a spokesperson for other people's feelings, dear. Every couple has their own pace and story, but my boy feels the same way you do. Even if he hasn't put it into words, I carried him for nine months and know my boy. Like his father, he only loves once, and you, my dear, are the chosen one."

Chapter 44

Christos

Return to Boston

Three Days Later

"How are you feeling?" I ask. We're almost arriving at the house I rented for her parents.

"Nervous. I know it's silly because I talk to them on the phone, but my dad and mom are all I have in the world. My real family, since the remnants of my biological family in Boston, apart from the cousin I told you about, Madeline, couldn't care less."

She mentioned she was related to the Turners of Boston. I had the displeasure of meeting the aunt she referred to, Adley, at a charity gala dinner a few years ago. She's unbearable, arrogant, and acts as if the universe should be grateful just for her breathing the same air as the rest of humanity.

"They're doing well," I say, referring to her parents.

"I know and I'm very grateful for that."

"Don't you understand that after everything we've been through, there's nothing I wouldn't do to see you happy, Zoe?"

I'm not joking, and I think she realizes that, but after a quick glance at me, she changes the subject.

"The streets look like something out of a *tv* show. Like an apocalypse, as if we're the only survivors."

"Those who have the privilege of working from home are being responsible."

We drive around, and my attention, which was entirely on her, shifts to check what she mentioned. Rarely does a car pass by us.

"Many have lost their jobs," she says.

In every direction we look, the few people on the streets are wearing masks.

The news that the first vaccine will start being produced within a month even surprised my mother, who is naturally optimistic. Odin was right again.

However, I think that even if people start getting vaccinated, the world will never be the same.

I believe it will take a long time before people feel safe again. Maybe it will never happen. Perhaps only in the next generation or beyond. My children will probably only talk about this as a bad phase, but for us, it's a new reality.

Children? Where did that come from?

Although it's something I want for the future, I never saw myself thinking about my descendants until now.

"Did you notice that even keeping a distance, people stop to greet each other?" she asks as we enter the familiar neighborhood where her parents are living.

"I think most people miss talking, especially those who live alone. Not everyone is lucky enough to be holed up with a *top model*."

I look at her, hiding a smile, and just in time to see her rolling her eyes.

"And me, with a *Greek CEO*. Lucky me, loss for others."

"What others?"

She glances at me quickly but then looks away again.

"It's none of my business. I was just talking."

"I haven't slept with anyone else since we met in Barcelona. I'm not driven by my cock. When I want a woman, she's the only one I want, but it usually doesn't last."

"I don't want to hear about it," she says, looking pissed at me.

"But you need to, because I know you feel insecure. I'm with you, Zoe, not because we have to stay locked up at home, but because I want to. If I were just after sex, a phone call would solve my problem. I want *more*."

"Can you pull over for a moment? I get nervous arguing while you're driving."

"Are we arguing?"

She doesn't answer, but as soon as I find a shoulder to pull over, she unfastens her seatbelt and comes onto my lap.

"I've never been good at interpreting text."

"What?"

"Are we really together? Like diving headfirst into a possibility of a future?"

Her hands hold my face so I won't look away.

There would be no need. I don't want to stop looking at her as I answer.

"Yes, we're together for real. Are you ready for that?"

My heart beats almost painfully. Even though she said she loves me, a thought crosses my mind.

What if the opposite is true and she's only with me because she has nowhere else to go?

"Ready for what? Words, Christos. Give me in plain terms what you want from me. From us both."

"Everything. A future. No more running away, either physically or mentally, Zoe. I want it all."

She looks at me as if trying to read all my thoughts. Seeming convinced, she then pulls me into a kiss that makes me forget where we are, making me want to bury myself deep inside her.

"As much as I like the idea of seeing your parents again, I'm dying to get home."

The corner of her mouth lifts.

"Do you have to work, Dr. Lykaios?"

"A lot. Inside you, deep. You're fully healed from the injuries to your feet and hands, so we can fuck with less care."

She blushes. I've noticed that whenever I act like I truly am, without using pretty words to say what I want, she turns red but also gets excited.

"Does that mean what we've done so far has been gentle?"

She seems breathless.

"You'll find out later."

"IF THERE'S BEEN ANYTHING good amidst all the death and fear, it's that people have started paying more attention to their loved ones," her mother says.

We've been talking outside the house for almost two hours, and I've realized that, unlike most people I interact with, I don't feel like leaving.

Socializing isn't usually natural for me. I do it in moderation. Zoe and I have that in common, but in my case, it's not shyness, it's just a lack of desire to chat. Her parents, however, are quite interesting, and Scott raised a hypothesis I had already considered: even when the vaccine starts being produced, it won't eradicate the disease due to the virus mutations. It's more likely that we'll be dealing with it for the rest of our lives, like the flu.

"I was like that too," I say, a bit embarrassed. "I barely had time to eat. I rarely had lunch, always involved in a thousand commitments."

"And what changed?" Zoe asks.

"I used to watch you from a distance; now I'm obsessed with doing it up close," I say, much more serious than playful.

I'm not sure how much she's told her parents about us, but they both start laughing while Zoe turns red.

"My personal stalker." She recovers and faces me.

"You can bet on that." I take her hand and kiss it. "But now I see things differently."

"How so?" Scott asks.

"I want to help people. I've always made generous donations to various causes, but I want something more effective, like building high-quality hospitals that are more accessible to those who can't afford a good plan."

"Yes, unfortunately, that's one of the ills of our country, my son. Access to healthcare for all citizens of less privileged social classes is still a dream. Even before this situation we're living through, some people would fall ill and refuse to seek treatment for fear of accumulating a huge debt afterward."

"I have some ideas," Zoe says.

"About helping people?"

"Yes. I've always been concerned about the future of humanity, but my focus is mainly on children and the elderly."

"The two extremes," I say.

"Exactly. The elderly deserve a dignified end of life and often don't have any family around. I've been researching in my spare time over the past few weeks and thought of recreational centers. A kind of free club where they can gather to play, talk, have a meal if they're hungry." She pauses to catch her breath. She looks beautiful at any moment, but watching her defend her ideas so passionately drives me wild. "I thought that when everything returns to normal, we could look for volunteers willing to give an hour of their day just to listen to them at this center. Sometimes, all a person needs is a kind word. Loneliness can be as lethal as a disease."

I offer my lap, inviting her to sit.

"Every time I think you couldn't fascinate me more, you prove me wrong."

She smiles, embarrassed, perhaps because we're in the presence of her parents, even though there's no reason for it. Scott and Macy were relieved to hear that her marriage is invalid, and my lawyers are already taking steps to ensure Zoe is never associated with that vermin again.

"I'm glad to know you have plans to help humanity, Christos. I hope other entrepreneurs like you become aware. Maybe the world needed this pause."

I agree in silence.

We lived so fast, thinking we were immortal—or at least had plenty of time left—and suddenly, God comes and shows us that our time on this planet might be shorter than we imagined.

"Did you mention you have plans to go to Greece for Zoe to do a photo shoot? When would that be?" Scott asks.

"We need to arrange everything to minimize the number of people involved, but I think within a month at the latest, we'll travel."

"Enjoy it for me," Macy says.

"Soon you'll be able to come with us."

Zoe turns to look at me, and I see thousands of questions on her face. She's transparent.

"Yes, *with us*," I reaffirm.

Chapter 45

Christos

Greece

A Month and a Half Later

"With all due respect, she's stunning," Yuri says from beside me as we watch my wife pose for the last photos of the shoot. After this, we'll officially be on vacation.

I'm not jealous of the men watching. How could I be, when admiring her is her profession? As long as they don't get too close, I'm fine with it.

Besides, I know Yuri isn't speaking out of malice. Like me, he's used to seeing beautiful women. Some are gorgeous after being made up, others in photographs with many effects, but I've seen Zoe in all states: wet hair, sweaty, in a sweatshirt, and dressed up like now. I can confidently say there's no woman more beautiful in the world to me.

Perhaps what fascinates me isn't just her physical appearance but the whole package.

She's shy, but also wild during sex. She doesn't ask or talk much, but she's all in, letting herself try everything.

I feel my cock get heavy when I remember how we fucked on the beach last night.

Zoe riding me by moonlight is a memory I'll always carry.

And then there's the other side. Something I've never found in a woman—maybe because I hadn't desired it before.

The blend of sweetness and determination. Her courage to intervene when she thinks I'm working too hard and need a break.

Without the slightest embarrassment, she comes to my lap and kisses me, barely concerned if I'm finalizing a deal.

As if that weren't enough, there are the little things, like calling my mother every day, just as she does with hers, to check if they're okay or need anything.

My parents are arriving tomorrow morning, but we've been here for a week already. It didn't make sense to bring them sooner when we couldn't give them the attention they deserved.

I had never participated in a photo shoot for a catalog. Mainly due to lack of interest, but I knew the work involved.

However, I hadn't considered the perspective of the models. She must be exhausted from being in heels and a bikini all day—which, by the way, is driving me crazy.

"Hey, boss, I didn't mean anything by it," Yuri says, misinterpreting my silence.

"What?" I look at him just in time to see a poorly concealed smile.

"Never mind, Christos. I get it. Your problem isn't jealousy of me but being mesmerized by your wife."

Half an hour later, Zoe finally comes over to us.

I notice the team's gaze on us and also the two other models who joined the shoot three days ago.

I ignore everyone.

Yuri summed it up well: I'm completely mesmerized by my mermaid.

"Do you want to swim? I'm dying of heat," she says, hugging me.

"Yes, but not at the beach. Let's go home."

"Everyone will leave today, right?"

"Yes. And the island will be ours."

"For twenty-four hours, until your parents arrive. Oh, and let's not forget about a dozen staff members."

"I told them they didn't need to come and take care of the house, but they didn't listen to me."

"Ah, poor Greek magnate. Here, you're not the all-powerful *CEO*, just a little boy."

I give her a playful smack on the ass for being so cheeky.

I mentioned that I was born on this island. Where my whole family lived their entire lives. My parents were employees, and when my grandmother died, it was the cue for us to leave. I returned as soon as I made enough money and bought it, knowing my father has an emotional connection to the place. What I didn't expect was to fall in love with my homeland again.

"They still see me as a kid. There's no convincing them that I'm now a god," I joke, though not entirely.

She laughs. The cheeky woman laughs at me.

"You should stroke my ego by saying something clichéd like 'You're my Greek god, Christos.'"

"You don't need ego stroking, miss. I'm sure you've had plenty of female attention before me. Besides, I have plans that involve massage, but not for your ego, and I guarantee you'll prefer it."

Her mischievous smile makes me certain these plans involve us both naked.

I kneel at her feet and free her from her high heels. Then, I pick her up and start heading home, not looking back.

"I guess I won't be seeing you guys again," Yuri says as we pass by.

"Goodbye, Yuri. Don't show your ugly face to me for the next two weeks."

"He's not ugly."

"Careful, woman, I might punish you for flirting with my assistant."

"Me, flirting with your assistant? How could I when I have my own Greek god to give me all the pleasure I desire?"— the cheeky one says, then winks. "Clichéd enough, my king?"

"Ah, Zoe, I'm going to love putting you on all fours on the bed and fucking you hard."

She swallows hard.

"I hope so," she says, with an enigmatic look.

I head straight to the bedroom. It's just the two of us in the house now, as the staff has already left.

"Put me on the floor and get naked."

I raise an eyebrow, surprised.

"Don't make me repeat that, Lykaios. I promise it will be worth it, but I'm not brave enough to make you a second invitation. Take off your clothes and lie face down on the bed."

"Why?"

Her cheeks flush red.

"I want to try something I read."

"Are you going to get naked too?"

A nod is her answer.

"Take off the bikini for me, Zoe."

She doesn't hesitate. She moves her hand behind her back and unties the bandeau top.

Her nipples are hard, just like my cock.

I lick my lower lip.

"The panties, now."

She slides them down her slender thighs.

"Jesus, Zoe, there's not a single time I see you naked that it doesn't drive me insane."

I threaten to step forward, but she stops me with a raised hand.

"No way you're ruining my plans. Naked, now, Lykaios."

Chapter 46

Christos

Without taking my eyes off her, I take off my white T-shirt, then lower my jeans and boxers. My cock springs up, hard and thick, pointing upwards, and she gasps.

"I asked you to lie on your back, but I'll have to adapt."

I can't hold back a smile.

"Do you have any idea how you drive me insane with this mix of innocence and boldness?"

"Go to bed or I'll forget the whole script, Christos."

I obey, curious about this massage.

She goes to the suite's bathroom and, when she returns, she has a bottle in her hand that looks like perfume.

"Scented oil," she says, as if she could read my mind.

"You're really committed to the massage idea," I say, trying to keep my tone neutral, even though I'm already crazy with desire, imagining those tiny hands on me.

"I do everything with commitment, Greek, and my goal today is..." she pauses, opening the bottle "to drive you crazy."

She comes to the bed and kneels by my ankles.

"I'm going to try a tantric massage," she says, but doesn't touch me yet.

"Really?" I can barely focus on what she's saying. Zoe drives me wild just by breathing, and seeing her so close and naked is stealing all my concentration.

"Yes. Do you know what it's for?"

"I'm not sure."

"I read that it's a good way to connect with your partner." Her hand finally touches my foot, and it's like getting a jolt of lust. The oil is warm.

She now uses both hands, slick with the oil. She begins to move them up my legs, and my heart races.

"Do whatever you want, Zoe, but later I'm going to fuck you so good... You'll scream my name every time I thrust into that tight little cunt."

She bites her lip, and I'm sure that if I touched her now, she'd be soaked.

Zoe wasn't kidding about being committed to the massage, as she presses into my skin. She's touching my thighs, very close to my cock, and I swear to God I feel physical pain from so much desire.

To my surprise, she opens the bottle again and applies oil to her breasts. She pulls and stretches her hard nipples, and I growl because I can't contain myself.

"Fuck!"

She smiles, head down, and leans forward.

I almost lose my mind when she holds both breasts, trapping my cock between them, and starts to masturbate me. I lift off the bed, and she stops.

"Don't move, or I'll go on a sex strike today."

I lie back down, and it's well worth it because her soft mouth opens and she starts alternating between sucking the head of my cock and masturbating me.

I grip the bed sheets, forcing myself to stay still.

She sucks me greedily, her tongue sliding along my entire length, and I have to think of everything I hate to hold back my climax.

I think she's playing some kind of game too because when she realizes I'm at the edge, she stops.

She gets back on her knees on the bed and applies the oil to her own body. Abdomen, thighs, and ass.

She lies on top of me and starts to grind, sliding. I lift her slightly to put her breasts at the height of my mouth.

She looks like she's going to protest, but I don't allow it, biting her nipple and sucking it hard.

She cries out and starts rubbing her clit against my length.

"So naughty. This delicious cunt is desperate to come, isn't it?"

"Yes, but as I said, Lykaios, I have plans."

She turns in my arms, lying on her back on top of me.

She looks back.

"Why don't you give me a massage too?"

"Only if it's on my terms."

Before she realizes what's happening, I use my feet to spread her thighs.

I finger her cunt. My thumb targets her pleasure spot while my middle finger slides all the way inside her, making her moan and writhe. My shaft fits snugly between her ass cheeks, and my breathing grows heavy.

"Play with your tits," I command.

I grip her belly, continuing to grind against her ass, while another finger joins the first, stretching her pussy.

Moving as well, she rises, making my head fit perfectly in her untouched opening. She pushes against me, and my cock grows even harder.

Am I understanding this correctly?

I test it, pulling my fingers out of her, sliding them between her legs to reach her from behind. I press one, and she writhes.

"*Fuck!*"

My fingers are slick with her fluids.

"Look at me. If you want this, you'll look at me, Zoe."

I'm crazy with desire.

I turn her to face me, and now we're face to face.

"Spread your legs wide."

Her breathing is rapid. When I press her from behind again, she bites and licks me.

"Do you want me to fuck you here?"

I insert the tip of my finger into her, and she writhes, eager.

"I don't want to hurt you."

"I'm dreaming of it. Of belonging to you completely."

Shit. This woman is going to be my undoing.

I move her body off mine, leaving her on the bed, face down. I place a pillow under her.

"Open that beautiful ass for me. I want to see you."

She hesitates but obeys.

Beautiful as hell, dying of desire, offering herself.

I lower myself and begin to lick her, my tongue playing where it has never been before. I use her fluids to lubricate her, but I don't think it will be enough, so I open the bottle of oil and coat a finger with it.

I tease the opening, pressing more than penetrating, letting her adjust while I bite the firm flesh of her ass and thighs.

She moans, and I can see the fluids dripping from her eager sex. I lean forward and position my cock at her cunt. I'm not gentle. I push all the way in to the base.

We both scream with desire.

I move her hair from her neck and bite hard. I want to mark her so she remembers she's mine.

"Harder."

"Harder what?"

"Harder. Don't hold back, show me I'm your woman."

I get on my knees and lift her, fucking her doggy style. I pound relentlessly, my hips driving her face into the bed.

She starts clenching around my cock. Her internal muscles drive me insane.

I touch her clit, pinching it lightly in the way I know makes her come, and as expected, within half a minute she moans, coming all over me, taking me to the balls.

She collapses on the bed, exhausted, but I'm nowhere near done.

I pull out of her, and with the head of my cock soaked with her fluids, I play with her untouched place.

"Tell me to stop," I command, completely out of my mind. Crazy with desire knowing we're about to break the last barrier between us.

"No. I want you inside me. I want you to take me in every way. I'm your woman."

She's still slick with oil, and I'm drenched with her juices. I position myself inside her, leaning forward but not releasing the weight. When she feels me touching her, she writhes.

"Shhhh... don't push yet. I don't want you to feel pain."

She stays still and waits. I thought I'd experienced all forms of madness with Zoe, but this new experience is sending me into orbit.

I push a little, and feeling her open makes me clench my teeth. It's so hot and tight.

I move my hand to her cunt, massaging her clit, and slowly but determinedly make my way into her body.

She screams, a mix of pain and pleasure, but she doesn't pull away. Instead, she pushes her ass up, and I enter further.

"So delicious, Zoe."

I wrap my arm around her neck and shoulder, giving a push that takes me halfway in.

She bites me.

"I'm going to fuck you so good! Fill you with my cum. I'm going to make it spill down your thighs and cunt."

"Oh my God!"

I slide two fingers into her sex, and she sucks me in.

"Do you like it? Being taken by me in every way at once?"

"I'm yours and you're mine. I love everything we do."

And with that, she wipes out my last shred of consciousness, and I thrust fully inside her.

She screams. Cries. Bites. Tenses beneath me.

"Mine. You're mine."

I think I needed to hear that because, a moment later, without me asking, she starts moving.

I get on my knees again, and the sight of my cock opening her has me milliseconds from coming, but I want to savor the sensation of being buried in her.

I begin a long, wild rhythm, equally driven by the pleasure of her muscles gripping me and seeing her whimper to be fucked harder.

My hands are like claws on her hips. I hold her still, lost in the sensation of her warmth.

I fuck her at a steady pace but lose the little control I had left when her hand starts to pleasure herself.

"Do you want to come, you little slut?"

"Please."

"Put two fingers inside your cunt."

I finger her clit as she obeys. In no time, she's pushing back.

I abandon any pretense of taking it easy and pound her hard.

The howls, screams, commands, and pleas we make simultaneously are probably echoing across the island.

There's no modesty or shame. Just delicious fucking between a couple madly in love with each other.

"I'm going to come," she warns, and I grab a handful of her blonde hair.

"I want it harder. Can you take it?"

"Yes," she says through moans of pleasure.

"Do you like this? I know you're loving it. You're soaking my hand, naughty girl."

"Ahhhhh..."

We lose ourselves for minutes, craving the prize, the little death. The journey as delightful as what we know will come at the finish line.

She arches one last time and comes all over me, making me a prisoner.

It's my end.

I thrust in and out. When I return, I fill her with my cum.

As promised, it spills down her thighs, dripping.

The caveman inside me wants to pound his chest.

My woman.

"I love you, Zoe. Always and forever."

Chapter 47

Zoe

"Did you say that in the heat of the moment?" I ask.
"No. I love you."

I open my eyes, finally awake. I'm still not recovered from everything that happened. A little discomfort in my body is nothing compared to the feeling of being taken by the man I love.

I shudder at the memory of his words and actions as he took me.

"I'm crazy about you. Love is too simple a concept to explain, but I'll borrow it until they invent a better one."

I lift my head from his shoulder and look back.

Christos has prepared a bath for me and has been holding me in the warm water for almost an hour.

We haven't talked because there was nothing that could explain what happened.

The surrender, the desire.

I am his. I always was his. How could I have thought there could be another?

"I'm okay with love," I say, turning around and straddling him, but sitting on his thighs to avoid provoking him.

"It's more than that, Zoe. I fought against it because my pride demanded that I not seek you out, but I knew."

"Knew what?"

"That no matter how much time passed... We belong to each other."

"If we hadn't seen each other again, you would eventually find someone else."

He shakes his head, indicating no.

"I never loved before you and I'll never love after. — He tucks a strand of my hair behind my ear. — I think I'm like my father. I can't imagine him marrying again if something happens to Mom. I knew there would be no replacement since I found you."

"I'M GOING TO SAY GOODBYE to Yuri," I say, pulling up my *shorts* but still without a top. He walks into the *closet* and, from the way he's looking at me, it doesn't seem like we just made love again after the bath.

"Yuri should be gone already," he responds with a stern expression.

We both know that's a lie. The yacht is still docked at the marina.

I turn my face to the side, trying to understand why he suddenly looks so angry.

"Are you jealous of your assistant?"

"Of course not."

I hide a smile.

"Don't be silly." I approach him, still topless. "I'm yours, Greek."

He grabs my breast and massages my nipple with his thumb.

I moan.

"Yes, all mine now."

I cling to him, my legs weak. It's incredible the power he has over my body.

"Are you sure you want to go?"

The confidence in his tone makes me, even against my will, pull away from him.

"Conceited."

He shrugs but doesn't deny it.

I put on my shirt.

"I just want to thank you for what you did for my parents. With all the chaos of the commercial shoots and the photo sessions, I didn't have time. He's a good friend, and I value people like that."

"He is. Just don't thank him too enthusiastically."

"Jesus!" I laugh loudly, shaking my head.

I finish dressing and untangle my hair with my fingers. I don't even put on my sandals.

I run down the stairs and head straight to the marina.

"Yuri!"

He's getting onto Christos's yacht, which will take the crew, including photographers, cameramen, makeup artists, and the two models, back to shore. He turns around when I call him.

"Zoe, is something wrong?"

"No," I reply, out of breath. "I just wanted to say thank you. You were so good to my parents, arranging both the clinic for Mom and the house for them to stay in between her treatments. I owe you a debt of eternal gratitude."

"It was nothing. I just did my job." He seems uncomfortable.

"That's my job. Taking care of them, I mean. But you were wonderful. Thank you so much."

I wave goodbye and turn to head back to the mansion, but before I can, I hear the captain shouting that someone is missing from boarding and that they need to leave before the storm that's predicted hits.

I skip down the entrance steps two at a time, and after wiping my feet on the mat, I start heading up to the second floor when I hear Christos's voice.

"Get dressed."

His tone is harsh, relentless.

Not knowing what's going on, I walk to where I think he is — the kitchen.

"You don't know what you're missing." I recognize that the person he's arguing with is one of the models from the shoot. My blood boils.

Get dressed?

What the hell is going on?

Before I can reach them, she says:

"If it's a woman you want for the holidays, why not me? I'm younger and prettier."

"Get out."

"She's crippled. Those scars on her feet and especially on her hand are disgusting."

For a moment, I'm shaken. I look at my feet. Yes, there are still marks from the burns because my skin is thin, but the makeup artist managed to cover most of them. The one on my hand is a bit worse, but not disgusting.

"Out, damn it! What don't you understand about what I said? You're fired!" Christos shouts.

I enter the kitchen and, at the same moment, the girl puts on the *top* she had taken off, exposing her breasts to my man.

"What do you think you're doing?" I ask.

I see her lower lip quivering.

"Get out!" my boyfriend orders again.

"Wait a minute. Let her answer me. What do you think you're doing, Hanna? You said you're younger than me, but you're at least eighteen or you wouldn't be here. I'll be twenty-one soon, but that's not the point. I've lived a life more than you."

"Zoe, I..." she starts, but I interrupt her.

"Do you think that by offering to have sex, by getting naked in front of a man, you'll make yourself valuable? In ten years, if not sooner, your ass and tits will start to sag. The force of gravity, love. No one escapes it. At this rate, you'll be known not for being photogenic but for sleeping with your bosses. An easy lay, as we call it in our circles."

"I'm sorry," the fake says.

"I'm not finished." I take two steps closer to her. "The one who talked to you just now was the old Zoe. There's still a trace of her in me. She's kind and compassionate. She forgives easily, too. But unfortunately for you, that silly girl is long gone. The one in charge now is the angry Zoe. Disgusting is *you*, who uses the fact that I have scars to try to bring me down."

"You're jealous because you know I spoke the truth. He's going to get tired of you," she sneers, her face twisted in hatred.

"Yes, I'm angry because he's *mine*, but Christos is big enough to know how to get rid of women like you."

Yuri enters, breathless.

"Hanna, what the hell are you doing here?"

"Offering myself to my boyfriend, but you missed the boat. Bye, Yuri."

I turn my back and run up the stairs. I'm furious, perhaps more at myself than at her for letting her make me lose control.

I barely reach the room when Christos grabs my arm.

"Zoe."

"I'm not upset with you. I've been modeling for almost two years. I know how this industry works. It's not the first time I've seen a girl show her breasts to a guy as a sort of calling card, but it's the first time I've seen someone do it to my man. I wanted to knock her face off."

He approaches, like someone approaching a wild animal, I think unsure of my reaction.

"Jealous?"

"No. Jealous doesn't cover it. I wanted to kill her, that's for sure."

"It wasn't what it seemed," he says, wrapping his arms around my waist. "I was worried when she mentioned your hand. I don't care at all. I..."

I put my fingers on his lips.

"I know. And I don't either. I could have lost my parents and my best friend, Christos. These scars are nothing. So it wasn't my self-esteem she hurt. It was fierce jealousy, but I wouldn't admit it."

He laughs, which helps me relax despite the stress of the moments before. However, seconds later, he becomes serious, pressing our foreheads together.

"I have a present. I was going to wait until your twenty-first birthday, but I don't want to leave anything hanging between us. — He gives me a light kiss on the lips and steps back. — Don't leave this spot."

"Yes, sir."

I hear him going down the stairs and he returns a minute later, holding a piece of paper.

"What's this?"

"Open it."

I read it, my mouth falling open in shock.

"A *farm*?"

"Yes. In North Carolina. Your dream of being a farmer is now coming true."

"It was a distant plan. I don't know what to do with a farm."

"We'll have plenty of help, but we can also learn together."

I look at him, incredulous, and I think he sees the question on my face because he shakes his head, agreeing.

"Yes, that's right. I'm asking you to be mine."

"I thought we had passed that point. I *am* yours."

"Let me try to do better, then."

He goes to the bedside table and takes out a jewelry box.

Then he kneels at my feet and my heart races wildly.

"I planned to do this with our parents present, but nothing between us follows a script, Zoe." He opens the Tiffany's box to reveal a diamond ring in a princess cut. "I needed to find you and then lose you to be sure you were the one I had been waiting for my whole life. I was your silent admirer. I loved you even when I didn't know it was love and..."

I don't wait for him to finish and pull him up by the hand.

"I love you and want to spend the rest of my life with you."

"You haven't answered yet."

"Yes. Yes. Yes! There's nothing I want more than to be your wife."

Chapter 48

Zoe

The Next Day

"Congratulations, daughter. Would I seem very presumptuous if I said I knew this was going to happen?"

"How so?" I ask, smiling.

"I'm old and maybe a bit out of shape, but I can recognize a couple in love when I see one."

"Oh, that's true. I noticed it too when you were at our house. I guess we know our kids well, don't we, Macy?" Danae chimes in.

I smile at her referring to her son as a kid. When I look at him, he's shaking his head too, probably for the same reason.

We're all gathered in the main house on the island, telling my parents, via video call, that we're getting married.

Danae and Alekos arrived earlier today, and my mother-in-law — yes, I think I can call her that now — was beaming when she heard the news.

I still can't believe it. I'm so happy that I'm afraid it's all been a dream.

This morning, Christos had a meeting with the legal team. They said that at most, in two months, the issue of the false marriage would be resolved. My fiancé wasn't happy and demanded a one-month deadline. He then told me he wanted us to marry as soon as a judge declared my marriage to Mike invalid.

"So, where do you plan to get married?"

"At our farm," I reply quickly, looking at Christos.

"You've got your answer, my mother-in-law. Zoe decides, I go there and say 'I do.'"

I roll my eyes.

"Yeah, right."

"Whoever sees it like this would believe it!" his mother says, laughing. "You and your father are just alike. If I let him, Alekos would even choose the color of my underwear."

"Too much information, Mrs. Danae," my fiancé says.

My mother bursts out laughing.

The atmosphere is one of camaraderie, and I find myself wishing for a future with a house full of children, family Christmases, and lots of love.

That part is already guaranteed. I feel loved and welcomed by both Christos and his parents. In my world, that's like winning the lottery.

"I'm going to talk to Yuri to see how he can help me with the wedding planning, and I'm sure Bia will want to be involved too."

"Speaking of which, how is she?" Mom asks.

"Well, but after what happened, she told me she plans to make a life change. She doesn't want to be a spy or an agent anymore. She's going to leave everything in Miguel's hands and take a sabbatical year. She's fully recovered from... our accident."

I look at Christos and see his jaw tighten.

"It's good that divine justice was served," his mother says. "That cruel man got the end he deserved," she adds, referring to Mike.

"Well, now we have to go, my daughter. We loved the news. I hope to be well enough to attend your wedding."

"You will be, Mom. I'm sure of it."

We chat for a little longer in the living room, but minutes later, I excuse myself and leave. There's something I need to do.

I head up to my room. With my phone and my little doll *Pauline* in hand, I run out of the house towards the beach.

Half an hour and many photos later, I sit on the sand, looking out at the sea.

"Hey, friend, I hope you can see, up there in heaven, how happy I am. I'm going to marry my Greek, or rather, my *Greek god*, according to his ego," I joke. "I didn't come to talk to you earlier because, right after the fire, my head was so messed up. I don't handle surprises well, and they came all at once. My parents' house destroyed, Bia in a coma, and in the midst of all this, I'm moving in with Christos."

I smile thinking about what he told me the other day: that life had come full circle, and in the end, we ended up in the same place — in each other's arms.

"I don't even need to say how relieved I am that my marriage to Mike, which never came to fruition, was also a lie before the law. He's so low-down that I can't even count which of his actions I hate the most. No, that's not true. Of everything he did to me, what I will never forgive him for is trying to kill my family. God might one day think he deserves a second chance and pull him out of hell, which I'm sure he's in, but I reserve the right to hate him for now. Anyway, I just wanted to say 'hi' and reaffirm that I haven't forgotten about our project. The photos will continue, but my modeling career won't last much longer, I hope. I will always carry you in my heart wherever I go, but it's time for me to live a little of my own life too, Pauline."

"Do you want some company?"

I look back and see Christos approaching.

I pat the sand beside me.

"Yours? Always."

"Taking photos with your friend?"

He positions himself behind me, wrapping me in his arms and legs. I feel trapped in a fortress. The sensation is delightful.

"Yes. I took a break from doing it because I like to send good vibes when I talk to Pauline, and at the beginning, right after the fire, I was very upset."

"Pissed off."

"What?"

"You don't need to moderate what you feel, Zoe. You're human and have the right to go crazy sometimes. You weren't just upset; you were pissed off because that bastard nearly destroyed your entire world. He lied by marrying you while already being married. Then he robbed you, and in the end, he tried to kill you. You have the right to express how you feel. Scream, allow yourself to curse and feel anger."

"I internalize my feelings."

"Most of the time, I do too. I'm not good with words. But I don't think it's healthy for you to keep it all in when you're angry."

"Even if it's at you?"

"Especially at me. We're a *forever*. I don't want a TV commercial relationship, but a real one. I'm Greek and have a fiery temper. Controlling, arrogant, and I have no doubt that we'll argue many times."

"You can count on it. Especially since I love making up afterward."

I feel his chest vibrate against my back and know he's laughing.

"Am I going to have to take you to a sex addict's treatment, future Mrs. Lykaios?"

"No, please. I'm fine with my addiction. In fact," I say, standing up, taking off my shorts and top, and remaining in just my bikini, "I want more."

New York

One Month Later

"ARE YOU TELLING ME I'm free now?" I ask the lawyer who is speaking with Christos and me over a video call.

"Yes. Actually, Miss Turner, you always were. It was just a matter of the law recognizing it."

Ignoring that we're in front of someone else, I run to Christos's lap and hug him.

I was working on a painting when he had the maid inform me that he wanted to see me. I enrolled in an *online* painting course to de-stress. I'm not a *Picasso*, but I like my creations. It's helped control my anxiety.

We're in New York now. We arrived three days ago. We came back from Greece to Boston because I wanted to see my parents, but Christos had to come here to deal with his company matters.

"Did you hear that? We're getting married," I tell my fiancé, as happy as can be.

"Thank you, Steve," Christos says, ending the call with the lawyer. "Tomorrow?" he asks with one of his rare smiles.

"Not so fast. I haven't given a final 'yes' to the dress yet. And there are details of the party still to be sorted out."

"Leave it to Yuri. I'm sure he'll sort everything out quickly."

"And to Bia as well. She already told me she wants to be the one to organize our party."

"That's fine with me, Miss Turner. As long as it means I won't have to wait long to see you walking towards me in a white dress."

"And me to have you naked on the wedding night."

"Slightly scandalous."

"*Your* slightly scandalous."

One Week Later

I FINISH THE FINAL brushstrokes on a painting that I want to give to my mother when my phone rings. I don't answer immediately because I don't recognize the number, but the caller insists and, sighing, I give up trying to ignore it.

"Hello?" I answer, grumpily.

"*Zoe?*"

"Who is this?"

"*Nelly Howard. Did I call at a bad time?*"

Mike's mother? What could she possibly want from me?

"Um... No. I'm sorry, I didn't recognize the number." *And not the voice, since you never made an effort to be in touch with me.* But I keep that last part to myself.

"*I couldn't have. We only met once.*"

Something about her tone annoys me, so I decide not to prolong the conversation.

"I don't want to be rude, but is there a specific reason you're calling me? When my parents lost everything, as far as I know, you said you didn't want to have contact with us."

"*Yes, I was very upset.*"

"Upset with me? Forgive my honesty, but it was your son who tried to kill me and my family. So if anyone should be furious, it would be me."

"*Yes, I know. I was depressed. The police notified me some time after the fire at your parents' house that my Mike had died in a car accident.*"

"If you're expecting me to apologize for not calling you to offer condolences, it's not going to happen. I have some flaws, but insincerity isn't one of them."

"*I didn't expect you to say you were sorry, and I didn't call to argue, but to have an honest conversation. I've started going to church again, and the priest advised me to try to mend the past. To fix my mistakes.*"

"I don't understand."

"*When Mike married you, I knew he was already married. That's why I didn't go to the courthouse on the day you got engaged. I couldn't be part of that farce.*"

"What? You're telling me you knew your son was committing a crime? Besides deceiving me and my family, you stayed silent?"

"*Yes. I know what I did wasn't right.*"

"Not right? You allowed your son to lead me into a relationship built on lies!"

"*I don't ask you to understand my reasons. I just wanted to apologize. When you become a mother, you'll see that there are no limits to what you would do for a child.*"

"I will never become that kind of mother. Loving a child means raising them with good principles, which includes showing what's right and what's wrong. By remaining silent, Mrs. Howard, you were complicit in Mike's wrongdoings. I wish you luck in seeking forgiveness from God, but you won't get it from me. Have a good afternoon."

I hang up feeling lighter. Maybe this is what Christos meant about externalizing when I'm angry. I could have offered her forgiveness, but it would have been insincere. I don't intend to harbor grudges, but I don't want any contact with anything related to Mike, including his mother.

Chapter 49

Christos

New York

Two Weeks Later

"*I have a gift for you. I think I'll even give it to you early, for the wedding.*"

"Rat cleanup?" I ask, excitedly.

I know he's telling me he found Howard.

I never doubted he would. Not for a second did I believe that story about the car fire. It was too convenient to die like that when the U.S. police were hunting the bastard.

"*Yes. You know how good I am at setting traps for rodents. Actually, at exterminating them too.*"

"That's not what we agreed on."

"*Agreed on? The cleaning business is mine, friend. I don't need a partner. Besides, in the current global scenario, it would be impossible. The cleanup wasn't done in the United States, but in Nicaragua.*"

"What?"

"*Enjoy your life, Christos. You have a beautiful woman at home. Your business is making money, not dealing with rodents. Let people like me handle the ugly side of life. I'll always be on watch.*"

I disagree with what he said. I'm capable of killing without remorse for those I love, and Zoe is my world.

I would have liked to make Howard suffer.

What comforts me is knowing that if his death came at the hands of Beau or his men, it took hours and was painful.

As if on cue, my phone rings, showing Odin's number.

"*Your wife has finally closed the book on her past. Ready to start writing a new story?*"

"Poetic, cousin?"

I assume he's talking about the annulment of the fake marriage, because I don't think he would know that Beau hunted and exterminated Mike. Or would he?

"*Excited, I would say. Getting the vaccine will allow me to proceed with my plans.*"

We learned today that the vaccination will start soon.

He doesn't elaborate on these plans. He's never spoken about them, but I know what they are. I don't try to dissuade him, though, because in his place, I would do the same.

"So, once you get the vaccine, you're going to Greece?"

"*Yes. To my island.*"

"Is it yours already?"

"*It is, along with everyone on it. Especially Leandros Argyros.*"

"And the rest of his family?"

"*I don't take revenge on women.*"

"Is revenge what you want?"

"*Why name it? But I would call it settling a score.*"

With the other part being eliminated, I have no doubts. But who am I to judge him when I'm currently satisfied with Mike Howard's death?

"How did you know Zoe's past was finally closed?"

"*Just because you asked me not to intervene doesn't mean I stopped investigating. You're my cousin. Your life is mine too. Anyone who threatens you is my enemy.*"

I'm moved by what he says. Odin is even more elusive than I am, and he's practically alone in the world. I know how much our friendship means to him.

"That goes both ways, so keep in mind that I'll be watching when you travel to Greece."

"*I had no doubt about that, but I have everything under control.*"

"Will you be attending our wedding?"

"*I wouldn't miss it for anything.*"

New York

Three Weeks Later

"WHAT ELSE IS LEFT?"

"There was an unexpected issue, but other than that, we need to do the sweet tasting. With all this social distancing, scheduling an appointment is a real mess."

"It could be worse. I didn't expect the vaccine to be ready this year. Your parents and mine will be the first to get it. As for us, I think only in group four."

"Maybe not," she says enigmatically.

"Why do I feel like you're keeping a secret?"

"Because I am, but unfortunately, I'm a terrible liar."

I was working in the library of my apartment when she came to talk to me, all mysterious. I thought it was something related to the ceremony, but now I realize there's more behind that beautiful, disingenuous smile."

"I can't disagree," I say, pushing my chair back and patting my thigh.

She sits down, facing me directly.

"That I'm a terrible liar?"

"Yep. The worst in the world. I'd go broke in a poker game."

"That's not great for my self-esteem."

"Being a liar isn't a quality, but to avoid completely ruining your ego, know that what gives you away is your eyes. They sparkle like precious stones when you're happy."

"In that case, a pair of sunglasses would solve the problem."

She's dodging the subject, and I'm more curious than ever.

"You said that besides the sweet tasting, there was an unexpected issue. What happened?"

"God, you don't miss a thing."

"No. So?"

"There's a problem with the dress."

"I thought you had already decided on the model. Didn't the Vanity designer promise to make it?"

"Yes, and he did. It's beautiful, but the size is wrong."

"What?"

She smiles.

"We'll need to adjust it. Make it a bit larger."

I stare at her, not understanding at first, but then I realize the barely concealed happiness.

"You've gained weight?" I ask to be sure, but my heart is already pounding against my chest.

"Yes. Two kilos, and I think I'll be even bigger in the near future."

"Words, Zoe. I want to hear it. I need to hear it," I say, holding her face.

My hand trembles a little. It's not easy for me to get emotional, but she seems to know all the right buttons to press.

"I'm pregnant," she says, and a tear rolls down her cheek. "We're going to have a baby. I know it wasn't what we planned, but..."

I kiss her because there's nothing I could say that would convey what I'm feeling.

We created a life.

My love for her is now going to be materialized through a piece of both of us.

When we pull away, she's smiling.

"I was afraid to tell you because we hadn't talked about it yet, but I'm so happy. Almost floating since I found out this morning."

"Did you think I wouldn't be?"

"I know you love me. I feel it in every cell of my body, but having a child is an eternal responsibility."

"I handle responsibilities well, but this," I say, placing my hand on her belly, "isn't just a responsibility for me; it's our love and our future. My world."

She snuggles into my arms and rests her head on my chest. I hold her tightly.

I believe that everything happens for a reason. It wasn't a coincidence, but the hand of fate intervened and made Beau discover and eliminate Mike Howard a few weeks ago. It happened at the right moment, as if the pieces of the board of life were finally falling into their rightful places.

Chapter 50

Zoe

Two Months Later

"You might have a sore arm, miss," the nurse who just administered my first vaccine dose says.

Contrary to what we initially thought, the vaccine is now available for everyone, even though they initially prioritized the elderly.

I decided to wait to get married until after taking it because, even though I risk being a bit fuller on the wedding day, I feel more at ease knowing that both I and the guests will be vaccinated.

Bia came with me. This is the first time we've met since the whole tragedy, even though we've talked on the phone almost every day. Especially now, concerning the wedding.

"I don't like feeling pain," she says to the attendant, rolling up her sleeve to get her dose.

"The other option is much worse," I ponder.

"Don't even talk about it. Thank God life is finally going back to normal. As soon as you get married, I'm finally going on vacation to the Caribbean, starting my long-awaited sabbatical year."

"Cruise?" I ask as we walk back to the car.

"No. A friend married a millionaire." She stops and smiles. "Another friend of mine, besides you," she corrects herself, "married a millionaire. After all, with Christos, the correct term is billionaire."

"And is he going to lend you an island? If you wanted to travel, you could go to Christos's in Greece."

"Jealous."

"I am."

"Maybe during my travels next year, I'll end up passing through there."

"Just let me know if you really want to go."

"Speaking of Greece, the commercial and the catalog you did on Christos's island are spread all over the world. Do you have any idea how many phone calls and *emails* Miguel gets every day from brands wanting him to represent them?"

"We're going to get rich," I joke.

"You're already rich. The contract you signed with Christos elevated you to a level envied by the elite of the runway, but according to Miguel, you received an offer from Vanity's competitor. They're willing to double Christos's offer for an exclusive contract and even cover your penalty with him if you decide to switch."

"Does this company know that my Greek isn't just an employer but also my future husband?"

"Probably, even though you haven't announced the wedding publicly yet."

"Because Christos decided to do that at our trip to the opera, in an exclusive performance for high society, in a little over a month. My belly will already be visible, and the gossipers will have two topics to discuss at once. It'll be good because when they find out I'm pregnant, they'll quickly stop offering me a fortune to model."

"I don't know. With how much this new Vanity commercial is being talked about, I believe they would even wait for you to have the baby."

"I highly doubt it's not known that Christos and I are together. Gossip runs rampant in our circles, and if that's the case, do they really think I'd break a contract with my future husband for more money?"

"Honey, you don't know what some people are capable of doing for a little extra cash."

"Some people, not me. Even if I weren't in love with Christos, no amount of money would make me break the contract. I'll stick exclusively with Vanity for the agreed five years and then quit modeling for good."

Opera Night in New York

A Month and a Half Later

"I'M A LITTLE ANXIOUS," I say before he opens the limousine door. "No, let me correct that. I'm *very* anxious."

"I know. I already know you, Zoe. You're so electric, it's shocking."

"They're going to devour me alive when I get out of the car. Especially because of the dress I chose."

He looks at my rounded belly. Since I'm thin, if I were wearing a loose dress, it could still be hidden, but with this fitted strapless one, there'll be no doubt.

"Did you do it on purpose?"

"Yes, I'm not ashamed of our boys."

We found out we're having twins. It was a surprise, and a joy as well. Two babies at once is a blessing. I just didn't understand how it was possible until talking to Madeline on the phone—my cousin, and I think the only blood relative who likes me—she told me that her mother had previously suffered a miscarriage with twins. Then she mentioned some cases in the family and thinks that's probably why I was rewarded.

She's a sweetheart and will be here tonight—unfortunately, her witch of a mother will be too, but life isn't perfect, right?

"Screw the gossips, Zoe. What matters is the two of us. Or rather, the four of us. No one will make us ashamed of our family."

"Never. I think the anxiety is greater because I don't like drawing attention."

"Not drawing attention in your case is impossible. You're beautiful. Walk in with your head held high. I'll be by your side every step of the way."

The car door opens and I see the bodyguards already positioned. Christos gets out, offers me his hand, and as I rise, I'm blinded by the *flashes* from the photographers. It's frightening because even with the human barrier formed by the security guards, they seem like flies on honey.

It's as if now that they're all vaccinated, they've given themselves the right to forget manners.

I'm used to the harassment, especially after the shows, but what's happening today is surreal.

It must be because of the Vanity commercials. Or because I'm arm-in-arm with Christos. Or maybe it's the whole package.

I keep a frozen, impersonal smile, and my face is hard from the tension. The only thing that reassures me a little is Christos's arm around my waist, while his other hand protects my abdomen.

I ignore the questions coming from all sides, focused on not tripping.

UNPLANNED OBSESSION

My heart is pounding fast, and my hands are cold. It's harder than I imagined, and I can only breathe a sigh of relief when we finally enter the building where the opera is located.

"Are you okay?" Christos asks.

"Yes," I lie and then correct myself. "Nervous."

He kisses my lips.

"I didn't want to be here either, but we needed this public appearance or the world would turn upside down when they found out about the wedding and the pregnancy. It'll be better this way. Tomorrow, Yuri will place an official announcement in the newspapers."

I nod, praying for the night to pass quickly.

"Zoe?" A hesitant voice calls me, and I turn to see who it is.

My cousin, Madeline Turner.

"I can't believe we finally reunited," she says.

We don't kiss or shake hands. It's awful, but people have been avoiding doing that even after being vaccinated. I think this will be another scar on the collective memory: the fear of hugging and kissing.

"Madeline, I'm so happy to see you. You look beautiful."

"Thank you," she says shyly.

She is truly beautiful. Fair skin, chocolate-colored hair, huge blue eyes, and delicate as a fairy.

She's wearing a long, bright red dress that doesn't match her personality at all. I'm sure she didn't pick it herself.

"Madeline, this is my future husband, Christos. Christos, this is my cousin I told you about, Madeline."

They exchange pleasantries, and a man approaches, catching my fiancé's attention. I turn back to talk to her, but freeze when I hear someone say:

"Zoe, how wonderful to see you again, dear!"

Oh, Jesus. Falseness has a name and surname: Adley Turner, my aunt. Or rather, Madeline's mother, since she was never really an aunt to me.

And "dear"? She offered me a maid's uniform the last time we met!

I turn towards the voice reluctantly.

The woman has such a wide— and fake—smile that it looks like she had it tattooed on her face.

"You never sought me out again, but I'm not one to hold grudges, so I'll overlook your ingratitude."

I can't help but roll my eyes.

"I'm very happy with the success of the campaign," she says, but her eyes keep drifting to my prominent pregnancy belly in the dress.

Maybe I'm being overly sensitive, but it feels like she's insinuating that I got the job due to my pregnancy, since Vanity is Christos's company.

"Thank you," I reply curtly.

"But I see you won't be able to model for quite some time from now on."

She takes a step forward with her hand outstretched, as if to pat my belly. I step back, but before I can move further away, Christos's voice thunders:

"No."

It's a definitive no, the kind that leaves no room for doubt, and it reads like a warning.

Don't come near.

Don't bother my wife.

Don't touch my children.

She freezes, her smile fading slightly.

"Christos Lykaios, I did hear some comments that my niece was..."— she pauses dramatically, and I want to hit her "working with you."

I hear a disgusted sigh from Madeline and feel sorry for her. She's probably embarrassed by her mother's behavior.

My fiancé wraps his arm around me.

"Not just working," he says in a tone loud enough for anyone in the VIP hall to hear. "She is mine in every way. Zoe will be my wife and the mother of my children."

An "ohhhhh" is heard, followed by almost half a minute of silence.

Adley is the first to recover.

"Oh, how wonderful!" she changes her tone completely. "Congratulations, Zoe. I'm very happy with the news. When is the wedding?"

I reach my quota of masochism for the day.

Ignoring the viper's question, I turn to Madeline.

"Could you accompany me to the restroom?"

"Of course."

I hold Christos's hand and kiss the back of it.

"I'll be right back."

He looks at me as if he wants to say something but stops. As we move away, I notice a bodyguard following us.

Chapter 51

Zoe

"I'm sorry about everything, Zoe."

"It's not your fault, Maddie," I say, using her nickname. "No one can choose their mother."

She lets out a laugh.

"I, more than anyone, know that."

"You're going to the wedding, right?"

"I am. I've never been to North Carolina. I'm very excited, but I wanted to ask a favor." I stop walking.

"Of course."

"Help me pick out a dress. My mother always criticizes all my clothes, and when she helps, they end up looking like this"— she says, pointing to her own outfit.

"It's beautiful, but it doesn't suit you."

"I know. I'm not extravagant, nor do I like showing too much skin. With all due respect," she says, glancing at my outfit, where a large slit exposes my left thigh.

"I'm used to dressing and undressing. I'm no longer ashamed of showing my body, but at the beginning of my career, I was much shyer. Therapy helped in the process of liberation."

"And speaking of liberation, I'm thinking of doing something crazy," she says.

"What kind?"

"Running away to London. Getting a job. Living life."

"What?"

"Do you think I'm not capable?"

"If you're asking me about mental strength, I think anyone is capable of anything. I just don't understand the reason for this sudden desire."

"I've been planning this for a long time. Getting out from under my mother's skirt and going to Europe, I mean. I can't stand the pressure she's putting on me to get married. I finished college, but I can't work because *it would shame the Turner name—*" she says, mimicking her mother. I laugh because it's quite accurate.

"What do you need to make this plan happen?"

"Moral support, mostly."

"You've got that. Count on me for whatever you need. Actually, I just had an idea. There's a friend of Christos's, Kamal. He's a *Sheikh*, but also a businessman. *CEO*, actually. My fiancé mentioned that he was looking for an assistant."

"Oh my God! Do you think I could get it?"

"Well, you have some qualifications. You know the world and have good taste. From what I understand, he wants someone who can travel with him and also give him some tips on Western etiquette."

"Etiquette tips? Is he a brute?"

"I can't say. But if you want, I can talk to Christos about it."

"Yes, please! Do you think this man would consider me for the position?"

I decide to be honest.

"I don't know. I've never met a *Sheikh* before. Unfortunately, he won't be able to attend my wedding because he has a commitment the same week; otherwise, Christos could introduce you. But I promise I'll talk to my fiancé about it."

The restroom is empty, and after using the stalls, we touch up our makeup, talking about a new lipstick brand that just launched and doesn't test on animals.

Suddenly, the door opens, and through the mirror, I see the last person I'd expect to see here.

Ernestine Lambert, Pauline's mother.

She's still a beautiful woman, though her beauty is just a shell. She's well-dressed in a long black gown, completely at ease as a high society lady.

She seems surprised to see me. I think we're both in shock, actually, but I recover first.

"Hello, you liar. What are you doing here?" I ask.

Yes, I think pregnancy hormones are making me act a bit crazy. I'm in a phase where if you piss me off, I want to rip your head off.

"Zoe, what a pleasure to see you again! As for your question, it wasn't just you who landed a billionaire, dear."

"I can't say the same. I feel no pleasure in seeing you again." I turn to my cousin. "Madeline, could you stay outside and make sure no one comes in?"

She leaves without arguing.

"We have nothing to talk about, Zoe. Or do you want to apologize for being the lover of that murderer?"

"If you open your mouth to speak about my fiancé, I'll hit you. Actually, you won't say anything. I will. How do you have the audacity to look at yourself in the mirror after what you've done? You're filthy, Ernestine. She was your little girl. Your child to love and protect. You knew who the man was who put her in that state, and yet you lied to all of us. You took advantage of the fact that Pauline was too young to remember the real culprit. Why? To gain people's sympathy? So that no one would know what a wretched, irresponsible person you are? As if that wasn't enough, you handed over the compensation to another boyfriend while your daughter was in need!"

"You don't know anything."

"Maybe not, but what I do know disgusts me. I never thought I'd say this, but Pauline was lucky to go to heaven. God took her because you didn't deserve her. Liar, gold-digger. You're a sketch of a human being. As filthy and vile as that rat who caused the accident. I hope that when you die, you two meet in hell. Have a shitty life, thinking about what your daughter suffered because of you. Or at least, because of the consequences of your actions."

I leave before I do something foolish, like putting my hand in her face. Don't get me wrong, it's not the fact that we're at a fancy party that stops me, but the concern for my babies. I don't want to harm them, so even though I'm extremely angry, I decide to leave.

When I reach the hallway, Maddie is still on guard like a soldier.

Christos is talking to a bodyguard, and a few steps away from him is an elderly man with white hair.

My intuition tells me this man is with Ernestine. When I see her leaving the restroom — thanks to my peripheral vision — and heading towards him, I follow.

"Nice to meet you, I'm Zoe Turner. I don't know what your relationship with Ernestine is, but if you want advice, run while you still can. If someone doesn't have love inside them to protect their own child, what would they do with a stranger? If you want to contact me, I'll tell you the whole story."

I pull out a business card from my purse and hand it to him.

I turn my back on them and go to my man.

He wraps his arm around my shoulders and begins to lead me back to the hall. We're followed by Maddie and the bodyguard.

"What just happened?" he asks, looking confused.

"Do you know who she is?"

"I'm not sure if I know her. Her face seems familiar, but..."

"The liar responsible for our separation. Pauline's mother."

His face transforms into fury, and he stops walking. He makes a move to turn back, but I hold his arm.

"No, love. It's over. It's finally over."

Chapter 52

Beau Carmouche–LeBlanc

Somewhere in Central America

One Day Before Christos' Wedding

"Why don't you just kill me already, damn it?" he screams.

There is no dignity left in what remains of him. Not a trace of the arrogant professor and woman-beater.

"So rude, doctor. Your former students would be shocked by your language. Not all of them, of course. Those you fucked over are probably used to it."

"What did I do to you, damn it?"

"To me? Nothing. But last time, you picked the wrong victim, Mike. Unfortunately for you, you messed with the wife of one of my close friends."

"Who? Why don't you at least tell me what I'm being accused of?"

"Because it wouldn't be as much fun," I reply, indifferent.

Howard doesn't know it yet, but today is his last day on this planet. I've let my men deal with him for months, but I've come personally to finish the job.

"Ahhhhhhhh... ahhhhhhhhhhh!" he screams in desperation, and I cross my arms, leaning against a wall.

"What's the matter? Not so fun when you're the victim, not two defenseless old folks? Or your ex-wife... oops, wait. She was never your wife. I just remembered. Not legally or biblically."

"I'm here because of that bitch Zoe? I never wanted her, was only interested in the money," he lies, because I doubt any living man could be indifferent to the beauty of Lykaios' bride.

"I don't believe that. However, it doesn't matter anymore, my friend. She's fine. The parents are too. Macy is recovered from cancer. Scott is in great health, and you, stuck in a basement in the middle of nowhere, being tortured for months. Was it worth it?"

A glimmer of hope appears in his eyes.

"No. I'm sorry."

I take the blade I like to work with and, in a single stroke, end his life.

"It was a rhetorical question, Mike. The moment you crossed my friend's path, you were already dead. You just didn't know it yet."

Chapter 53

Christos

North Carolina

Christos and Zoe's Wedding Day

She is coming towards me.
 Beautiful, smiling.
Mine.

We've crossed a lifetime to get here, but from today on, only death can separate us. Maybe not even that.

Zoe has blossomed, yet remains that beautiful blend of girl and woman.

She's been laughing and playing a lot lately, and I believe Macy's recovery is an important factor in that equation.

Oh, and our boys, of course. She loves being pregnant and is happy to see her belly growing.

She's also become more confident. Brave enough to displease the occasional person.

Mom, my mother-in-law, she, and Bia organized the entire wedding, using Yuri as a last resort. I suspect he thanked God, because when the four of them start talking at once, only a translator can make sense of it.

When I asked why she didn't hire a specialized company, she replied that this would be her one and only true wedding, so she wanted to do everything as she had always dreamed.

A few days ago, we made the farm here in North Carolina our permanent residence. The move was discussed with the whole family, and when my parents said they would move to Chapel Hill to be closer to us, she cried.

However, I knew her happiness would never be complete without Scott and Macy nearby, so after talking to my in-laws, I gifted them a house next to my parents'. That way, the four of them can watch the grandchildren grow up. Not just the twins that are coming, but many others, as we plan to contribute diligently to the planet's population growth.

Zoe walks arm in arm with her father, and Scott seems very proud of his girl. He whispers something to her, and she smiles.

God, the woman is so beautiful. I am completely in love with her, with everything about her.

We have our disagreements like any couple — usually due to my overprotectiveness and fear of something happening to her — but the fights don't last. Zoe has the power to calm my combative nature.

She continues with her therapy and her anxiety attacks have decreased, although they still occur sometimes.

The other day, she woke up in the middle of the night and asked me what would happen to the babies if we died.

I know it's her mind playing tricks. It's not something that can be avoided. I've read about it. Anxiety is not *just a fuss*, as most people think, but a real issue.

I even took an *online* course to learn how to help her deal with it.

I learned that they are triggered by certain stimuli. Talking with her about it, we try to create strategies to avoid them, but it's not always possible.

Anyway, she hardly has any moments of sadness now, and every day spent by her side is a discovery.

Zoe has a kindness and inner beauty that rivals her outer beauty.

She finally stands before me, and Scott hugs her, squeezing her cheek. Dad steps down from the pulpit, breaking protocol, to kiss her on the forehead.

I think my wife needed this. The feeling of being welcomed into a family that loves her. Together with Macy and Scott, we are a whole, and our children are coming to join us.

We opted for a small ceremony, with only fifty guests — mostly family, like Odin.

Beau apologized but said weddings weren't his thing. I didn't take it badly. He has already proven to be a loyal friend. Everyone handles what they can.

I was convinced by my assistant to allow some journalists and photographers, carefully selected.

Although I wasn't very pleased with it, Yuri argued that if we didn't let them come, the press would speculate and turn the start of our marriage into a hell, trying to find news.

After Macy and mom also hug her, I go to meet the woman of my life.

I kiss her, satisfying a bit of the eternal hunger for her, instead of just taking her hand to complete the walk to the altar.

I don't pay attention to what the celebrant, from our faith, the Orthodox Church, is saying.

The ceremony to me is just a social protocol, like the piece of paper we'll sign.

Zoe is mine, and I am hers.

There is nothing and no one that could change that fact.

Her small hand grips mine, holding me tightly, and I can feel how emotional she is.

She turns to me, and I know the time for the vows has come.

She smiles and kisses my hand before speaking.

"I was very anxious..." She pauses. "Actually, I *am* very anxious, but I was a bit more because, in addition to never having spoken to an audience" she turns to the guests, smiling "I wanted everything to be perfect. At the same time, I didn't want anything rehearsed, because my story with my love has never followed a script."

Shaking her head, she points to her own face, which is red. I know how difficult it must be to be the center of attention.

"I love you," I say.

"I love you too." She gives me a light kiss. "When I met my Greek, the one you call Christos Lykaios, I was sure from the very first moment that he was my Prince Charming. A rather reluctant, gruff prince, but my heart knew, before we even realized, that he would be my *forever*. Unlike fairy tales, the prince and princess were separated for a time. She was lost, scared, but the prince was not a man to give up easily. He found me once and then, found me again. He loved and protected me. Thank you all for being with us on this special day. Soon you will witness the true beginning of our story and say: and they lived happily ever after."

Zoe throws herself into my arms in a long kiss.

When we finally part, I prepare to declare my devotion to her in public.

"I had planned to recite a poem, but I've decided to go with something more real and not echo what thousands of couples might have repeated around the world. There are no words to express what you are to me, Zoe. Woman, lover, mother of my children, my home and my soul. The one, the first, the eternal. My love."

Epilogue 1

Zoe

Wedding Night

I thought that after so much time together, the excitement of making love with Christos would diminish, but I feel overwhelmed just like the first time.

I love everything about him, especially the way he looks at me. His gaze is deep, full of unspoken words, but radiates so much love and desire that it makes me dizzy.

I'm only a few steps away. I feel beautiful, despite having gained a few pounds.

"Do you have any idea how crazy it drives me to see you exposing yourself to me with that rounded belly of our babies?"

I shake my head as if to say no, but it's a lie.

The corner of my mouth lifts, and he knows I'm teasing him. We undress each other, but while my husband is naked, gorgeous, his erect member inviting me to a delightful night, I still keep my panties on.

I run my fingers over my sensitive nipples and hear a hoarse sound from his throat.

"Are you going to let me play with your body?"

"I'm yours, woman."

I move closer.

"Take off the panties." But right after giving the order, he kneels in front of me. "No, I'll do it."

He slowly pulls down the garment, and feeling his fingers on my warm skin sends shivers of pleasure through me.

I'm naked now and don't spread my legs, but the lips of my sex. He sucks on my most sensitive spot, and I need to lean on him to avoid falling.

"You told me you were mine," I moan, desperate. My plan to seduce him is going downhill.

"Yeah, and I am, but I never promised to stay still."

He places one of my thighs over his shoulder and tastes me with his open mouth, devouring me, hungry.

In no time, trembling, I melt into his lips.

He carries me in his arms and takes us to the bed.

"Playing dirty, Lykaios."

"I can't resist, Zoe. You're a delight," he says, running his tongue over his lower lip.

He lies on his back and I, straddling his thighs, but without our sexes touching yet.

I close my eyes, the strength of my love for him making them fill with tears.

"Look at me," he commands, holding my hips, aligning our sexes.

He enters me slowly, as if savoring, and I moan loudly.

When he fills me completely, he doesn't move, just feeling me open for him — soul, body, and heart.

One of his hands caresses my erect nipple, while the other rests on my belly.

"Ride me," he commands.

Now, he holds me by my butt cheeks, lifting me. I let my body go, taking him slowly.

The fit between us is difficult. My small sex stretching to accommodate every inch of him, making us moan as he moves inch by inch within my walls.

"I love you," he repeats every time I descend onto his thick rigidity.

My hands rest on his shoulders. I'm crazy with pleasure but also overwhelmed by a love so intense it robs me of the ability to speak.

Perhaps sensing this, he takes control, leading us into a ride that is also an unbreakable connection, claiming me deeply, and all I can think about is the perfection of us together.

"More," I plead.

He touches my clit and sits on the bed, sucking on my nipples, the movements accelerating to a wild speed.

"You're so delicious," he says, and when he moves his hips, hitting the perfect angle, I scream his name and climax.

I grind, determined to drag him with me, and I feel victorious when I see his tense face, a sign that he is close to his own release.

"I'm going to come."

"Give me everything. Fill me."

"Zoe..." he howls.

Our bodies create their own cadence, seeking each other incessantly in constant thrusts for several minutes.

He thickens inside me and when the first jets of his orgasm fill me, I feel complete.

He lies down, withdrawing from me and positioning me on my back on top of him. Minutes pass and I still feel the beat of his heart... or rather, our accelerated hearts.

"How is it always getting better?" I ask.

"Because it's not just physical, my Zoe, or a perfect fit of sexes seeking pleasure, but a meeting of skins, scents, mouths, tongues, and, above all, our souls."

"WHO IS SHE IN ODIN'S life?"

We're on our way to New York. Christos has a meeting there. I want to shop for the babies and also get a haircut from a Brazilian hairdresser that Bia recommended. She's becoming quite popular in the *Big Apple*. I'm tired of my current haircut.

When I found out we were going, his cousin invited us to dinner at his house, and according to Christos, there will be a woman there: Elina Argyros.

"If I had to guess, I'd say she's his girlfriend. What other name can you give to a couple living together?"

"Roommates?"

He smiles.

"Odin, with a roommate? My cousin is the most individualistic person who ever existed."

"You used to be, Mr. Lykaios, and yet here we are."

He becomes serious for a moment, then unbuckles my seatbelt and takes my hand to the bedroom of his — of *our* — plane.

He lies on the bed and pulls me to lie beside him.

"Because you were missing, Zoe. I always knew, before I met you, that I hadn't found the right person yet."

"How could you know?"

"The soul recognizes its other half, even if the brain doesn't realize it."

"Even when we fight?"

"Sharing a life with someone isn't simple, but everything about us is worth it. Even your mess."

"I'm not messy. You're the one obsessed with order."

"I don't deny it, but I don't mind picking up your panties scattered on the floor of the *closet*. They smell nice."

I laugh so hard that I lose my breath.

"I don't even have words to express how that sounded perverted, husband."

"I thought that point was already established. I'm a pervert, but only when it comes to you, woman."

"Well put, Christos. I've been more jealous than usual. Guard your life."

"I'm crazy about you, Zoe Lykaios. How can you feel insecure?"

"Because sometimes I still can't believe it."

"Believe what?"

"That we've turned the fairy tale into real life."

Epilogue 2

Christos

Day of Birth

It feels as though all the emotions I didn't allow myself to feel throughout my life had been accumulated in a mileage account for me to experience with Zoe.

I look at my wife in the hospital bed with a baby in each arm, while the nurse takes photos as requested. I can't move, paralyzed by the flood of love that overwhelms me seeing the three of them together.

Adonis and Demetrius came into the world just as the Lykaios are: shouting at the top of their lungs, announcing their debut so that no one doubts there is another generation of arrogant Greeks in sight.

Zoe smiles as she looks from one to the other. Happiness radiates from her like light.

My wife shines. Complete, beautiful, a mother.

My heart pounds in my chest and I silently pray, thanking God for my family.

The nurse now asks us all to pose for a photo. I do so automatically, my brain functioning outside its normal capacity because, at this moment, I am all feelings.

After taking our photo, she steps back, giving us privacy, and I kiss my wife and each of the babies, holding them in a protective embrace.

"You're very quiet, Mr. Lykaios," she says as the nurses take my boys back to the nursery.

"Because I can't find the right words."

"For what?"

"To show what I'm feeling, so I'd rather just hold you and thank the universe, God, fate, whatever brought us together. I love you, my Zoe."

Ten Years Later

LYING ON A BLANKET, we watch our children sit at the picnic table with their grandparents.

We have a team of five in total, but we weren't satisfied yet, so we've ordered another little girl, who should arrive next Christmas.

We have four biological children — two sets of twins, boys — and one from the heart, Elijah, the youngest.

Our parents are in love with the children, and although Zoe's mother's health still requires care, she is cured of cancer, and it hasn't returned. It's a sword over our heads, as we're always expecting it might come back, but as Macy herself says, why live suffering in anticipation?

The second set of twins gave us quite a scare. Yes, I know it's a blessing, but four babies with such a short time apart basically requires a military operation: an army of employees and lots of love from the grandparents, because both Zoe and I continue with our careers.

I've adjusted my life to be closer to the kids because I miss my family.

Zoe has been off the runways for over five years, when our contract ended, as she was determined to see it through. Now, she runs two non-profit organizations, each separately aimed at caring for children and the elderly in need.

The current pregnancy, of our Athina, was a surprise but also very desired after we confirmed, because we wanted a girl.

I wonder how she will handle our five little boys.

For better or for worse, they all take after me in temperament, and even Elijah, at just two years old, has absorbed his brothers' behavior.

They're always trying to mark their territory and are somewhat controlling.

"Athina wants to join in the fun with her brothers," she says, probably because our little girl has moved.

"Really?" I cuddle her more in my arms.

She shakes her head, agreeing.

"I think we're going to have a surprise with this one."

"God, don't say that. I was hoping she'd be born with your temperament."

She laughs.

"I think your genes are stronger, but I'm okay with that. I enjoy keeping all the Lykaios in line."

"I don't mind. Keep trying."

She looks back, lost in an expression of indignation and laughter.

"You're so arrogant," she says, pulling me in for a kiss, "but in a way that drives me crazy."

"All yours, woman. Use me as you please."

"That's exactly what I intend, Greek. Our parents will take care of the kids. Get ready for a sleepless night."

"Was that supposed to be a threat? Because it sounds like paradise to me. Take everything you want from me, Zoe. I'm yours."

The End!

Did you love *Unplanned Obsession*? Then you should read *The Ballerina's Keeper* by Amara Holt!

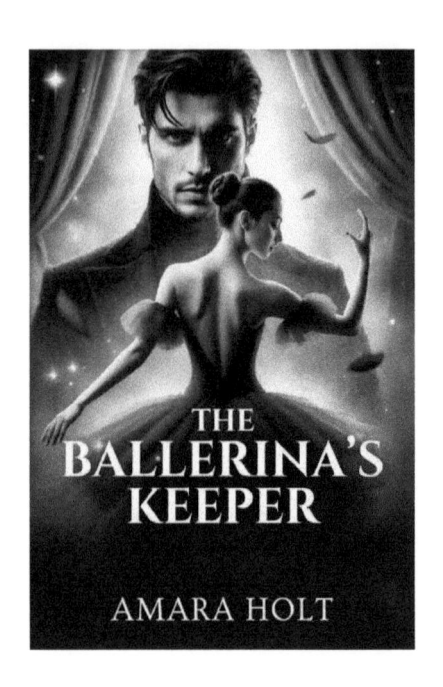

The Ballerina's Keeper

In a world of **wealth**, **secrets**, and **forbidden desires**, one man's **obsession** could be her **salvation**—or her **undoing**.

Julian, the **reclusive billionaire** shrouded in **mystery**, has built an empire on **power** and **fear**. Few have seen his face, and even fewer have dared to cross him. But when a **tragic accident** leaves him the sole heir to a vast fortune, Julian's world is turned upside down by the arrival of someone he never expected—Lorena.

Lorena, once a **graceful ballerina**, now lives in the shadows of her former life, her **dreams shattered** by a **devastating accident**. **Innocent** yet **resilient**, she pours her heart into teaching children, trying to find peace after the loss of her family. But peace is elusive, especially when she learns the truth about Julian, the man she's been taught to despise.

Their worlds collide when Lorena finds herself in **danger**, and Julian becomes her unexpected **protector**. Whisked away to his **isolated mansion**, Lorena is caught between **fear** and **fascination**, unsure whether she is a prisoner or a guest, a captive or a cherished treasure.

As she unravels the layers of Julian's **dark past**, Lorena must confront her own feelings. Is Julian the **villain** she imagined—or the only one who can save her? In **The Ballerina's Keeper**, love and danger intertwine in a gripping tale of passion, power, and the delicate balance between **trust** and **betrayal**.

Get lost in a story where **passion** knows no bounds and **love** becomes a game of **life and death**. **The Ballerina's Keeper** will keep you on the edge of your seat until the very last page.

About the Author

Amara Holt is a storyteller whose novels immerse readers in a whirlwind of suspense, action, romance and adventure. With a keen eye for detail and a talent for crafting intricate plots, Amara captivates her audience with every twist and turn. Her compelling characters and atmospheric settings transport readers to thrilling worlds where danger lurks around every corner.

Milton Keynes UK
Ingram Content Group UK Ltd.
UKHW030903011224
451693UK00001B/143